LIMITED
TIME
OFFER

KELLY JAMIESON

Limited Time Offer
Copyright © 2017 by Kelly Jamieson

ISBN: 978-1-988600-30-7

Cover by Scott Carpenter and Kanaxa
Interior Formatting by Author E.M.S.

Published in the United States of America.

PRAISE FOR THE NOVELS OF KELLY JAMIESON

"Kelly Jamieson delivers a blazing passionate read that tugs at the heartstrings!"
~ **Carly Phillips,** *New York Times* **Bestselling Author**

"seductive and bewitching from the very start… Softly romantic and wickedly provocative"
~ *RT Book Reviews* **on Rule of Three**

"Kelly Jamieson now has a permanent place on my keeper shelf and I can't wait to see what she writes next."
~ *Joyfully Reviewed*

"Ms. Jamieson once again gives the reader a richly detailed story that is brimming over with sexual tension, intoxicating desires and intriguing carnal needs that is edgy and psychologically intense…"
~ *The Romance Studio*

"…I love Kelly Jamieson's books and the way that she depicts her characters…"
~ *Sizzling Hot Book Reviews*

*Super big thanks to editor Christa —
obviously I could not have written this without your help.
Thank you for giving me this opportunity and trusting me
to write these stories.*

1

What the hell was going on in that room next door?
The doors that could turn the two hotel rooms into adjoining rooms were closed and locked, but the noise filtered through them as if they were tissue. "Yeah!" a male voice shouted. "Do it!" Loud laughter erupted.

Sloane frowned, punching her pillow into a different shape beneath her head. She buried her face in the pillow, squeezed her eyes closed and tried to ignore the noise.

Another male voice hooted and more laughter assaulted Sloane's ears.

Oh my God. Could this day get any worse? She clenched her teeth. She willed sleep to come back but it ignored her, and she opened her eyes and stared into the dark hotel room. Crap. She was wide-awake. Now, all she could hear was the noise from the other side of the wall.

Sloane flung back the covers and approached the door. Leaning in, she listened. She heard several male voices, all loud, obviously drunk, and a lot of laughter. She leaned her forehead briefly against the door and considered calling the front desk to complain.

Surely this wouldn't go on much longer. The clock on the bedside table said 1:20 a.m. She padded across the carpet and slid back into bed, then pulled the pillow over her head. It helped, but she couldn't get any oxygen. She adjusted it and focused on her breathing.

She needed sleep. She *really* needed sleep. She'd been working late every night this week and had been sleeping in a strange bed, displaced from her home by the bathroom reno from hell. On top of that, she'd been called into the CEO's office at five o'clock that afternoon. A meeting with the CEO at five o'clock on a Friday was never a good thing.

Just because a new client had done a drive-by visit that afternoon and found their creative team sitting on the floor playing with LEGO bricks rather than working on their ad campaign, Joseph Huxworth, CEO of Huxworth Packard, one of Chicago's top advertising agencies, had flipped shit. And she was the one he'd picked to fix things.

She replayed their meeting in her mind, her frustration resurfacing. But he was the boss.

And she'd worked too hard to get where she was not to deliver exactly what Joe asked for.

She groaned and flopped onto her back. A loud burst of male laughter from the other side of the wall had her body tensing even more. Now the clock said 3:05 a.m. Christ. They were still going at whatever it was they were doing.

That was it. She needed to sleep and for what she was paying for this damn hotel room, she *deserved* to sleep. She threw back the covers again and climbed out of bed. She stomped across the room, then paused at the door that separated the two rooms. Curiosity about what the hell they were doing had her listening. Now she could hear a female voice.

One female voice and several male voices. Sloane couldn't make out many actual words, although the woman did seem to be giving the men instructions.

Then she heard, clear as anything, "And then you can come on my tits."

Sloane's eyes popped open wide, then closed briefly. Oh sweet loving Lord.

She listened more intently. Yes, there were at least four or five male voices, and only the one very distinct feminine voice. Oh my God. What was that woman doing in there?

"Do you just do this for bachelor parties?" one of the male voices asked.

Sloane thunked her head against the wall. A bachelor party. *Of course.* She couldn't quite make out the words of the woman's reply.

Her stomach knotted up a bit, thinking about a lone woman in a hotel room with a bunch of strange men. God. She supposed this was what this woman did, but holy hell, she was putting herself at incredible risk.

For that reason only, Sloane continued to strain her ears to hear what was going on. Okay, and maybe a little prurient curiosity. Still she couldn't make out many words, just a lot of hoots and hollers and laughter, and "the bachelor should go first" *(oh dear God, first at what?).* She heard the woman give a little shriek but then laugh and issue what sounded like more instructions, as if they were playing some kind of dirty game.

"Why do you even have your shirt on, dude?" a male voice asked quite clearly, his question followed by more indistinct talk.

God, she was so tired. She did not want to listen to these guys do whatever it was they were doing with that woman. Who was she? A hooker? A stripper? An escort? How had they found her? And what were they doing with her? Were they actually having sex? What would the bride-to-be think if she knew this was going on? Or did she know?

If it were *her* husband-to-be in that room there'd be hell to pay. Geezus.

Sloane was far from innocent. She knew guys liked to go out and go wild for bachelor parties, one last crazy fling before they settled down, but God, having sex with

3

another woman, no matter if it was paid for, was really quite…disturbing.

The noise was getting louder. She listened carefully for any signs the guys were…well, close to hurting the woman. Even if she was willingly having paid sex with them, she was still at risk. But there weren't any what she would consider "sex noises". It seemed they were having a lot of fun, even the woman giving shrieks of what sounded like delight, and then trilling a feminine laugh.

Now Sloane had second thoughts about actually going and knocking on the door and telling them to keep it down. The better plan would be to call the front desk and have them deal with it. She was just reaching for the phone when a loud banging on the door reverberated through the room.

She froze. Geezus! Was that *her* door?

Again she padded to the door. She peered through the peephole. Nothing.

More knocking. "Security!"

The knocking was on the door next to hers. Thank the baby deity. Someone else must have complained, saving her the trouble.

Security had to knock and call out a few more times, while silence fell in the room. Sloane leaned against the wall, imagining all the naked guys panicking, trying to get dressed. Finally someone opened the door.

Again, she couldn't hear all the words, but the security guard from the hotel was clearly telling them they were making too much noise. The man who spoke to him in a low, deep voice sounded apologetic, and actually respectful, not drunkenly belligerent as she'd been afraid. She heard him say, "Yeah, yeah, got it. Sorry, man."

The door closed again.

Okay. Finally. Things would quiet down now and she could get some sleep.

Back in bed, she pulled the feather duvet up under her chin and got comfy, closing her eyes. But another burst of laughter made her sigh. The male voices had quieted for a while but were gradually growing louder and louder. Oh my God. Security hadn't helped at all.

Around four o'clock she got up again, listening. She heard the woman say something about who was going to pay her. Maybe they were done. Then the door of the adjoining room opened and closed. And opened and closed again. Okay. People were leaving that room.

Hopefully the guys were taking taxis and not drinking and driving.

Christ, why did she even care? They'd hired a hooker to come to a hotel room and do who knew what.

Finally, silence. Sloane sighed.

It was still hard to get to sleep, imagining what had been going on in that room. Was someone still in there going to sleep? The bachelor, perhaps? Or had he gone home to his unsuspecting fiancée?

Argh. She arranged her pillow again. She had to stop thinking about it.

Finally, she drifted into sleep.

Saturday morning when she awoke, she blinked bleary eyes. Blackout drapes on the windows kept out most of the June sun, but brightness around the edges told her it was already late. She turned her head on the pillow toward the clock. Crap. Nearly ten o'clock. That few hours of interrupted sleep had messed her up. Her appointment at the spa was at ten thirty. She needed to get moving.

She dragged herself out of bed, started coffee in the small coffee maker and stumbled into the bathroom. Shower. Coffee. Then she could go get pampered. Since she'd been kicked out of her condo by the contractors doing bathroom renovations, she'd been staying with her brother all week, but he'd been pretty clear that she needed to be out of his condo Friday night for his hot date. So she'd booked a night in the hotel and decided to spoil herself with a facial and mani/pedi in the elegant spa. A small indulgent reward after the crap week she'd had. After that she'd go home to her newly renovated bathroom. The contractors had promised it would be usable today, even if not completely finished.

The hotel invoice had been slipped under the door and she didn't need to check out. She dressed in a pair of yoga pants, a loose, thin T-shirt and flip-flops. She pulled her hair up into a messy knot and didn't bother with contact lenses or makeup since she was going for a facial. When she'd packed, she backed out of the hotel room, pulling her small carry-on sized suitcase behind her, struggling a little with the heavy door. As she did this, the door of the room next to hers opened and a man stepped out, slinging a duffel bag over his shoulder.

They came face-to-face in the hall.

Ugh. One of the bachelor party dudes. As if she wanted to actually see any of them after listening to them all night.

She met his gaze with raised eyebrows.

He was probably about her age, thirtyish. His dark hair was messy, stubble shadowed his cheeks and jaw, and dark circles hugged his lower lids. He blinked bloodshot eyes at her. Beautiful eyes, probably, when they weren't red—deep-set and a clear light blue, with thick dark lashes. Crap, even though he looked a little rough, he was one of the most gorgeous guys she'd ever seen.

She lifted her chin. "So, did you boys have fun last night?"

Color washed up into his face and he briefly closed his eyes. "Christ. You could hear us."

"Oh yeah. Pretty much everything."

That was an exaggeration, but she had a damn good idea of what had been going on.

"Fuck," he muttered, rubbing a hand over those bloodshot eyes. "Sorry."

"You should be. I'm a few hours short of sleep and that makes me cranky." She narrowed her eyes at him. "Also, I don't know you or the bride-to-be, but I hope she never finds out what you were doing at the bachelor party."

She turned her back on him and stalked down the carpeted hall toward the elevator, tugging her suitcase along behind her.

Of course, he was heading the same direction and they ended up waiting for the elevator together. He shoved his hands into the pockets of baggy cargo shorts, his big shoulders hunched under a wrinkled Cubs T-shirt. The air around them hummed with discomfort.

She adjusted the strap of her purse on her shoulder. Stared at the small table and chairs arranged nearby. Bit her upper lip. Tapped her foot in its flip-flop.

The guy cleared his throat. "It wasn't like we were doing something illegal," he muttered.

Her eyebrows flew up. "Prostitution is legal in Illinois now?"

The man choked. "She wasn't a prostitute!"

"Whatever." That poor woman. Sloane didn't want to be all judgy. Who knew what would move someone to do such a thing. She just hoped the woman was okay. It hadn't sounded violent but...her active imagination had been creating scenarios where the police arrived at her door in the morning to question her on what she'd heard because they'd found the woman's raped and mangled body somewhere.

Finally the elevator dinged its arrival. Maybe she should take the stairs...but they were on the twenty-fourth floor and she was just being ridiculous. The police had not found any body. She stepped in first, poked the button labeled L for lobby, and faced the doors as they slid shut. She edged farther away from the man in the elevator, eyeing him warily.

The man leaned against the opposite wall. She heard his sigh.

Poor baby. All tired and hungover. Beh.

She let out a breath of relief when the elevator stopped on fifteen and another couple, probably in their fifties, got on. They stood in the middle of the elevator holding hands and smiling at each other.

Cute.

When the elevator arrived on the main floor, she let the couple precede her out, and the other man held out a hand to let her go before him. Polite. Huh.

She watched him smile at the doorman too as he walked out, and geezus, he wasn't even trying to be charming and sexy — but he was, and she felt that smile in her girl parts.

Lovely.

She was obviously overtired. And undersexed. Her fatigue had disappeared, thanks to seeing her neighbor, and was now replaced with an Energizer Bunny buzz of annoyance.

She headed into the spa, unreasonably disturbed by having run into that man. It was bad enough having heard them. He was irksomely normal looking, handsome and polite to the hotel staff. She would have expected someone more skeevy.

She tried to put him out of her head as she relaxed in the steam room before having her face cleansed, buffed and polished, then her toes and fingers done. Hopefully the contractor was correct and she'd be able to move back in. Being out of her home for over a week was a pain in the ass. It wasn't supposed to take this long, but her building was old and every time they did one thing they ran into another unforeseen problem that added time to the reno. She'd been harassing Lando every day about it and he was probably as eager to have this job done as she was, so he wouldn't have to put up with her anymore.

Monday morning, Levi inspected his appearance in his bedroom mirror. He brushed a hand over the lapel of his perfectly fitted Armani jacket, adjusted the collar of the golf shirt beneath it, turned his head to check the hair and his shave job. Sideburns perfect, hair back off his face. All good. First day on the new job. Hopefully he'd nailed the casual but professional vibe he'd gotten when he'd been at the office for his interview. He needed to make a good impression.

He wasn't really worried. They wanted him at Huxworth Packard. They wanted him so fucking bad they'd recruited him from AdMix after they'd won that Cannes Lion and One Show pencil for their Mercedes commercials. He grinned. He was a star copywriter and Huxworth Packard was goddamn lucky to get him.

He checked the time on his cell phone as he unplugged it from the charger on his dresser. The distance from his Streeterville condo to the Lachman Building on South Wacker wasn't that far, but he wanted to be sure to have time to locate his new parking spot, one of the perks of the new job, along with a substantial increase in pay.

Not that he'd ever outwardly show it, but he was damn excited about this new job. Huxworth Packard had the coveted Verhoeven Brewery account. Beer! Everyone wanted to work on a beer account. And *he* was going to be working on that account. *Fucking yeah!*

"Okay, Chuck." He looked at his King Charles Spaniel lying on the rug near the door, chin on his paws. Big brown eyes gazed up him. "Gotta go to work, dude. Come on now, don't look at me like that. You know I have to go to work. Happens every day." He'd already taken Chuck out to the dog run across the street. He reached down and gave the silky head a rub, then left his condo still with a smile on his face.

He negotiated traffic along East Illinois in his beloved Mercedes SL Roadster, onto Michigan and across the river. In the Lachman Building he rode the elevator to the thirty-fifth floor where the offices of Huxworth Packard occupied the entire floor. Gorgeous building, gorgeous views in every direction. Levi loved Chicago. Born and raised there, he'd even gone to college there. He'd traveled, sure, he loved traveling, but he never wanted to live anywhere else.

He was greeted by the receptionist, a smokin' hot blonde with a nice rack, sitting behind a curved white desk. On the black wall behind her in white script was a quote from Dr. Seuss — *Think left and think right and think low and think high. Oh, the thinks you can think up if only you try!*

What was her name again? He'd met her when he'd been there for his interview with Mason Ward. That had been so fucking cool. Mason Ward, executive creative director at Huxworth Packard, was approaching the status of advertising legend at the ripe old age of thirty-six.

"Good morning, Mr. Wolcott." The receptionist's smile held feminine appreciation and just a hint of flirtation. Clearly she was expecting him. The nameplate on the desk said Carly. Yeah, that was it.

"Good morning, Carly." He smiled in return. "Good to see you again. And please, call me Levi."

"Of course. Come this way, Mr. Ward is waiting for you in his office."

"Great, thanks."

He followed her past a big potted palm and through glass doors, admiring the fit of her pale pink pencil skirt on her nicely rounded ass. She tapped in her high heels across the big open area with shiny hardwood floors, past desks, chairs, couches, benches and plants, and down a carpeted hall to the office he remembered from the last interview nearly three weeks ago. Mason Ward sat behind his desk frowning at a computer, but the frown vanished as Carly knocked on his open door to announce their presence and he looked up at them.

"Good morning." Mason pushed back his chair and rose.

The guy'd been a college football player and it still showed. His custom suit was clearly tailored to his tall, broad-shouldered frame. He'd apparently blown out a shoulder, which had cost him a pro ball career, but that was the advertising world's gain, in Levi's opinion. He smiled at his new boss and moved into the office to shake his hand.

"Glad you're here," Mason said with a bone-crunching grip. "Thanks, Carly."

"Let me know if there's anything at all you need, Mr. Wol...I mean, Levi." She gave him a brief wink as she departed.

"Thanks." He winked back and her cheeks turned pink.

"Come on, let's introduce you to everyone and get you settled in your office," Mason said. "Once we've done that, we'll have a chat about a few things."

"Sure. Sounds good."

He was eager to meet his new colleagues. He'd met Scott McCrae, the art director he'd be working with. Leaving his AD partner Fergus behind at AdMix had sucked balls. They'd been a good team and had worked together for nearly five years. It kind of felt like he'd gotten a divorce. Not that he'd know what that felt like, since he'd never been married and had never even been in a long-term relationship. But getting a divorce probably sucked.

Mason paused at the office next door to his and stuck his head in. "Hey, Sloane. Levi Wolcott is here."

"Come in," a female voice said, and Levi again followed Mason into an office, a smile at the ready. He'd also heard of Sloane Granderson but hadn't yet had the pleasure of meeting her. She too was acquiring a reputation in the biz as a tough but brilliant account director.

As Mason stepped aside, Levi moved forward with an outstretched hand. Oh no. Wait just a goddamn minute. The woman who walked toward him had his blood freezing in his veins. It couldn't be...

It was. The woman who'd been in the room next door at the hotel Friday night was Sloane Granderson.

2

She looked different than she had Saturday morning, but he was sure it was her. She'd pissed him off that morning with her judgy attitude, looking at him down her tiny little nose through dark-rimmed glasses, pretty lips dipping at the corners in disapproval.

On Saturday morning, he'd thought she looked like a teenager. Now, he wasn't so sure—maybe she was closer to his age, twenty-nine. She'd seemed tiny standing next to him waiting for the elevator, but now heels gave her added height. The glasses were gone. Makeup emphasized dark blue eyes with extravagant eyelashes and a small, lush mouth. Her shoulder-length blonde hair was shiny and perfect, and she wore a sleeveless ivory and black dress that fit her slender body from shoulder to knee. She extended a sleek, toned arm to him.

Then she hesitated.

She recognized him too. Her gorgeous eyes widened. Pink lips parted.

Levi had to admit part of the reason she'd pissed him off was because he'd felt a twinge of guilt at the fact that they *had* been making a lot of noise. After his first few attempts to get the guys to tone it down, he'd given up. Then security had come and lectured them, which of course he had to deal with. Even that hadn't been enough to get the guys to dial down the noise level.

They'd been having fun. Innocent, pre-wedding, bachelor fun. Okay, maybe innocent wasn't the right word, but like he'd said to Sloane that morning, it wasn't like they were doing something illegal. Boys will be boys, right?

So he pushed away that guilt. They hadn't done anything wrong. She'd lost a little sleep that night, but it wasn't the fucking end of the world. He stepped toward her with a smile on his face and reached for her hand. "Pleased to meet you," he said as if they'd never met. "I've heard great things about you."

Now those sexy eyes narrowed. "Likewise." She appraised him with a chilly and decidedly unamused look. She'd lost her composure for about, oh, 3.2 seconds but was now back in control. This impressed him.

Mason was talking and Sloane was answering him, but he wasn't paying attention. He was taking in the way her breasts were outlined in the soft fabric of her dress, the way the black stripe of fabric emphasized her narrow waist and curve of hips, how those shoes made her calves and ankles look slender and sexy.

Fuck, get a grip, man. This was one chick who was seriously off limits. Even *he* had rules about who he'd sleep with and who he wouldn't. Not many rules, but some.

He focused on the conversation, the plans to meet with the entire team later after he'd been taken around and introduced.

The rest of the introductions were a bit of a blur. He was usually good with names and faces but it was going to take a while to get everyone straight. He did make a mental note of Account Manager Noah Cavanaugh, who he would be working with directly. He met a bunch of guys, copywriters and art directors, forgetting who was who…Isaiah, Owen, Hunter, Ravi, Dash and Renzo. Two cute media buyers, Bailey and Phoebe, and Kaleb, media planner. Producer…what was her name again? Ah well, he'd get it eventually. And Scott McCrae, who shook hands with him.

"Welcome." Scott gave him a coolly assessing look.

"Thanks. Happy to be here."

He and Scott had met during the interview process, and Levi knew Scott had been consulted on whether or not he wanted to work with Levi. The agency would never pair them together without Scott's blessing, since the success of their partnership was so vital to the agency's success. So Scott had to have been positively impressed…but that didn't show at this moment.

Levi studied the guy. Not bad looking. Shaggy blond hair gave him a laid-back surfer dude look. Well, they'd have to get to know each other and see how things went.

Later, after he'd been shown to his office—yes, he had his own fucking office—and he and Mason had talked more, the other creatives took him for lunch at a nearby restaurant, Bon Vivant, which turned into two hours of interrogation and extensive sampling of their clients' products.

"So you worked at AdMix," Hunter said. "Why'd you leave?"

Levi grinned and slid his cold glass of Ammen lager closer. "Got a better offer."

"They've got a good rep," Owen said.

"Yeah," Levi agreed. "Small boutique agency. There are pros and cons."

"You won a shit ton of awards there," Owen commented with narrowed eyes.

His chest swelled a little. "Yep." He might be the new guy but he wasn't a rookie. Good for them to all know that.

"We've won awards too," Ravi said with a chin lift.

"True that." Levi acknowledged that by raising his own chin.

A cute waitress arrived to take their food order. They sat at two tables pushed together in the bar, on high stools. Most of the guys ordered the classic burger. Levi observed Dash requesting his burger done medium, grilled onions instead of raw, horseradish Havarti cheese, Dijon mustard instead of yellow, no tomatoes. The waitress patiently noted his requests. Scott requested sweet potato fries instead of regular, and Owen ordered a bunless burger, which had the other guys gaping.

"Dude." Hunter's forehead wrinkled. "No bun? How is that even a burger?"

"Shut up," Owen muttered. "I'm cutting back on carbs."

Levi wasn't going to judge the guy. Cutting carbs sucked, but you did what you had to do to stay in shape. Then the waitress looked at Levi. Her smile changed, going warm and flirty. "What can I get you?"

He smiled back. "Classic burger also, with bacon."

"You got it. Do you need some ice water?"

"Uh, sure, that'd be great."

She collected the menus and he watched her walk away, swinging her ass in a short, tight skirt.

He turned back to see all the guys staring at him. "What?"

They exchanged frowns and shook their heads. "She didn't offer any of *us* ice water," Owen said.

Levi laughed. "What the fuck ever."

Owen sighed.

"So who does what?" Levi asked, looking at them around the table.

"Copywriter," Ravi said, putting a hand up. "So are Hunt and Dash."

"Renzo, Owen and I are art directors," Isaiah said. "And Scott, of course. Renzo and Dash work together. Me and Hunt, Owen and Ravi."

"What's it like working for Mason?"

"Great," Scott said. "Mason's the shit. I mean, he has his moments, who doesn't. Can be a bit moody, but he gets over it and he's fair. He's great at knowing exactly what clients want."

"And Sloane Granderson?" Levi casually traced a finger through condensation on his glass.

A couple of the guys made appreciative noises. "Smokin' hot," Owen said. "But totally hands off."

Levi rolled his eyes. "Yeah, I already got that. I mean, what's she like to work with?"

"She's smart. Knows her clients really well."

"The type to throw you under the bus when the client doesn't like your work?"

"Fuck no."

Levi nodded.

"She and Mason are pretty tight," Owen said.

Levi frowned. "What does that mean?" Sloane and Mason? *Fuck.*

Owen shrugged. "Who knows? They're friends. Rumor has it they're more than friends, but they don't show it if that's true."

Why did that annoy him?

"Can't be true," Ravi said. "Mason is a serial dater. He's always out with a different woman."

Levi lifted his glass and drained the last of his beer. "That was good."

"You should try another one," Scott suggested. "You need to know the client, right?"

"Right. Absolutely." He picked up the menu card that listed the beers available. He'd already researched Verhoeven and knew all their brands. "What should I have next? IPA? Stout?"

"Let's work our way through the list," Owen said. "The brown ale is really good."

"Okay." He caught the waitress's eye and she hustled

over to him with a bright smile. "I'll have the Barking Bear Brown Ale."

"You bet." She turned away, then paused and looked back at the other guys. "Anyone else?"

"I'll have one of those too," Owen said. The others declined.

"So what's the deal with Verhoeven?" Levi asked.

"They're going to fill us in this afternoon. There are projects ongoing on their existing brands," Dash said. "Renzo and I have Ammen and Ammen Light. They want a big new TV campaign for the Cerone brand." Which Levi already knew was being assigned to him and Scott. "And they need new campaigns for these new craft beers. Verhoeven just bought out a few craft breweries."

Levi knew that too. He was eager to get started. He knew he had a lot to learn, but he'd be a sponge later at the meeting, taking it all in. He was so going to wow them with his ideas. He knew it.

"So give us your story," Ravi said. "Hometown, college, married or single?"

"Born and raised in Chicago. Went to U of C for undergrad, then Portfolio Center. Single and staying that way."

"What part of town did you grow up in?"

"Lake Forest."

Eyebrows all lifted. Levi shrugged. "Yeah, my dad is John Wolcott."

After a short pause, Owen said, "You didn't want to go into the family business? Christ, you could be pulling down a lot more cake than you are as a copywriter."

"Yeah, Dad was disappointed, but it just wasn't for me. I started taking business and finance courses in college, and I did okay, but they just bored me."

They all nodded. He'd hated disappointing his dad, but luckily he'd gotten over it and was proud of what Levi'd accomplished. For a while he'd been uncustomarily and uncomfortably in the doghouse. Usually he could do no wrong in his family's eyes.

"If Mount Rushmore was made up of cartoon characters, who would your picks be?" Scott demanded.

Levi grinned. "Uh. Let me think. Homer Simpson."

This was met with chin lifts of reluctant approval.

"Stewie."

Nods.

"Scooby Doo. And...Wonder Woman."

"Wonder Woman?"

"Hell yeah. She's hot. She wears cuffs." The idea of a strong, smart woman cuffed to his bed was one of his favorite fantasies.

"Huh," Dash said.

"What was your favorite food when you were a child?"

"Steak and lobster."

More frowns greeted this news. Maybe he shouldn't be so honest.

"What's the most played song on your iPod?"

"What is this? An inquisition?"

"We're getting to know you. Answer the question."

Levi thought. "Right now, 'Jumper'. Third Eye Blind."

"What's your favorite indoor or outdoor activity?"

Levi grinned. "Sex."

Dash bent his head to hide his grin while the others groaned. "Of course," Scott said.

"You're reminding me of this drinking game I was playing on the weekend," Dash said. "I got so fucking hammered. It was stupid."

"What drinking game?"

Dash rolled his eyes. "It's a bunch of sick questions, like would you rather snort sand off a monkey's balls or ingest a bag of elephant shit. Or, if everyone playing the game had an orgy, would you rather give oral sex to everyone, or receive an oversized anal sex toy. You guess how the other person's going to answer and if you're wrong, you drink."

"How can you guess the answers to questions like that?" Hunter frowned. "Those are crap choices."

"I know, I know, right?"

"Tough choices," Levi mused. "I assume there were guys and girls playing the game?"

"Yeah." Dash grinned.

"I guess I'd have to go with the anal sex toy," Levi said. "I love giving oral, but not to guys."

"Dude." Dash high-fived him.

"Nobody's fucking me up the ass with anything," Ravi said.

"Don't knock it till you've tried it," Scott said. "Haven't you ever heard of the prostate?"

A bunch of guys groaned. Levi eyed Scott. This made him wonder what team Scott played for. Whatever. That didn't matter.

Cute Waitress arrived with his beer. "Here you go, hon," she purred, brushing her tits across his shoulder as she set the drink in front of him. Then she served Owen his and again checked in with the others. "Your lunch should be up shortly."

"What did *you* do on the weekend?" Scott asked him in a challenging tone.

"Friday night I hosted a little bachelor party for my buddy. He's getting married in a few weeks. Rest his soul." He lifted his drink and the other guys all toasted. "We hired a girl from the Kitten Club. Topless waitress came and served us drinks and did a few lap dances and played some games."

"Shut the fuck up," Dash breathed. "That's fucking awesome."

"She was cool," Levi agreed. He didn't tell them he'd been a reluctant participant in the whole thing, but the other guys had insisted they had to do something raunchy for poor Jacob. It had turned out okay. The Kitten Club had strict rules about what the girls would and would not

KELLY JAMIESON

do, and he'd made sure they followed the rules. He did not
want any kind of sick trouble, especially with Jacob's
fiancée Tara who would rip him a new one if Jacob got
in any kind of trouble right before the wedding. Or any
time.

Levi actually really liked Tara. She was damn near
perfect. Smart and pretty and fun, she didn't take crap but
she also wasn't a bitch. She let Jacob have his time with the
guys, and the times she joined them she laughed at their
crude and rude jokes and could drink some of them under
the table. Levi had no desire for a relationship or marriage
at this point in his life, but he understood why Jacob had
fallen hard for Tara and was willing to forgo sex with any
other woman for the rest of his life to be with her.

To Levi, sex with only one woman for the rest of his life
sounded like wretched, torturous hell. He enjoyed variety.

Their burgers arrived. Cute Waitress again leaned in
close as she served him his and whispered, "I gave you
premium Wisconsin cheddar, no extra charge."

"Thanks, doll," he murmured back.

He picked up his burger and took a big bite. "This is
fantastic," he said a moment later.

"Yeah, we like this place. We come here a lot.
Sometimes we come and brainstorm over a beer."

"Excellent." He approved of getting out of the office to
get creative. And he'd done the alcohol-fuelled
brainstorming a few times, but you had to be careful with
that. Sometimes the ideas that seemed genius after several
shots of tequila were just plain stupid the next day.

They ate and talked and ordered more beers, moving
on to the Natural Belgian Blonde—heh—then the
Albatross Ale and the Grasshopper Wheat. The wheat beer
came with a slice of fresh orange. Fuck, that was good.
They were all damn fine beers. Not like he'd never drunk
Verhoeven Beer before—anyone who lived in Illinois
drank Verhoeven beer; okay, anyone in America drank

Verhoeven beer — but some of these newer specialty beers were ones he hadn't tried.

Around one thirty he suggested it might be time to get back to the office. They were having a big meeting at two thirty. The guys all waved that idea away and ordered another round, so he shrugged and went with it. Flying Pigs Pale Ale.

"I should hit the john before we leave," he ventured.

"Don't do it, man," Ravi said. "Once you break the seal..."

Levi laughed. "I know, right?"

"That's an actual fact," Dash said. "Because it's not just the volume of liquid you drink, but with alcohol there's the added diuretic effect."

"For every gram of alcohol you drink urine excretion increases by ten milliliters. Also alcohol reduces the production of the hormone vasopressin, which tells your kidneys to reabsorb water rather than flush it," Ravi said.

Jesus, nerd much? But Levi grinned. He'd consumed a fair amount of liquid. "Verhoeven now has an extensive collection of beer," he mused as he knocked the last of that one back.

"They do," Scott agreed. "Okay, we better get going."

They paid their tabs, though it seemed to take forever since they wanted separate checks. When Cute Waitress handed Levi his bill he smiled to see that she'd written *Thanks so much, my name's Piper and here's my number...* He caught her eye and winked as he handed over his credit card, slipping the check into his wallet. Hey, you never knew.

He checked his cell phone for calls, messages and emails as they walked back to the Lachman Building. Jesus Christ! It was nearly two thirty and they weren't even in the building yet.

"Uh, hey guys," he said uneasily. "We need to move our tails."

21

"Relax," Owen said. "They can't start without us."

"True that." He smiled and straightened his shoulders. But despite his bravado, this was his first day on the job and he didn't want to screw up. He wasn't alone though, so there was that.

They rode the elevator to the thirty-fifth floor and piled out into the lobby. Carly greeted them all casually. "Hey guys. Um, they're waiting for you in the meeting room."

"Thanks, Carly darling," Dash said, striding through the glass doors.

Fuck, this wasn't the way Levi wanted to show up. He needed to grab his notepad and a pen from his new office, which he hadn't even settled into yet. And he wasn't even sure where the meeting room was. Probably that big glassed-in room he'd noticed earlier. He veered into his office, grabbed a leather portfolio from his briefcase and a pen, and headed to what he hoped was the meeting room.

Fuck, he needed to take a piss. All that beer...

Yep, that was where the meeting was. Mason and Sloane sat at a long, sleek light maple table surrounded by funky black chairs. Sunlight poured through floor-to-ceiling windows along one side of the room, illuminating big green potted plants in the corner. Others Levi'd met earlier—account manager, producer, media planner, media buyers—sat there too, along with some people he hadn't met, and everyone turned and looked at the seven guys who crowded through the door.

"Thanks for joining us," Sloane murmured with an edge to her tone that made Levi's skin tingle.

"Only a few minutes late." Scott beamed at Noah, the account manager. Noah's lips tightened.

Levi caught Mason's eye, taking in the notch between his brows.

"Uh, guys," Mason said. "Where the hell were you?"

"We took Levi out for lunch," Scott said. "We have to get to know him."

"Yeah," Mason agreed, with a glance at the watch on his wrist.

"We were doing research," Dash said with a smirk, dropping into an empty chair. "Beersploring. Testing the client's products."

"Oh my God," Sloane muttered.

"I do have to know the client's products," Levi said earnestly, also taking a seat. Christ, his bladder was about to burst. Why hadn't he insisted on using the can before they left the restaurant?

All the others burst out laughing. Well, not Sloane and Noah and Mason. But the guys he'd been with.

"Jesus fucking Christ," Mason said. "You fucking assholes."

They all laughed again and Levi looked around the room.

Fuck me sideways.

They'd done it on purpose. Taken him out and got him drunk and made him late. And now he had to sit there in agony through a two-hour meeting.

He pulled in a deep breath through his nostrils. He needed to handle this the right way. For one thing, he wasn't going to make it through two hours without taking a leak.

He pushed back his chair and rose to his feet. "My apologies." He looked at Mason then Sloane. Christ, she was glaring at him as if he'd walked in with dog shit stuck to his shoe. "I'm going to have to delay things another couple of minutes while I, uh, take care of some business. Please excuse me."

He walked out of the meeting room with his jaw clenched and eyes closed. Christ.

He legged it to the fucking men's room. Luckily he knew where it was. Then he sprinted back, slowing his pace as he neared the meeting room and they could see him through the glass wall. He closed the door behind him and took his seat again, looking around the table and smiling. "My apologies again. And guys...thanks...*for a great lunch.*" He nodded so they got his meaning. He wouldn't forget this. But he had to admire their balls.

"Levi, let us introduce you to the others here you haven't met," Mason said. He went around the table until finally he arrived at an older guy with silver hair who frowned at him. "Levi, you haven't yet met our CEO, Joseph Huxworth."

Fuck me again. Levi summoned a smile for the old guy, rising from his chair to round the table. "Mr. Huxworth. Pleased to meet you. I'm sure you've gotten a great impression of me so far."

Joseph Huxworth also rose and shook his hand, his grip firm for a guy with white hair. He frowned and Levi's heart dropped. "Indeed," he murmured, studying Levi's face with unnerving scrutiny.

Levi felt a sudden need to pee again.

3

"Υou have got to get these guys to tone down their behavior."

Sloane sat across from her CEO in his office later that day. She resisted the need to rub her throbbing temples.

Just effing great. They'd taken the new guy out for lunch and got him drunk and made him late for a meeting that included the CEO, *and* it was the first business day after said CEO had already talked to her about this issue.

She swallowed a sigh. These guys were the best and brightest creatives in the advertising business in Chicago. Yeah, they were all puffed up ego and strutting my-dick-is-bigger-than-your-dick males, but dammit, they were good at their jobs. For every time they pulled a stunt like they had today, there was a time they'd gone to the wall to get something done, pulling solutions out of their asses at the last minute, wowing clients with their brilliance. She sometimes shook her head at them, but at the end of the day, they got it done.

"They're immature and irresponsible. Things have changed in the advertising business. Our clients don't appreciate knowing we're spending their money on a bunch of frat boys drinking beer all afternoon."

She swallowed a sigh. She got what he was saying, but... "We weren't spending their money on that. Those guys picked up their own tab. Yes, they took a long lunch, and technically that was work time, but...it's not like that cost our clients anything. And team building is important. We have a new copywriter. They need to get to know each other. Bond."

Even as she said it, she repressed a shudder. What she said was true, but team building didn't have to happen in a bar and the guys had kind of hazed the new dude. Which was all kinds of wrong. She knew that.

Levi Wolcott.

She still could not believe he was the guy in the room next door Friday night. What the hell? She rubbed her index finger across her forehead, looking down at the carpet in Joe's office.

It didn't matter. Did. Not. Matter. He was their new copywriter. He had to perform, like everyone else.

Oh, that was the wrong choice of words. Imagining him performing in bed flashed through her heated imagination. He was sexy and charming and utterly full of himself. He'd totally deserved that little fun the other guys had had with him. But dammit, he'd handled it beautifully. He'd even charmed Joe, despite Joe's annoyance with the team's antics.

"Okay, Joe," she said. "I understand. It's the optics. I haven't had a chance to talk to them yet, but I will."

"Thank you, Sloane. I know I can count on you."

The old guy beamed at her and her heart softened. She owed a lot to Joseph Huxworth. She'd been with the firm for just over five years now, working her way up. He'd given her a lot. Not that she didn't deserve it.

It wasn't only the guys who could be cocky.

She smiled and rose from the chair to leave his office. It was six o'clock. Joe didn't spend the long hours in the office that he used to, but she still did. She had a gazillion emails to answer, clients to call, staff to deal with. As the account director, she was the go-to person for every detail of every project she oversaw.

Her office on the east side of the building was already dimmer, but the low summer sun illuminated the glass façade of skyscrapers facing the Lachman Building and they glittered against the clear blue sky. She spent the next few hours working until finally her stomach gave a hungry rumble. She lifted her head from her computer and used her right hand to massage the tense muscles of her left shoulder, then vice versa. She rolled her head around several times. Okay, maybe time to call it day.

She shut down her computer. At nearly eight o'clock on Monday night, most people had left. When they had a tight deadline some nights the office would be full of people going crazy, but not tonight.

But as she passed by Levi Wolcott's office, he was still there. She hesitated, then took two steps backward to the open door. "You're here late."

He'd shed the designer jacket and sprawled in the chair behind the desk, outstretched hand on the computer mouse. The golf shirt was casual but clearly expensive, hugging broad shoulders and a muscled chest, and revealing nice biceps. The arm holding the mouse was lean and sinewy, with veins tracing their way down to the back of his long-fingered hand. Narrow-fitting pants emphasized his long, long legs. The perfectly styled hair he'd arrived with that morning was now tousled. She closed her eyes briefly. She shouldn't be noticing his body. Then he flashed a smile at her, and she felt a flutter down low inside her belly.

Christ, that smile. He probably had women falling to their knees in front of him just because of that smile. But he apparently was getting married.

"Yeah," he said easily. "Getting up to speed."

She nodded, impressed in spite of her earlier

27

disapproval. Should she say anything about how they'd met? Or ignore that little detail? No, that wasn't her style. She opened her mouth to speak, but he beat her to it.

"I apologize again for disturbing you Friday night," he said, eyebrows drawing down over those gorgeous blue eyes. He straightened and leaned forward, conveying sincere regret. "I was trying to keep the guys quiet, but it was impossible." He grimaced. "I'm sure we disturbed more people than just you."

"You were trying to keep the guys quiet," she repeated. "Uh-huh." Easy for him to say that now. Sure hadn't sounded like it Friday night.

One corner of his mouth lifted. "You don't believe me. That's okay. That wasn't the best foot for us to start off on, and I'm sorry. But I know you're professional enough to set that aside and judge me on my work."

She pursed her lips, running her tongue over her teeth. "Good one." She nodded, a smile tugging at her lips. He was playing her.

He grinned.

That smile again nearly made her knees go weak. The dimples in his cheeks, the sparkle in his eyes, the white gleam of his teeth…it was lethal.

"But you're right," she acknowledged. "What you do in your private life is your business. What you do here is *our* business. And that is what you'll be judged on. Good night, Levi."

She caught the answering admiration in his eyes before she turned away.

"Good night, Ms. Granderson."

She should tell him to call her Sloane. Maybe tomorrow. Or next year.

She rode the elevator to the underground parking garage and climbed into her car for the short drive home, wondering how long Levi would stay at the office before heading home to his no doubt gorgeous fiancée. Again, she wondered if the fiancée knew the details of that bachelor party.

She replayed her conversation with Joe, rubbing her aching forehead. She'd need to nip this in the bud, given they had a new guy. They certainly didn't want him thinking that two-hour liquid lunches were acceptable, no matter that they were drinking the client's products.

Although, as she'd tried to suggest to Joe, there were worse things they could have done.

She let herself into her condo, her haven that had turned into hell the last few weeks. The construction guys were gone for the day, but some of their tools and supplies remained in a corner of the hall. She hated the chaos her home had become, the lack of privacy, most of all the utter lack of control she'd had over things. She knew she'd probably been the bitch client from hell, constantly on the contractor to make things happen *now*. It had driven her crazy when the vanity and sink she'd ordered had been delayed in shipping, meaning days had gone by where nothing could be done. When they'd finally arrived, the contractor had started another job and had to finish something there before they could get back to her place. There'd been days she'd thought she was going to explode from frustration.

She'd also hated the week when there was no plumbing and she'd been forced out of her home. Eric had let her stay with him but she probably would have been better off spending the week at a hotel since living with his personal chaos wasn't much better. He meandered in and out of his apartment without concern for moldy food in the fridge, the floor that needed sweeping or dirty towels in the bathroom. The time she'd spent cleaning and doing laundry had gone unnoticed. So much for trying to show her appreciation.

She headed straight to her beautiful new bathroom to inspect the latest work. Today they'd painted. The smell of fresh paint didn't help her headache, though she was glad this project was finally nearing completion. The baseboards and door casings had been painted off-site and would hopefully be put up tomorrow and that would be it.

She surveyed the tile floor, the big new shower, the old-fashioned claw-foot tub and sighed with pleasure. The condo didn't have an en suite bathroom and there wasn't enough room to have one built, so she'd compromised by giving up some closet space to enlarge this bathroom and add a door into the master bedroom. Her condo still had only one bathroom, but it was big and beautiful, with the toilet area and a small pedestal sink separate from the shower and bathtub area, which had another sink and a long vanity. This way, guests would see what appeared to be a powder room, while she could access all of it from her bedroom.

She'd lived here for three years now and she loved, loved, loved her home. She loved the old duplex with its red stone front, high ceilings, arched doorways and hardwood floors. She loved the fireplaces in the living room *and* bedroom, the kitchen that she'd renovated last year with its pristine white cupboards and granite counters, and she especially loved the tiny courtyard out back that was her own little green space. She loved the Gold Coast neighborhood too, so close to restaurants and shopping and even the beach and Lakefront Trail.

She changed into a pair of shorts and a tank top in her bedroom. The weather had been hot and humid for days now. She couldn't wait to get out into her tiny yard. In her kitchen, she pulled out some leftovers and set them in the microwave to reheat.

She moved to the back door and looked out into the courtyard. She'd spent much of yesterday out there pruning and deadheading. She hadn't known much about gardening when she bought this place, but it had developed into a hobby that gave her peace and satisfaction. She wasn't one to sit and do nothing, but there were moments when she poured herself a nice glass of red wine and sat in one of the comfy chairs on her patio admiring her plants and flowers. And she was going to do that tonight.

Eating by herself was more of a nuisance than a pleasure. She liked food, but living alone meant she usually tried to multitask while eating. Well, the truth was, she tried to multitask doing pretty much everything. She flipped through her mail while forking the leftovers into her mouth. She knew she should be more mindful and spend a few minutes enjoying her food, but who had time for mindfulness? Not her.

As she tidied the kitchen her phone rang. Eric. "Hey you," she answered.

"I need help."

She smiled as she wiped the counter. "What kind of help? I guess I sort of owe you."

"It's not that big. How do you get mustard out of a white dress shirt?"

"Oooh." She made a face. "I think your shirt might be toast."

"Shit."

"Did you try a stain remover?"

"That spray stuff?"

"Yes. What kind of fabric is it? You could also try bleach."

They discussed his laundry issue, she asked about the date he'd had on the weekend and if he was seeing her again—no—and then Eric ended the call to go try to salvage his shirt. She poured that glass of Cab and walked outside. The warm humid air caressed her bare skin.

Her mom had liked to garden.

For years after her mom had gone missing, Sloane hadn't thought about the big yard they'd had in Oakville. Her mom had spent a lot of time out there planting flowers and pruning shrubs. As a kid, Sloane hadn't had much interest in or appreciation for it. But when she'd bought this condo and had a small yard, she'd found herself researching plants on the Internet and visiting garden centers. Now she could see it was an attempt to bring back a little of her mom, to maybe connect with her and keep her with her.

She plucked a dead petunia, brushed her hand over a pot of impatiens, checked the soil to see if it was dry. In this hot weather, the smaller pots needed watering nearly every day. She set her wineglass on the glass-topped table and reached for the watering can to fill it from the rain barrel tucked in the corner.

The brick wall between her unit and the neighbors', the wall at the back of the property and the wall of the house on the other side created an outdoor room. The bay window of her kitchen with mullioned windows added character, and the neighbors' maple tree shaded the yard with big leafy branches. She'd coaxed vines to grow up the walls and had discovered through trial and error that there wasn't enough sun to grow some of the first flowers she'd attempted. She now had gorgeous hostas and exotic grasses, some columbine, day lilies, lamium and hydrangeas around the perimeter.

When the watering was done, she picked up her glass of wine and settled into one of the wicker chairs beside the table. Voices drifted over the brick wall between her yard and the one next door—low words, a soft laugh. The young couple who lived there, newly married and in love. Lovely for them.

Yes, there were moments when she felt very alone. Despite her love for her home, sometimes she wished she had someone to share it. But dating and relationships had never gone very well for her. In the last couple of years, she'd pretty much given up on that. She had a fulfilling career, which she loved, that required a lot of socializing with clients, and lots of acquaintances. At work she had Mason, her closest work friend. The two of them were so alike. They didn't talk about a lot of personal stuff, but they got each other.

She didn't believe a woman needed a man to be complete.

She sipped her wine and looked up at the blue sky above, turning a paler blue as the sun set—the color of Levi Wolcott's eyes.

◯﷼◯

Sloane was talking to Bailey Harris, one of their media buyers, about a problem with some advertising space in *Sports Illustrated* that was a part of a media plan Kaleb had developed when Levi Wolcott arrived at work the next morning. Late.

Very late.

She glanced at her watch, then at him with a raised eyebrow.

"Good morning." He flashed that devastating smile.

Bailey let out a soft little sigh.

Sloane cast her an irritated frown, though the smile gave her the same reaction. But he could not coast through life using that smile as a way to get away with whatever the hell he pleased.

"Good morning, Levi," she said crisply. "I'll be in my office in five minutes. Join me there."

"Sure." He gave Bailey a wink and continued into his own office.

"Find Kaleb and Noah," she said to Bailey. "We'll meet in my office in half an hour."

"Okay, Sloane. Thanks."

Bailey tapped away in high-heeled sandals. The advertising business wasn't one that had strict dress codes, but Sloane had taken Bailey aside shortly after she'd started at Huxworth Packard about a year ago to talk about her wardrobe. All the guys thought she was a cute, blonde ditz, and if that was the image she wanted, fine, but Sloane had seen that she was a bright young woman, and had teased out that she wanted to move up in the business. She wanted to work on the account side. Bailey hadn't realized the impression she was creating with the short skirts, tight tops and high heels she'd been wearing. Sloane had given her some advice, telling her she could still be feminine and stylish, but it was better if people noticed her brains rather than her…boobs.

The guys still noticed her boobs, of course. No getting around that when you were built like Bailey. Sloane smiled ruefully as she headed to her office.

Levi.

Damn him, he was going to make her do this on his second day there.

She got to her office before he did and took the seat behind her desk. Levi strode in moments later with the cup of Starbucks coffee he'd been carrying when he walked in. He looked just as good as he had yesterday, a casual sports jacket over a button-down shirt that he'd left untucked. The air of self-assurance and his confident smile made her…crazy. It made her chest tighten and her breathing go uneven.

This was ridiculous. She was an experienced businesswoman, an account executive who'd worked with swaggering creatives like him for many years. What was it about this guy that was pushing her buttons? She was better than this. Not only that, he was about to be married.

"Have a seat," she said with a sharp gesture. "And you might want to close the door."

"Sure." He did as she asked. "What's up?"

"You were late this morning."

He lifted his eyebrows. "Uh…a few minutes."

"We start at nine."

"I was here until nine last night."

His steady gaze almost made her throw her hands up. "That doesn't matter. Joseph Huxworth didn't see you here at nine last night. But he did see you come in at nearly ten this morning." She leaned forward. "I just want expectations to be very clear. We don't make our own hours here. There may be times we work long and hard, and sometimes that gives us the flexibility to have some time off. But you have to earn that. It's your second day here. You haven't earned it yet."

He held her gaze for a long, intense moment. His smile had faded but his face was neutral. "I understand," he said. "I apologize. It won't happen again."

"Thank you. That's all."

He rose, all tall and gorgeous, and left her office.

Crap. She resisted the urge to lay her head on her desk. Now she had to go give the other guys shit for the lunch stunt they'd pulled the day before.

4

Levi ground his back teeth together as he strode out of Sloane's office. What. The. Fuck. He'd never been treated like a child at AdMix. Was this what he'd signed on for? Christ. In his office, he threw himself down into his chair and let himself stew in anger for a few minutes, heat washing over him, rushing through his veins.

Just last night she'd assured him their first meeting would be left in the past and he'd be judged on his work. So much for that bullshit. She was clearly still pissed at him for Friday night, but come on. Seriously? A few hours of sleep and she was going to hold a grudge? For how long? Was he supposed to do penance for that?

Or was it for the sin of holding a bachelor party for his best friend? Again, seriously? He rolled his eyes. Was she that much of a pruda cuda that she couldn't tolerate some guys having a little fun? Jesus.

Maybe they'd cut him some slack at AdMix because he was their star, not minding when he came in late after a late night, or laid off early the odd Friday afternoon. Why they couldn't see that here at Huxworth Packard he had no fucking clue. Did they not see that One Show pencil sitting right there on his shelf?

Okay. Okay. He let out a long breath. He couldn't dwell

on this and let it interfere with work. He had shit to do.

He rolled up to his desk and tapped his keyboard to bring the screen to life. *There we go.* He and Scott were meeting at ten thirty to start throwing out some ideas. He had a few things to get done...a few emails already... He frowned at his computer. What the fuck? The cursor was out of control. He gave his mouse a hard shake and tried again. He stared in confusion as the cursor jumped around the screen. What was going on?

He sat back and frowned. He picked up his mouse and examined it. It looked fine. He rapped it on the desk a couple of times. Suddenly a Word document he had minimized appeared on the screen. He blinked.

His computer was going nuts. Fucking great. He'd have to call that IT guy, what was his name...He'd met him briefly yesterday when they got him set up on the network. Fuck, he couldn't remember his name.

He pushed his chair back, stood and strode out into the open area. He spotted Noah. "Hey Noah," he called. "My computer's acting weird. Who should I call?"

Noah turned to him. "Huh. Call Yoshi. His extension is 4819."

"Thanks."

Back in his office he made the call. Yoshi promised to be right up. Levi sat back down and watched his computer. It seemed fine now. He reached for the mouse and tried to minimize the Word document. It worked! Okay good, he'd call back Yoshi...then the Word document appeared again. Shit! What was he doing wrong? Then his email program appeared. And closed. Then Internet Explorer opened...and the image of a naked brunette on her knees being nailed from behind by some muscular dude appeared full screen.

"Jesus Christ!" he yelled.

"Problems, Levi?"

Fuck no! He closed his eyes, his heart giving a

sickeningly hard kick against his ribs. Not Sloane. But yes, it was. He turned to her. "No, no! Everything's fine."

"I heard you cursing as I walked by." She stepped into his office.

He threw out a hand. "Stay back!"

She frowned at him. "What is wrong with you?"

Dammit, she moved closer. Levi grabbed his mouse and frantically circled it on the desk. Nothing! Fucking *fucking* hell!

"What are you doing?" Again she came closer, still frowning, and then she froze as she saw his monitor.

"I don't know how that happened!" Levi said. "Seriously! My computer is doing weird things, it was out of control and it opened this site all by itself."

She crossed her arms and lifted an eyebrow, her chin lowered. "Oh my God."

"I'm not lying." Heat washed up from under his shirt and into his face. "Fuck me, something is wrong with my computer."

"I cannot believe this," she said tightly, turning and striding out of his office on those fucking sexy-as-hell legs, though how he could even notice that at this point when his career was spiraling downward like a turd in a toilet, he could not fathom.

At that point he became aware of distant laughter. He looked out the glass wall on one side of his office and saw Scott, Ravi, Owen and Dash collapsed over a desk. Tears were literally running down Owen's face. Dash rolled off the desk and hit the floor next to an upholstered chair. He pounded his fist on the seat, laying his face against it, still howling.

With a flash of realization, Levi knew…he'd been set up.

Oh for fuck's sake.

He was pretty tech savvy and couldn't believe he'd fallen for this. He bent his head to the computer and pulled out a tiny USB. He held it up to the guys and, with a grin, Scott held up the wireless mouse they'd been using to fuck him up. Levi reached beneath the desk and found the cord of his own mouse, disconnected.

He nodded. Once again, they'd got him. He was going to have to up his game here.

Reluctant admiration coursed through him. If it weren't for the fact that Sloane Granderson thought he was a total asshole, he'd be laughing right now. Had they planned that part too? Or was that just his fucked-up luck that she'd come by in the middle of his humiliation?

What to do, what to do?

He stood and strolled out of his office. "Nice one, guys," he said with a friendly smile. "You got me again."

They were still laughing so hard they couldn't speak.

Mason walked by and stopped at seeing the four men collapsed in laughter. "What the hell is going on?"

"Small joke." Levi pocketed the tiny USB. He was sure as shit not going to be the one to tattle to the boss.

"You should've seen your face," Ravi chortled. "And then Sloane walked in…"

Levi gritted his teeth again. "Yeah, about that—"

"What the hell did Sloane walk in on?" Mason demanded.

Oh yeah, right. Mason and Sloane were "tight". Whatever that meant. Levi eyed his boss, his mind racing as he tried to figure out how to handle this without throwing his coworkers under the bus. Though right then he personally wanted give each of them a hard fucking shove.

"You're gonna love this." Scott held up the wireless mouse to show Mason. "We took control of his computer. Opened up his browser to a porn site. Bwhahahaha!" He shook with mirth again.

Mason's lips twitched. He swallowed. "And that's when Sloane walked in?"

"Yep." Levi sighed. He didn't want to mention that she already thought he was a dickhead.

"Well, Levi, you're getting quite the initiation here with these assholes."

"Yes, I am."

"I'll explain it to Sloane," Mason said. "Now please, get to work, gentlemen."

Their hilarity passing, the guys managed to pull themselves upright and wipe away their tears.

"Did you plan for Sloane to come by then?" Levi demanded. "Or was that just my good luck?"

"We couldn't plan that," Owen admitted. "But damn, it couldn't have worked out better."

"We were gonna send in Bailey or Phoebe." Ravi named the two media buyers on the team. "But Sloane got there first."

Levi gave them a disbelieving look. "That's kind of asshole-ish to the ladies."

They frowned at him. "They can take a joke," Ravi said.

Well, he wasn't going to argue with them, but the last guy who'd said that to him had been slapped with a sexual harassment suit the next day. Jesus.

A short time later, once everyone had calmed down, Levi and Scott occupied two of the bright red armchairs in a far corner of the open space. Levi had another cup of coffee and he set it on the small table as he opened his notepad.

"Okay," he said. "Let's talk beer."

"I'd rather drink it," Scott said. "Ha."

Levi had studied the creative briefs they'd been given yesterday afternoon by Noah, signed off by the clients just last week. He'd done a shit ton of his own research too after learning what the problem was they were being asked to solve.

"So we have these 'craft beers'." He did air quotes with his fingers. "That now aren't really craft beers but we have to market them as craft beers."

"Yep."

Verhoeven had recently bought a number smaller craft breweries in an attempt to expand their market. All these newly acquired craft breweries required their own advertising strategies, and on top of that there was the ongoing work on Verhoeven's existing lines.

He was aware of a backlash another big beer company had experienced by marketing their so-called craft beers as such, claiming they were locally made and so on when they really weren't.

"Verhoeven wants us to target Millennials," Scott said. "Which I don't disagree with."

"Stats show that cohort is less likely to drink beer than Gen Xers."

Scott frowned.

"But," Levi continued. "Nearly half of all *craft* beers are drunk by Millennials. Millennials are more adventurous. When it comes to craft beers, they're more likely to try something new."

"How the hell do you know all this?" Scott fixed a narrow-eyed gaze on him.

Levi smirked inwardly. Scott thought he knew more about beer than him. "I did some research," he said casually.

"I guess that's true," Scott said slowly. "My dad drinks the same kind of beer he did when he was in his twenties. That's all he drinks. Ever. I take over a new kind of beer for him to try and he drinks one bottle, says it's good, and goes back to his Bud Light."

"Right. So Millennials are more adventurous. I get that. I'm a Millennial." Levi rolled his eyes. "Or close, anyway. I haven't picked one kind of beer and stuck to it. I like to try new things."

"As we clearly saw yesterday." Scott smirked.

Levi wasn't sure whether to laugh or punch him. He decided to laugh. "Fuck you." He shook his head. "We need to reach Millennials through a combination of traditional and social media. Not just billboards and magazine ads."

"I know that." Scott frowned.

"Of course you do," Levi said easily. "Just saying."

"We need to build their loyalty." Scott held up a Sharpie he was using to doodle on the notebook in front of him. "How do we reconcile that adventurous attitude with getting them to stick with our brands?"

"Great question. Even when they do commit to a brand, they're still interested in trying new things. But considering how many craft beers Verhoeven has now, they could try a new one every day for…well, a long time."

"I'm not sure of the exact numbers either, but yeah."

Levi scribbled some notes to himself. That was a point he wanted to spend more time thinking about. "Last year craft beers were the only beer category that had double digit growth in sales. Despite the higher prices."

Scott met his eyes with a challenging glare. "And nearly half the growth was from new drinkers, which was way up from the year before."

Yeah, yeah, you did some research too. I got it.

They continued to throw out random facts, trying to best each other. Thank Christ he'd stayed late last night to do some research.

"We know that craft beer drinkers expect a brewery to have numerous beers, not just one," Levi said.

"Seasonal beers," Scott said. "Lighter for summer. Different ones for fall and winter."

"Why do people drink craft beers?" Levi posed the question as he picked up some notes he'd made. "Fifty percent of people polled said they like to experiment with different flavors. Forty-six percent said they bought craft beers because they taste better."

Scott snorted. "Well, duh."

Levi smiled. "Thirty-six percent said they buy craft beers as a treat, sometimes as a gift."

"Definitely more impressive than a dozen light beer if you're giving someone a gift."

"Eighty percent of craft beers are drunk by white consumers in the twenty- to forty-five-year-old age bracket. The majority earn at least fifty grand a year and are college-educated."

"Meaning growth is with multicultural and lower income beer drinkers."

"Possibly." Levi did a doodle of his own. "So white male Millennials and Gen Xers are the number one consumers of craft beers. Our natural tendency is to market to that group, but there's still potential in other groups. What about women?"

"We'll never target a beer campaign to women. No client will ever go there." He gave him a you-are-an-idiot look.

Levi agreed inside, but shrugged. He knew better than to rule anything out in the early stages. "Consumption by women is about a quarter of all beer consumption. It's not growing, but there are indicators that women are more interested in beer. Especially craft beer."

Scott shook his head. "Okay, I'll give you that. But anything marketed to women is the kiss of death. Women hate that shit."

Levi grinned. "Yeah. Patronizing bullshit about light beer, low cal, fruity beer…that's not gonna go well."

"It has to be focused on quality and taste."

Levi sat back in his chair, not sure how this was going. It almost seemed like Scott didn't want to work with him. Or maybe he just felt he had something to prove… "So let's talk about men," Levi said.

"Huh?"

"As opposed to women who don't want beer to be fluffy and feminine, we men like manly things." Levi printed the word "manly" on his pad. "We're childish and immature. Witness the shenanigans that have occurred here over the last two days."

"Heh."

"Also we like women and we like to be flattered. Told

how great we are." He knew this to be true, because, hey, he was a guy. Nothing he liked more than beautiful women who stroked his ego. "We also like a challenge."

"And to win."

"Word."

"And we don't like to have our masculinity questioned. Is there anything unmasculine about drinking beer? If there is, we need to address that."

Again, Levi knew better than to dismiss the obvious. Beer was obviously a man's drink. He tipped his figurative hat to the most interesting man in the world. And those fucking "legends". Goddammit!

A surge of adrenaline flashed through his veins thinking of those amazingly successful campaigns. He wanted that. He wanted to do better than that. He fucking *would* do better than that.

"Competitive," he muttered, reflecting back on this whole discussion.

"Huh?"

"Men are competitive. As for anything unmasculine...the guys who drink spirits...sophisticated, tuxedo-wearing, shaken-not-stirred spirits...they make us beer drinkers look like rednecks."

Scott rubbed his chin.

"So how do we want to see ourselves?"

"Sexy."

Levi lifted an eyebrow.

"Chick magnet," Scott elaborated. "Like you." He rolled his eyes.

Levi frowned.

"Did or did not that waitress slip you her phone number yesterday?" Scott demanded.

"She did."

"There you go."

"Sophisticated?"

Scott considered that. "Maybe."

"So sexy, sophisticated, masculine, competent, the best at what we do."

"We want our egos stroked."

"Yeah, dammit." He paused. "Dominant."

Scott's eyebrows flew up.

Levi shrugged. His thoughts spiraled. He scribbled more notes. Things needed to percolate—or maybe that was ferment, ha—in his brain for a while.

"Time for lunch," he said.

He was on his way back to his office, when he ran into Sloane. "Hey," he said. "Listen, about earlier—"

"In my office," she snapped. "Now."

"Uh...okay, but did Mason talk to you?"

"About what? I haven't seen him."

Shit. Levi followed her into his office feeling like a truant schoolboy about to get spanked by the principal. Not that he was in any way opposed to spanking, but he preferred it to be done in the bedroom and liked to be the one delivering the spanking, preferably to a sweet little female ass.

Imagining Sloane naked and stretched over his lap with that round little ass right there immediately made things heat up down south and he clenched his jaw. Goddamn his inability to not think about sex.

She shut the door herself this time and leaned against it, arms crossed. Again, she looked amazing. Today's dress was pale gray with pink and blue flowers, cap sleeves and a deep V-neck, draped and fitted to her curves. The shoes were gray suede platforms with a killer heel. "Look," she said. "We give you guys lots of flexibility and freedom to do your job. We don't have lockdowns on our Internet access like some companies do. Facebook? Fine. Twitter? Part of the job. Do all the research you need to do. But watching porn during office hours? Not acceptable."

He tilted his head and pursed his lips. "Watching it outside of office hours is okay, though?"

Her eyes widened.

Fuck his smart-ass mouth. He sighed. "Sorry. I was making a joke. I wasn't watching porn earlier. Mason said he'd talk to you about it."

"What the hell were you doing? It's going to take a lot to convince me that was research!"

He swallowed a laugh. "The guys set me up. It was a practical joke. They had a wireless mouse and they jacked my computer from outside my office."

Her pretty eyes narrowed. "Are you kidding me?"

"Nope."

After a brief pause, she snapped, "I am going to kick their asses."

"No!" He held up a hand. "Christ, I don't want to get them in trouble. It was…kind of funny."

"It was juvenile and immature and unprofessional. This kind of behavior cannot continue."

Now his own eyes widened. "It was a joke," he said slowly. "No harm done."

She made a sound that almost was a growl, which oddly, made his dick stir again. She was fucking gorgeous with flushed cheeks and glittering eyes. She pushed away from the door. His eyes dropped to her bare legs. Damn, those shoes made him hard.

Oh man. This was not good.

5

"Who the hell hired that idiot?" Mason leaned back in his chair and regarded Sloane, looking calm and at ease in contrast to the anger and frustration simmering inside her. "Which particular idiot are you referring to?"

"Levi Wolcott."

"Ah. Well, that would be me. I hired him. And I'm pretty sure he's not an idiot. Is this about that incident this morning?"

"Yes!" She dropped onto the chair across from Mason's desk, perching on the edge. "I walked into his cube and my eyeballs were seared by what I saw."

"Come on, hon, you've never watched porn?"

"Mason."

His lips twitched. "It was a practical joke, Sloane."

"I know." She blew out a breath and her shoulders slumped. "That has to stop."

His eyes tightened at the corners. "Why? It's not like you to be so hard-ass. I mean, you totally *can* be a hard-ass." Her lips quirked. "But even though you're a suit, I know you have a sense of humor."

She sucked briefly on her bottom lip. "Joe wants me to clean up their 'bad boys of beer' reputation."

Mason blinked. "Ah."

"I get that he's worried about optics," she said, even though she despised that word. "How we're perceived by the client. Last week, the marketing guys from Wrigley did a drive-by." Their newest client. *Big* client. "They found the creatives sitting on the floor playing with LEGO."

"The dreaded drive-by," Mason murmured, setting his fingertips together.

"Yeah. I know they were trying to spur their creativity." She sighed again. "And I get that. So should Joe."

"He's been removed from the front lines for a while," Mason said. "His concern now is the bottom line."

"We're making money!"

"I know, I know. Relax, Sloane. Look at you. Your hands are about to snap the arms of that chair. You're wound so tight when you release everybody better stand back."

"That could be true," she murmured, loosening her grip on the chair. She rubbed at the tightness behind her breastbone. "I wish people would just do what I say!"

Mason laughed. "Oh, honey, I know. It drives you crazy when you can't control everything, doesn't it?"

"Yes."

She gave Mason a wry smile. He got her. With him, she felt like she could let down her guard a little and let him see the real her inside. And yet…there was only friendship between them.

Not that he wasn't an attractive man. Only five years older than her, he had a sexy, mature handsomeness, fine lines at the corners of his eyes that fanned out when he smiled, a muscular and solid build with a flat abdomen and broad shoulders. There were shadows in his eyes, though, hints of a darkness he kept locked up behind his easygoing façade that she recognized…because she had them too. They'd never shared a lot of details but understood that about each other. Of anyone at Huxworth Packard, he was the one she was closest too, but it had never been anything sexual or romantic. Mason was a serial dater and made it clear he had no intention of ever settling down with one woman or starting a family. Her intuition told her something in his past had made him that way, and she got it because she'd never been able to commit to someone either.

"I've always appreciated working for a company that valued quality work above billings," she said slowly. "I don't want that to change."

"I don't think it is."

"You know how shitty that is," she mused. "When the team comes up with something, something *great*, and we're sitting in a meeting with the client and they don't like it and suddenly I'm all, yeah, that idea never really worked—taking their side."

"You don't do that," he murmured.

"Sure I have. And hated myself after. I still do it, but I've learned to do it more diplomatically."

He smiled.

"But I feel caught in the middle," she said. "Between the client and the creatives. The client is always right. Right?"

"You know they're not always right."

She exhaled again. "Yes, but in the end, they're always right. And same with Joe. He's the boss. He's always right. We do what he says. He says clean up their image, I clean up their image."

"I get it, Sloane." His dark eyes softened. "Look, I'll talk to the guys, okay?"

She hesitated. Joe had asked her to deal with it. But Mason was directly responsible for them. And she trusted him. "Okay."

"I've always got your back, hon."

She slumped back into the chair. "I know. And thank you."

"Wanna get lunch?"

"Yeah. Let's do that."

They went to the restaurant on the main floor of the building, and were shown to a table out on the patio right next to the Chicago River. Pots of bright flowers decorated the railing, and colorful umbrellas shaded tables from the brilliant midday sun.

As they took their seats, Sloane glanced around and spotted Levi sitting at a table with Phoebe, Bailey and Carly. Her eyebrows flew up but she quickly schooled her features into a neutral smile, acknowledging them with a lift of her hand and a smile.

"Geezus," she muttered, menu up in front of her face. "Second day on the job and he's having lunch with *three women*?"

"Um, Sloane, honey…is there something else you want to tell me?"

She lowered her laminated menu and frowned at Mason. "What do you mean?"

He leaned closer across the table and lowered his voice. "You seem to have a hate on for Levi Wolcott. Yeah, he was the victim of a bit of hazing, but…he hasn't actually done anything wrong."

She blinked and lowered her gaze back to the menu. Damn. She swallowed.

"Give the guy a break," Mason continued.

"For one thing, he's engaged to be married," she muttered.

Mason just shrugged. "He's having lunch. Probably safer with three girls than one."

"And I don't like his attitude," she continued. "All cocky and confident and…" Charming. Sexy. "Strutting like he's Prince Levi of Wolcott."

Mason choked on a laugh. "Uh. Okay. Again, though, you know if he walks into Huxworth Packard *without* that kind of attitude, he's gonna get crapped on. Those pranks the guys did would've been way worse. He handled them like a champ. You know he's gotta have a little attitude or they'll steamroll right over him."

She pursed her lips. "I think I'll have the Southwest blackened chicken salad."

Mason grinned. "Way to change the subject. You know you're only piquing my curiosity."

"There's nothing to tell. Like I said, he just rubbed me the wrong way, the way he strutted in here."

Rubbed me the wrong way. That made her think of Levi's hands on her, rubbing, petting, stroking... She blinked rapidly and turned to look at a tour boat cruising along the river. She could not be thinking things like that about Levi Wolcott. That was just...eeeeew.

Well, not exactly. It was actually disturbingly erotic.

It wasn't her fault. How could she not associate him with sex after listening to him and his friends and that...that hooker, or whatever, Friday night, doing sexy things? Since she'd met him, the images her mind conjured up were even more vivid and erotic. Him naked.

She made a sound in her throat and then turned at Mason's chuckle.

"You okay?"

"I'm fine. So. How are things going with the new campaigns?"

"They're working on them. All four teams. Levi and Scott seem to be hitting it off."

"That's good," she said crisply.

The waitress appeared to take their orders, and they spent the rest of their lunch talking shop. Sloane tried not to be aware of Levi lunching with the three girls, but every time she heard his low laugh or one of the ladies' higher pitched laughs, her muscles tightened. When she and Mason left the patio, the four of them were still there.

She paused by their table. "Hey all," she said with a smile. "Heading back to work now?"

"Yes, just waiting for Levi's credit card," Bailey said quickly.

She caught the way Levi's mouth tightened at her question.

"He bought us lunch," Carly said. "Isn't that nice?"

"Lovely." She gave Levi a smile that was just a crinkling of her eyes. "See you back in the office."

In the elevator, Mason rubbed his forehead. "Jesus. I'm not sure if *I* want to work here anymore."

She stared at him. "What?"

"It's lunch, Sloane."

She frowned. "Yeah, says you, famous for four-hour lunches."

"Working lunches. And don't tell me you've never had a long lunch with a client. Because I've been right there with you."

She was being a bitch. She knew it. Dammit.

The Verhoeven account was important. They were a huge client with tight delivery dates and big expectations. Verhoeven had made it clear that if this ad campaign didn't meet their expectations they would be putting the account up for review, meaning they could potentially lose it. So not only did they have to deliver, they had to do it quickly and they had to do it spectacularly. She was dealing with communications people and management from several different brands of beer now under the Verhoeven umbrella, which had been a pretty damn big umbrella to start with. She was still working to get to know some of these new businesses. Joe counted on her to keep everyone happy. And that meant keeping the boys out of trouble.

She'd bemoaned the lack of women creatives at Huxworth Packard before. Would things be different if they had more females on the team? She'd never wanted to accuse the company of sexism in hiring; she knew Mason for sure wasn't sexist. She herself was a testament to the fact that they did hire and retain women, but she was the only female on the beer account. There'd been a few female copywriters over the years but for various reasons they always moved on. Mason was right. You did have to be tough to survive in this world. If women ran the world... She laughed at herself as she walked into her office. If she ran the company... *Oh stop.* She had things to worry about here and now, not crazy ideas like that.

She stopped at the ladies' room before going to her office and was in a stall when the outer door opened and female voices reached her ears.

"He is soooo hot," she heard Carly say.

Oh sweet loving Lord.

"I know!" Phoebe chirped as she entered a stall and shut the door. "Gorgeous but really nice too. Hillary Bayard is so jealous he's working in our department."

"He's okay," Bailey said.

Sloane blinked.

"Oh come on," Phoebe said. "He's way more than just okay. And he's single, so hey, all's fair."

Single? He told them he was single? What the hell! What kind of douche bag was he?

"He seems like a player," Bailey said. "I mean, he's nice, but from what he was saying, he seems like the kind of guy who just likes to sleep around a lot."

Sloane frowned.

"Every guy is like that until he meets the right woman," Carly said.

Sloane rolled her eyes.

"I agree," Carly continued. "All's fair. And I like him."

Oh for Chrissakes. Sloane repressed a groan and exited the stall to quickly wash her hands and escape before the girls included her in their little Levi love fest.

A week later, Levi was about to admit defeat.

It was eight o'clock on Wednesday evening. What a long fucking day.

Had taking this job been a mistake?

He ordered a beer — yes, a Cerone lager — sitting at the bar at Hugo's, located across the street from the Lachman Building. It wasn't full, but there were still a number of guys in suits and professional-looking women occupying tables and stools at the long polished oak bar.

He leaned his elbows on the bar and gulped a fizzy mouthful of beer. His head throbbed and his body felt like he'd been worked over by Floyd Mayweather. Repeatedly.

In the last week he'd been the victim of countless practical jokes. When the guys had tampered with his mouse, they'd also set autocorrect in Word so that it replaced the word "client" with "nutsucker". The first time he'd typed up a fast document and sent it off to Mason and Noah, all proud of his research for the Cedar Springs brand, Noah had forwarded it to Sloane before reading it, and then shit had hit the fan.

Mason had apparently had a chat with the boys about their bad behavior, and then they'd been even pissier. The next day Levi had walked into his office and sat on his chair, and it had immediately dropped to the lowest level, damn near giving him a heart attack. The fuckers had somehow rigged the lever with a pencil and as soon as he put weight on it, it popped out and the seat dropped. Of course this didn't happen when he was alone. It happened when Mason was in his office. At least that time it wasn't Sloane.

Why was he such a target? He was a great guy. He got along with everyone. Well, barring Sloane. Scott seemed to be softening up. And okay, he was kinda not feeling Owen so much. The pranks from the other guys felt like just innocent fun, but Levi sensed Owen had a nasty streak in him. Maybe jealousy. Sure there was competition between all of them. But come on, they were adults.

Well. Sort of adults. He couldn't resist a tiny little payback. He'd waited for the perfect moment when Scott's computer had been left unattended. It didn't take long before people were howling. Every time they emailed Scott, his auto-reply gave the message *I will be out of the office for the next two weeks for medical reasons. When I return, I will be known as Nancy rather than Scott.*

Of course Sloane had heard about all these things and freaked the fuck out, calling *all* of them into a meeting and reaming their asses out. The saddest part of that was, she was so fucking gorgeous in her wrath he'd gotten a semi during the meeting. He'd had to slouch lower in his chair so the board table would hide it, and then Sloane had looked at him with slitty eyes that had raked over his slouched posture and said, "Are you listening to me?"

She'd also continued to ride his ass about showing up at work on time and not taking long lunches. And he'd gotten the distinct impression she wasn't happy about him taking out Bailey, Carly and Phoebe for lunch that day. Well, fuck that bullshit. He'd have lunch with whomever he wanted.

He downed the beer and rested his head on one hand.

Not only that, he still hadn't come up with the genius ideas that were going to blow everyone's boxers off. Especially for the big Cerone television ads. They were there, teasing the edges of his mind, so close. He and Scott had come up with some great ideas, sure. But he and Scott were...different. It wasn't easy, like things had been with Fergus. But fuck, if those assholes would just leave him alone and quit messing with his head, maybe he'd get this done.

No doubt that was their intent. New guy in the office had to learn his place.

Well, maybe his place was out the goddamn door.

He'd wanted so much to be one of the "Brew Crew", as

they called themselves. He'd gotten the narrow-eyed looks from copywriters in other departments who'd clearly wanted his job. The guys working on fucking cereal. Everyone wanted to work on the beer account. Now he was starting to wonder why.

Someone slid onto the stool beside him. He turned and his heart lurched at the sight of Sloane.

She met his eyes, a veil of wariness in hers. "Hey," she said. "I thought that was you."

He straightened. "Uh, hi." She thought it was him and still came to sit with him? That was weird.

"You okay?"

He blinked at her, not moving any other muscle in his face. As usual, her beauty rendered him an idiot. Her blonde hair brushed her shoulders, curving under her chin. Her eyes were big and shadowy, and her small pouty lips made him want to bite them. Today she wore a sleeveless pink blouse tucked into a pale gray pencil skirt and her usual spiky heels.

"Of course." Usually his smile was easy to summon up no matter how shitty he felt, but at that moment, it had deserted him.

She lifted one shoulder. The bartender appeared and she glanced at Levi's empty glass. "I'll buy you a drink." She turned to the bartender. "Another of those. And I'll have the same."

"Never would have pegged you as a beer drinker," Levi said.

The corners of her sexy mouth lifted. "Why not?"

He shrugged. "You strike me as an expensive red wine kind of girl. Say, a nice bottle of Château Canon-la-Gaffelière Saint-Émilion."

Her perfectly arched eyebrows rose. "Wow. I'm impressed. Although I don't even know what that is, so you could totally be bullshitting me."

"Yeah, I could be. I'm a good bullshitter."

Her lips twitched and she shook her head. "And so modest."

"Modesty's for pussies." He was screwed no matter what. Might as well say what he was really thinking.

Her scent drifted to him, something luscious and expensive-smelling...raspberry and flowers and some kind of exotic spice...carnal passion in a fragrance. His cock stirred. What the fuck kind of perfume was that? It made him crazy.

Where was that damn beer?

"Seriously," she said. "Is that a real wine?"

"Yeah."

"How'd you know that?"

He tilted his head to look at her. "My mom used to put it in my baby bottle."

She choked on a laugh.

"Okay, maybe not," he conceded. "But my folks drink shit like that all the time."

"Shit like that." Amusement gleamed in her beautiful blues. "Who are your folks?"

"My dad owns Wolcott International."

Her eyes widened briefly. "Ah. No wonder, then."

Yeah, his parents were filthy rich. Yeah, he'd grown up drinking hundred-dollar bottles of wine for Sunday dinner. Whatever.

Their beers arrived and he picked his up and chugged back half of it. Sloane took a delicate sip. She was no fucking beer drinker.

"How is it?" he asked.

"Good. Um...it's a lager, right?"

One corner of his mouth kicked up. "Good guess."

"Hey, I'm no expert, but I'm learning."

"Of course you are. Part of the job, right?"

"Right." She eyed him with a hint of uncertainty. "You sure you're okay? You seem kind of...down."

He inspected his beer. He wasn't about to admit that

57

he'd been feeling defeated, wondering if he'd made a huge fucking mistake giving up a great job at AdMix. "I'm good," he finally said. "Long day."

She was silent for a few moments, then said, "Look, I'm sorry about that meeting earlier."

His eyebrows pulled together. "You don't have to be sorry about anything," he said slowly. "You're the boss. You tell us what to do. We do it."

"That's not the kind of boss I want to be."

Her words surprised him. And when he glanced at her, he thought maybe she'd surprised herself.

"And anyway, I'm not your boss. We all know the account people are here to serve you...the creatives."

He liked hearing that. It was true, but some suits didn't get that. He appreciated that Sloane did.

"I know you're used to being number one. The star."

He pursed his lips and gave a very brief nod of acknowledgement.

"You're very good at what you do." She further surprised him. "Give it time."

"I was actually just thinking maybe I made a big mistake coming to Huxworth Packard."

She sighed. "Here's the thing. I shouldn't be telling you this, but I want you to know it's not personal. Joseph Huxworth is concerned about the reputation you guys have. You, as in the Brew Crew. He's concerned that it doesn't reflect well on the company."

Levi turned and stared at her. "This is coming from him?"

"Yes."

He thought about that. "Is it because of me?" He knew he hadn't made a great impression that first day.

She rolled her eyes. "No, Levi, the world doesn't revolve around you, much as you might think it does."

A slow smile spread across his face. "You're really bursting my bubble here."

She laughed, and it was a feminine, lighthearted sounded that tugged at something inside his chest. His skin tingled everywhere.

"You're really pretty when you smile," he blurted.

One eyebrow shot up. "Now there's backhanded compliment."

"Fuck! I didn't mean...I mean, you're always pretty. Shit." He shook his head. He was usually way better at this. Compliments generally flowed smoothly from his lips. But this was Sloane and he should not be telling her she was pretty. "You know that's not what I meant."

She grinned. "I know. I'm yanking your chain."

Her sexy grin had his blood running hot in his veins. "You actually have a sense of humor."

Her lips tightened. Oops. "Of course I do."

He exhaled sharply. "I'm sorry. I didn't mean to insult you again." He held up his glass. "I'm blaming the booze."

"How many have you had?"

"This is my second."

She snorted. "Lightweight."

It took a second for his brain to process the teasing insult. Not because of the booze. Just because...it was Sloane. And because fuck, he liked it. "I'll have you know I was the boat racing champion of Omega Kappa Kappa."

She shook her head slowly from side to side, a smile tweaking her sweet lips. "Frat boy," she murmured. "I should have known."

"And proud of it." He toasted her with his glass.

"Where'd you go to college?"

"U of C."

"Of course."

He grinned. "Don't give me that. I worked hard in college."

"While mastering boat racing."

He shrugged. "I have many talents."

Okay, that sounded kind of dirty. If he'd been with any other chick, he would've accompanied it with a wink and maybe a shoulder nudge. But...this was Sloane.

Their eyes met with a flash of sparks that told him she was also thinking about what his many other talents might be. And dammit, he wanted to show her.

6

"I'm sure you do," Sloane murmured.

Oh God.

She wasn't even sure why she'd approached Levi at the bar. She'd just finished having dinner with clients and had spotted him sitting there. She'd paused and taken in how dejected he'd looked. Something had turned over in her chest and she'd found herself walking across the bar toward him.

He'd put on a good face, of course, denying anything was wrong, but the slump in his shoulders and the absence of his usual cocky smile gave him away. And she found herself wanting to make him feel better.

She should have known better than that. She'd learned early in her career that caring too much about the people you worked with only got you booted in the chops. The person you cared about and helped today was the person who'd steal a promotion or a client away from you tomorrow.

Wow, when had she gotten so cynical? She gave herself a mental shake.

Somehow she'd coaxed a smile and a joke out of him and now they were sitting there, the air around them buzzing with tension, and her thighs tightening.

Damn, he was gorgeous. He knew it too, but his confidence had enough humor that he came across as charming and not an asshole. Every girl in the office had a crush on him, and he was winning the guys over. Those mesmerizing light blue eyes reminded her of a blue zircon ring her mother had owned, and his mouth…holy hell, the firm shape of his lips and the way they curved into a smile made her girl parts squeeze.

He was also getting married. Although others in the office seemed to think differently.

"That night at the hotel," she began.

He grimaced. "Yeah."

"Was that *your* bachelor party?"

His forehead creased. "No. It was for my buddy Jacob. Christ! I'm not getting married!"

She nodded. So he *was* single.

"You thought that was *my* bachelor party?"

She shrugged. "I assumed, yeah."

"You know, it really was pretty innocent."

"I was there, remember?"

"Yeah, I remember. But I don't know what you heard. We hired this topless waitress from the Kitten Club— Scarlet. She came and served us drinks and did a few lap dances. We played some games, but there was no sex. There are strict rules when you hire a girl from the Kitten Club. It's a classy place. You can't even touch her."

For some reason, this earnest speech made her chest go weirdly soft and warm. She tipped her head to one side and slowly shook it, smiling. "You're serious."

"Yeah." The notch between his thick eyebrows deepened.

"I believe you," she assured him, and she did. What had she really heard? Although she'd been listening for any sounds of trouble, there'd mainly been a lot of laughter, including from, er, Scarlet. "It's just sort of…cute."

Now his eyes flew open. "Cute? Uh, that wasn't what you were thinking that morning when I ran into you in the hall."

"No. It's cute that you say it was all innocent when really, anything could have happened. I mean...sure, they have strict rules, but come on. Who's there to enforce them? That young woman was there all alone in a hotel room with a group of men she didn't know. Completely vulnerable. Anything could have happened to her."

"Not with us," he protested. "We're great guys."

His firm belief that that girl had been completely safe with them touched her. She huffed out a little laugh. "I did hear...something about..." She stopped.

"What?"

"She told someone he could come on her breasts."

He grimaced. "Uh, yeah. That was Jacob. The bachelor. But he couldn't touch her. He was just, you know...pumping gas at the self-serve island."

After a beat, she burst out laughing. "Oh my God."

He grinned. "If you get my meaning."

"I get it."

Their eyes met again and the way he looked at her, the focused intensity of those pale blue eyes, made her stomach do a slow roll of lust. Heat built between them. She picked up her beer and took a big gulp of the cold brew.

"My buddy Tucker was the one who hired her," Levi continued. "I booked the hotel room. I wasn't sold on the idea, but Tucker and Cam insisted we had to do something really good for Jacob's bachelor party."

"So that was you who dealt with hotel security?"

One corner of his mouth kicked up. "Yeah. I kept trying to get them to quiet the hell down, but they were all hammered and having fun." He paused. "I'm sorry we disturbed you."

"You said so that morning."

"It was thoughtless and stupid and a whole lot of alcohol and testosterone and…what can I say? We were having fun. Guys are idiots."

She smiled, more heat pooling low in her belly. She licked her bottom lip and when his gaze dropped there, she realized that had been a mistake. The way he looked at her mouth, as if he was famished, made her toes curl.

"Have you eaten?" she asked.

"Uh, no." He met her eyes again. "Why?"

She closed her eyes briefly. "I just wondered."

"I thought maybe you were going to offer to buy me dinner *and* a drink."

"I just had dinner."

"Oh."

She'd thought he was teasing but was that a flash of disappointment in his eyes? "But you should probably eat something."

"Yeah, probably."

And she should probably leave him to it. "So, order something. I'll keep you company."

He reached for a menu, leaning closer to her so that his chest brushed her shoulder. Again the air crackled with excitement and ripples danced through her stomach.

"Will you share some mussels with me?" he murmured a moment later, looking at the laminated card of food items available in the bar.

"I could eat a few, I guess."

He caught the eye of the bartender and ordered, and Sloane wasn't oblivious to how fast the female bartender hustled over and fluttered her eyelashes at Levi.

"So the guys have been giving you a hard time this week."

Now, he turned on his stool so he was directly facing her. His knees brushed her hip. "I can handle it."

"I know what's going on. We may have gotten off to a

rough start, but I know you're not calling our clients dicklickers on purpose."

"It was nutsuckers," he said, correcting her.

"My mistake." She paused. "It *was* kind of funny."

"You didn't think it was funny when you walked into my office and saw that chick on my computer, getting nailed from behind."

She bent her head, setting her fingertips to her forehead. "I have to admit I was a bit stunned. Especially after I'd just heard what I thought was either an orgy or a gang bang in the hotel room next door to me and knew you were part of it."

He choked on his beer. "Jesus Christ."

"But Mason talked me down," she added. "And then I was reluctantly admiring of their evil genius."

"It wasn't so genius," he scoffed. "It was just dumb luck that you happened to walk in at that moment. If nobody else had seen it, it would have been a fail."

"True." She drank more of her beer.

"So, uh, you and Mason…"

She turned her head and gave him a look. "Me and Mason what?"

"The guys tell me you two are…what was the word…tight."

God, even that word made her think dirty thoughts, coming out of his mouth. "We're friends."

He nodded. "That's it?"

"Yes."

"You don't wear a ring so I gather you're not married."

"No."

"Boyfriend?"

"No." She hitched one shoulder. "No time for a relationship."

"Ah ah ah. That's no good."

She swiveled her stool so that her knees were alongside his and they were now both facing each other.

"From what I hear about you, you don't have time for a relationship either." She'd felt sorry for his nonexistent fiancée.

He grinned. "I have time. I just don't want one."

"Ah."

"You know what they say about all work and no play."

"All work and no play makes Jill financially independent."

He laughed. "Well, there is that. But you still gotta have time for fun."

"I have fun."

"How?"

She blinked. "I, um, garden."

"Sounds exciting."

"I have other hobbies." Not many. Ugh. "I work out. In the winter, I teach figure skating."

His chin lowered. "Figure skating?"

"Yeah." She shrugged. "I competed when I was younger. I teach kids on weekends."

"Huh. That's cool." His blue eyes glowed with hot sexuality. "But still. I get the feeling you need to have more fun, Sloane."

She sucked in a long breath through her nose. He was turning her on and making her want things she shouldn't. Especially with him.

The mussels arrived along with some warm crusty bread. She hadn't eaten a huge meal at dinner so she was able to sample a few of them.

"These are really good," she said a few moments later.

"Are mussels supposed to be an aphrodisiac?" Levi asked, holding a shell in one hand and a fork in the other.

"I think that's oysters."

"Oh. Okay. Because looking at these is totally making me think of something else." He held out the shell and she looked at the flesh inside it. Yep, a definite resemblance to female genitalia.

She rolled her lips in and met his dancing eyes. "You have a dirty mind."

"Yeah. I eat perv cereal for breakfast."

She laughed. "So, frat boy. When's your friend getting married?"

"In two weeks. I'm the best man."

"Of course you are."

"What does that mean?"

"The day after you started, I told Mason you strutted around like Prince Levi of Wolcott." She eyed him. "Though little did I know, that's pretty much true. I guess growing up in the Wolcott family was kind of like growing up as royalty."

"Eh. I don't know about that."

She nodded, appreciating that he didn't launch into a description of their mansion or how many maids they had or their European vacations. In fact, he said nothing.

And again, she found herself warming to him.

When the mussels had been eaten, they turned on their stools to face each other and finish their beers, and now somehow her knees ended up between his spread ones. She looked down at his big thighs in black dress pants on either side of her bare knees primly pressed together and it was…erotic.

They'd flirted and laughed and talked a little dirty. Attraction hummed between them, and she sensed he was feeling it too, a warm buzz of sexual tension. Of course, from what she knew of him, she could have been a potato and he'd be humming with sexual tension. The alcohol from the glass of wine she'd had at dinner and the beer also created a tiny buzz, which was probably why she didn't slap his hand away when he reached out to move a strand of hair off her face.

"You have gorgeous hair," Levi said. "But then, you're pretty much gorgeous all over."

This was what she expected from him…confidence and

67

warm flattery that made her insides flutter. To distract herself from that, she said, "Earlier you told me I'm only pretty when I smile."

He'd been flustered then, as if he'd lodged one of his Prada shoes in his throat, but she was teasing him. Now he just smiled. A slow smile that radiated sex and sin. Temptation. "I did not say that."

When he lowered his hand, he set it on her bare knee. Tingles raced up her thigh, then up her spine. She breathed in. And out. She should be moving his hand away. She should be running out of there. His palm was warm on her skin, and his thumb brushed back and forth on the inside of her knee. She imagined his touch sliding higher up her thigh…and she wanted that. Heat washed down through her and she almost moaned out loud.

Their eyes met again. "Are we going to do this?" he asked, his voice low and rough.

She again swiped her tongue over her bottom lip. Her nipples tightened into hard, tingling points. Heat shimmered between them.

This was crazy. She was so attracted to him, on so many levels. She knew it was wrong. But the vulnerability he'd displayed, so at odds with his usual confident, cocky air, pretty much obliterated her good sense, and any resistance to him had vanished. "We need to pay the bill."

Without a word, he reached for his wallet, pulled out several bills and tossed them onto the bar.

"I was going to buy *you* a drink," she protested even as he was sliding off his stool. He took her hand to help her down, melting her insides a little more.

"Fuck it," he muttered. "Let's go."

"Where are we going?" He held her hand as he led them out of the bar. She tapped along with him in her heels.

"My place."

She couldn't believe she was going to say this… "The office is closer."

He halted. Paused. Then kept going. "No way. No fucking way."

She hurried to keep up with his long strides down the sidewalk. The sun had just set and the lights of the skyscrapers twinkled around them against the pale blue sky. "You're probably right."

They entered the building lobby and he punched the elevator button to go down. At this time of day, the elevator car was right there, and they stepped in and descended to the parking garage. He led her straight to a gorgeous silver Mercedes convertible.

"Nice car."

"Thanks."

Copywriters didn't make *that* much money. But oh yeah…he was a Wolcott. And also, he'd worked on the Mercedes account.

He drove with the same casual confidence he did everything else, zooming out of the parking garage and onto South Wacker, negotiating traffic across the bridge then turning right.

"Where do you live?" she asked, while in the back of her mind a little voice chanted, *You're crazy, don't do this, you're crazy, don't do this.*

She ignored the pesky voice, buzzing attraction and the warm ache in her pussy overriding good sense.

"East Illinois. Near Lake Shore."

"Nice."

"It's decent."

And it wasn't far, luckily. Minutes later they were again in an elevator, riding to the twenty-first floor. When he unlocked the door to his condo, she halted as a small shape hurtled at them in the darkness.

"Chuck!" Levi flicked a light switch and bent to pick up a dog.

The dog wriggled and whined and swiped his tongue at Levi. He paused, looked at Sloane, then went back to attacking Levi with kisses.

"This is Chuck," Levi said. "Chuck, this is Sloane."

"You just introduced me to a dog."

"Of course. He needs to know who you are."

She rolled her eyes, smiling. "A spaniel?"

"King Charles. Hence the unimaginative name." Levi set the dog down and Chuck approached her, feathery tail wagging. She leaned down and held out the back of her fingers for him to sniff. "Do you like dogs?"

She stared at the dog, her throat going tight. "Sure," she said casually. "He's adorable." The middle of his face was white, with a cute black button nose and big brown eyes, his ears were brown and his body was patched with brown and white. She wanted to pick him up and squeeze the breath out of him. He wasn't the same kind of dog Teddy had been, but the face was so similar it made her stomach hurt.

She straightened. "How do you look after him, working such long hours?"

"I hired a kid to take him out for a walk every day." Levi moved into his condo. "Hang on, I have to get him a treat." He strode over to the counter separating kitchen from living room and lifted the lid off a container to pull out a dog biscuit. "Colin's fourteen. He was looking for a way to make money. I saw a flyer posted in the store on the corner and gave him a call. Turns out he lives right in this building. So every day after school he comes and gets Chuck and takes him over to the park. Sit."

"Well, okay."

It was a joke—sort of, because when he said "sit" in that commanding voice, she really wanted to...sit. He'd been talking to Chuck. But he sent her such a scorching hot look she thought her panties might have melted.

Chuck's wiggling butt hit the hardwood floor. Levi tossed him the small biscuit and he caught it.

"Good boy," Levi praised, with a smile for the pup that hurt her chest. Then he looked up at her and the smile changed from affectionate to carnal. "Okay, now where were we?"

She resisted the urge to hurl herself into his arms as Chuck had. Second thoughts crowded the back of her brain, but Levi walked toward her with lazy masculine grace, oozing charm and sex, pushing those thoughts aside.

He closed the distance between them and set his hands lightly on her hips. "Oh yeah. Now I remember. I was about to do this." He bent his head and kissed her.

Her brain sizzled and snapped into emptiness. His mouth was warm and firm and tasted delicious. He didn't rush it. He gave her one long, soft kiss, lifted his lips from hers then kissed her again, gently opening wider and deepening the kiss. His tongue licked over her bottom lip and then his teeth gently nipped her there.

"I've wanted to do that since the first time I saw you." He stroked over her lip with his tongue again. "You have a very biteable mouth."

She swallowed, her knees wobbling a little. She set her hands on his chest. "Thank you."

"Not to mention other parts of you." He kissed her again, this time his tongue fully sliding into her mouth. She licked him back and curled her fingers into his shirt. Fire spread through her body.

"I wanna make a confession," he murmured long moments later, his lips on her cheek.

"What's that?"

"This afternoon, when you were chewing us out, I got hard." He sucked gently on the skin just below her jaw. "That's why I was slouching."

"Oh my God." Her fingers flexed in his shirt as sparks

rushed through her veins and her stomach did a lusty little flip.

"You were all fiery and bossy and all I wanted to do was punish you for making me hard in the boardroom."

She sucked in air sharply.

"I wanted to turn you over my knee and spank that tight little ass, and then make you come so hard."

That was it. Her knees gave out. Luckily his hands were on her and he pulled her up hard against him. Oh sweet geezus, that felt good. She breathed in his scent, deliciously male and citrus-spicy, savoring the feel of his muscular body against hers. And his erection.

God, he'd just articulated one of her most secret fantasies.

A moan slipped out from her lips as he wrapped his arms around her, crushing her breasts to his chest, and kissed her again, this time harder, with forceful tongue and voracious desire. She kissed him back, out of her mind, yes, but damn, he was a good kisser and he tasted good and smelled good and felt so good... *God.*

The room spun around her. Levi's hands went to her ass, then lifted her against him. She tried to wrap her legs around him, but the result was a ripping sound from the back of her skirt.

"Shit."

"Love the tight skirt," Levi muttered. "But right now it's in the way." He lowered her feet back to the floor, tugged the zipper down, then worked the skirt down over her hips. It dropped to the floor and then he lifted her again and this time she was able to hook her legs around his hips. "Keep the heels on. They're fucking hot as hell."

With their mouths fused and hands all over each other, he carried her across the room and down a short hall into his bedroom.

7

Levi was dying, burning up, Sloane's ass in his hands, her hands in his hair. Her thong panties left her curves bare for his pleasure, and he carried her into his bedroom and reluctantly sat her on the side of the bed while he turned on the lamp.

Gorgeous. Her normally smooth blonde hair was tousled around her face, her lips even poutier than usual. She set her hands on the bed on either side of her, legs bare from the hem of her blouse to her toe cleavage, knees together, high heeled shoes flat on the floor.

"Look at you," he said, voice coming out husky. He moved back to her and nudged her knees apart so he could stand between her legs. His fingers slid into her hair to push it back. "Such a sexy girl. That mouth." He brushed his thumb over her bottom lip. She gazed back up at him with those beautiful big eyes. He held her gaze steadily, then reached for her hands and pulled them around his waist. She held on, and as he bent to kiss her, her eyelashes fluttered down.

He tasted her again. Oh man, she was sweet. Hot and sweet. He wanted her against him again so he reached for her and hoisted her up. She wrapped her arms around his neck as they continued to kiss, fast, deep and wet kisses.

He loved how it felt like she was trying to climb up his body, get closer and closer. Her shoes hit the floor behind him as she toed them off.

Impatient, he set her back down on the bed, pushed her to her back and climbed on himself, his knees between her legs. He got a glimpse of her panties as he moved over her, the tiny pink triangle darkened with moisture. "Sloane," he groaned as he lowered his body on top of hers. "Your panties are wet."

She just moaned.

"Tell me I did that to you. Made your panties wet."

"Yes." She sighed against his lips. "You made me wet. Dammit."

His lips curved against hers. "Damn right." He slid his hand around the soft skin of her neck, thumb stroking her jaw, then cupping her throat. Gently. He kept his gaze fastened on her, lifted her thigh up to his hip and rocked into her.

Her breath stuttered and her eyes went dark. Pretty lips parted, she stared up at him. One of his hands was still at her throat, and the other cupped a breast. Oh fuck yeah. Soft and firm, she filled his palm, and he gave her gentle squeezes as he kissed her again. And again. Their mouths moved together, then apart, then clung again. She made soft sounds of pleasure as he rubbed his thumb over her nipple. His hand slid around to the back of her neck to hold her in place for his devouring mouth.

"You smell fantastic," he whispered, rubbing his nose alongside hers. "So fucking sexy. Just breathing in your scent made me hard."

"What *doesn't* make you hard?" she murmured, and he drew back to meet her eyes again. They shared a smile.

"There is a long list of things that don't make me hard," he said. "But let's not go there. Right now it's all you."

She sank her teeth briefly into her bottom lip.

He kissed her again, rolling his hard, aching cock

against her soft, damp pussy. Sensation burned and twisted inside him.

Then he rose back up onto his knees, pulling her with him so she sat up. As he hastily unbuttoned his shirt, she went to work on the button and fly of his pants. He got rid of the shirt and then bent to kiss her as he reached behind him to shove off his shoes and socks.

She kept making sexy little sounds that had his blood scalding his veins. He pushed her back down, but then rolled, taking her on top of him. Oh yeah. Very nice. She straddled him and he slipped a hand down inside the back strings of her panties to cup one cheek, fingertips grazing the crease of her ass. Her buttocks clenched at that touch, whether with fear or excitement he wasn't sure, but he couldn't wait to find out. His other arm wrapped around her and tangled in her hair. Their mouths met again, just barely touching as they stared into each other's eyes.

It was intense. Electric. Intimate.

She rose onto her knees and unbuttoned her pink blouse. The light fabric floated off her shoulders, leaving her in a pink lace bra that sweetly cupped her tits. He traced a finger down her chest, between her breasts, hooked the finger in behind the satin bow and tugged. Still holding his gaze, she reached behind to unfasten the bra and slowly slipped the straps down her arms.

"Let me see those beauties," he murmured, tugging again on the bra. This time it came away from her and he tossed it aside. "Oh yeah. Gorgeous. Wanna taste those pretty pink nipples."

She sucked in a shaky breath as he sat up and, holding her on his lap, bent his head to taste. "Mmm." He circled his tongue over one stiff peak, then drew it into his mouth in a firm pull. In the sexiest move he'd ever seen, she lifted both arms to run her hands through her hair, shaking it out, then lowered her hands to the bed behind her, arching her back. He cupped her breasts with both hands, sucking one nipple then the other, plumping them up for his mouth. "Feel good, baby?"

"Oh God yeah." Her whimpers sounded in his ears as he closed his eyes and worshipped her lush feminine curves. "Feels so good. Oh yeah." She approved as he gently used his teeth on one nipple.

"Biteable," he murmured. "Suckable. Christ, you're hot." They were fucking beautiful nipples, small tight points. He admired them again.

He licked the curve of her breasts, kissed his way down to her stomach, then used his abs to lower himself not quite flat on his back so he could tug her panties off. She bent and lifted her legs to help, and he swallowed hard as he tossed them aside, her pussy right there for his viewing pleasure, her legs spread, hands on the bed behind her supporting her.

"Beautiful," he murmured, stroking one fingertip over soft flesh. "So fucking beautiful."

Women's bodies were amazing and lovely and sexy, but Sloane was making him nuts. He stroked over her snatch, petting it, exploring how wet and hot she was for him. He found her clit with his thumb and worked it, his gaze going back up to her face.

Her eyes were heavy lidded, her chest rising and falling in quick breaths. She lifted one foot and placed it flat on his chest. They smiled at each other, sultry and seductive.

Enough of the slowness. He was hard and horny and hungry for her. He turned her and pushed her down to her back again, head now on the pillows, following her with his body. He stretched out beside her. He kept his hand on her pussy, stroking slick tender flesh while he ate at her mouth again in long, devouring kisses, then kissed his way across her jaw to the side of her neck. Both of them breathing faster, he paused to meet her eyes again, nose to nose, mouths a breath apart. Her hips moved against his hand in a needy rhythm.

"Hot sexy girl," he breathed. "You want to come, don't you?"

She whimpered. "Yes."

"Gonna put my cock inside you," he promised. "Gonna make you come."

He gave her mouth one more hard, quick kiss before rolling away from her to tear his pants and underwear off. He reached for a condom in the drawer next to the bed and had his dick suited up in seconds. He was dying to be inside her, excitement pounding through him, his cock a throbbing spike.

He pulled her leg forward and up, so she was on her side, facing him. He fisted his cock and slid it up and down through her sweet cream, getting nice and wet before pushing into her. Christ, this was moving fast, but they were both so hot for it, out of control.

His bottom arm slid beneath her shoulders, that hand twisting into her hair again, and his other hand gripped her hip. She moaned as he penetrated her. Hot. So hot and tight around him. Fucking heaven. He groaned too. "Holy hell, baby," he whispered.

She lifted a hand to cup his face and he moved inside her. The sweet friction of her pussy on his dick had his blood racing hot, electricity sizzling up and down his spine. Once again, he rubbed his nose alongside hers as he fucked her, deeper, harder, pushing sweet little sounds out of her throat. Before he could stop himself, he gave her ass a little pop and she gasped. Still he held her gaze and knew she liked it.

"Like it hard, baby?" he muttered. "'Cause don't know if I can slow down now."

"I like it." Her voice was breathy. "I like it hard."

Oh yeah, *that* was what he wanted to hear.

He was close. So damn close. His body buzzed and tingled. Pressure built in his balls. He eased her onto her back so he could access her clit. He settled wet fingertips

over it and rubbed in small circles. Her whimpers turned
to cries, her hands tightening on him, and then her head
went back and her pussy contracted around him as she
came. He watched her, enthralled by her expression of
utter bliss and the sexy noises she made.

He let it happen, pumping faster, his balls so tight. The
mattress rocked beneath them and fiery sensation
exploded in him, sizzling up his spine right to the top of
his head and down to his toes. He grunted his pleasure,
teeth gritted, eyes closed, still breathing in the seductive
scent of Sloane's hair where his nose was buried.

"Christ, yeah," he groaned. "Fuck, yeah."

He pulsed inside her powerfully, hand still on her
pussy, waves of intense savage pleasure crashing over
him. He pressed his nose against her, panting harshly,
heart thudding against his ribs.

"Holy hell," he muttered long moments later. "That
was intense."

"Yeah." She gave a long, voluptuous sigh and
masculine pride swelled in his chest.

"Too fast, though. Man." He brushed his lips over her
cheek. "I didn't even get a chance to taste your pretty pussy."

She quivered against him.

"I have to get rid of this rubber," he said regretfully,
slowly withdrawing from her clinging heat. "Be right back."

He used his attached bathroom and returned to find
Sloane rolled up in the duvet.

He slid in next to her. "Cold, baby?"

"Mmm."

"Let me take care of that." He unwrapped her and
settled them both beneath the covers, pulling her into his
arms. She fit there perfectly. For some reason that
disturbed him. He wasn't one to cuddle a lot after sex. He
closed his eyes and just absorbed the feel of her, soft skin
and silky hair, and her amazing scent. His body started to
tighten again and his mouth watered to taste her.

He rolled her beneath him to kiss her again.

"You're a very good kisser," she murmured.

"So are you." He sealed his mouth over hers again, then started sexploring, letting his tongue taste the sensitive skin of her neck, kissing her breasts, breathing in the scent of her skin. He teased those pert little nipples again. She liked that.

He closed his eyes as he suckled, the tight bud fitting perfectly against his tongue. His fingers toyed with the other nipple and her breathing quickened. Then he kissed his way lower still, long, open-mouthed kisses with tongue on her smooth belly.

He tossed the covers behind him as he shifted lower, nuzzling the neat landing strip of dark gold hair, kissing the crease of her thigh on one side, then the other. She parted her legs willingly for him to lie between them.

He took his time. He loved oral sex. Giving *and* receiving, natch, but he really did enjoy going down on a woman. Sloane's arousal was thick and sweet and he lapped it up, tracing her soft folds with his tongue, gently pulling her flesh into his mouth in tiny suckling kisses, stiffening his tongue to probe deeper. He drew back to use his hands, running his thumbs up over her outer lips in a deep massage, then slipping in to find the slick inner lips and take them between thumbs and forefingers in small, tender pinches. He set his fingertips on her mound and massaged there too for a moment. Her body twitched hard as he applied pressure to that sensitive area. Then he used both hands to pinch up her flesh, gently pushing it up away from her clit.

Her eyes flew open wide and she lifted her head. "What are you doing?"

"Does it feel good?" He moved her flesh carefully but firmly, up and down, knowing her clit was feeling that friction.

"Oh my God, yes!" Her head fell back.

He studied her with warm appreciation. Shades of pink and rose and crimson, shiny and slick, smooth and soft. Yum.

"God," she gasped, her hands landing in his hair. "You're good at that too."

"Damn right." With a smug smile he dove back in, circling her clit with his tongue with torturous slowness. Her hips lifted to his mouth. He licked slowly up the center of her, again and again, and she made little begging sounds that went straight to his dick. Hard again, already.

He wasn't done, though. Not even close. He lifted her legs so her feet were on his shoulders, then cupped her ass, bringing her to his hungry mouth. He licked lower, nipped at her ass cheeks. She gasped.

"Gonna turn you over, baby," he said, rising to his knees. He lifted her easily and flipped her onto her stomach. She mewled a sound. He gripped her hips and elevated them, going down for more of her delectable taste, this time from the back. He paused for a few seconds to take in the view. Damn that was gorgeous, firm rounded cheeks and soft pussy lips plumped up between her thighs. He opened his mouth on her ass, nipped with his teeth, soothed with his tongue. His fingers now played in the wet folds, rubbing through them, his long middle finger slipping inside her tight sheath. His thumb brushed over her anus and she shuddered.

"So sweet," he murmured. "You taste good, Sloane. I just wanna eat you up."

She moaned into the mattress.

He played and tasted, gave her a sharp little tap on each butt cheek, then flipped her over again. He pushed her knees high and wide and buried his face in her pussy, her scent filling his head, the taste of her delicate spice tingling on his tongue.

He licked his lips, circled his tongue around her clit, and then over it. With his finger inside her, he bent it to find her good spot and her soft cry told him when he did. "Is that good?"

"Oh yeah. Oh God yeah."

"You want to come now, don't you, beautiful?"

Another moan.

Her body shuddered and her pussy clenched on his finger. He licked her straining clit, moved his finger in her. Her fingers curled into the sheets and he looked up at her over her flat stomach and sweet tits. Her eyes were closed, chin lifted. Oh yeah. Beautiful.

He sucked her clit into his mouth, still fingering her, and her body convulsed. Her cries of delight excited him, as did her clit swelling and pulsing on his tongue. His dick throbbed once again but he worked her through her orgasm, drawing it out until she was limp and quivering, pushing at his head.

"Stop," she begged in a weak voice. "God."

He kissed her just above the patch of hair then rolled away for another condom. In seconds he was inside her again, on top of her, one hand under her neck, the other pushing her hair off her face. He stared intently down at her as he thrust inside her. She met his eyes, hers dazed and so pretty. "There," he said. "That was a beautiful orgasm. Can you do that again?"

"No..."

"Let's see." This time he was going to last longer, not all frantic and desperate for her. Pleasure swelled in him, heat burning across his skin. He kissed her mouth, her jaw, sucked her earlobe, licked her neck. He pushed up onto his knees and found her breasts, cupping them and gently squeezing, taking her nipples in his fingertips. Then he took one of her hands and slipped it between them. "Touch yourself, baby. While I'm fucking you. Come again."

She swiped her tongue over her bottom lip and did as he told her, finding her clit. He pushed her legs back, rolling his hips against her, his dick sliding in and out of her sweet pussy. Tingles slid down his neck and spine, centering in his low back and balls. Oh yeah. There it was...

He watched her eyes drift closed, watched her pretty lips part as her breathing quickened. Hot whimpers spilled from her lips and then she cried out again. The sound of her orgasm was already familiar to him and he grimaced as he let his own climax pound through him.

Fuck yeah. Her hand flopped to the bed and he fell over her and gave one last, deep thrust, holding himself there as he pulsed inside her, face buried in her neck, almost unbearable pleasure coursing through him.

"You're amazing," he groaned. "Fucking amazing."

Her mouth pressed against his shoulder in a long kiss and her hands landed on his back. "Yes," she murmured. "I am."

He shook with laughter, still breathing fast and hard, and lifted his head to lay a hard kiss on her mouth. Damn, he liked this woman. And damn, he liked fucking her.

8

Sloane was not in the best of moods the next morning. After an early-morning taxi ride to her condo to shower and change, and a rush to get to the office, she was all kinds of annoyed with herself for what she'd done last night.

Geezus. She'd slept with Levi Wolcott.

Not only that, she'd stayed all night at his place. They'd probably only gotten a few hours of sleep between several rounds of hot, dirty sex. Now she was tired, whisker-burnt not only on her face but her inner thighs and breasts, and...still hungry for him.

No no no. She shook her head as she stood in line at Starbucks. That was never going to happen again. *Never never never.*

Her thighs ached with a delicious pain that made her pussy squeeze every time she felt it. Her nipples were still sensitive from the attention Levi had paid to them. She closed her eyes at the dart of heat she felt low in her belly, remembering everything he'd done.

And everything he'd said. Holy hotness, the man was a sweet dirty talker. He'd turned up the heat a hundred degrees with his frank, sexy words.

Forget that. She grabbed her coffee and muffin and

strode to the office. It was still a few minutes before nine and only a few people were there. In her office she set her coffee and muffin on her desk and turned on her computer. While she ate the muffin she flipped through morning newspapers looking for client ads—as well as ads of their competitors. Keeping an eye on things. Then she dealt with client and internal emails. She went to talk to Noah about the Herstal account, and was standing in the door of his office when Levi walked in.

Late.

He stopped to talk to Phoebe and Bailey, smiling that panty-melting smile at them as he said something that made them laugh. With a wink, he moved away from them and started toward her. His expression warmed when he saw her, and her heart gave a flutter, which she savagely tamped down. She looked pointedly at her watch and then back up at him.

"And once again Levi makes his own hours," she snapped. Bailey and Phoebe's heads turned toward her and they exchanged glances. Sloane ignored them.

Levi paused close to her and said in a low voice, "Are you shitting me?"

She stepped back, keeping her expression severe. "I've talked to you a number of times about our hours of work."

She sensed Noah's surprise.

"My apologies," Levi said. "I had a...late night. Overslept a little." He shot another wink at Bailey and Phoebe that made Sloane's skin tighten, then sauntered down the hall to his cubicle.

Sloane paused, drew in a breath and let it out. She turned back to Noah. "Okay, so we're meeting with Kirk and Alex at eleven o'clock. They're not entirely happy with the copy Dash wrote for the new magazine ads for Ammen Light."

"I'll swing by your office around twenty to eleven and we can walk over there."

"Sounds good."

She returned to her own office to get a few other things done before going to the meeting. Her concentration was shot, though. She was all tingling and shaky from seeing Levi, pissed off at him and at herself and…and…she was an idiot.

She pulled herself together and made it through the meeting with the client's marketing team. She got what they were saying, and they agreed to another meeting with Dash to try to clarify the script they wanted. She and Noah went back to the office and she ate a sandwich at her desk while she dealt with more emails, then met with Hunter and Isaiah on a presentation they were doing for Herstal, one of Verhoeven's old brands, that afternoon at three, finalizing their boards and presentation materials. Then she and Noah met with Dash about their earlier meeting, giving him some of the feedback they'd heard from the client. He was frustrated at the lack of clear guidelines and she assured him that the Ammen marketing team was aware of the issue and was working on it.

Keeping busy kept her mind away from Levi. The three o'clock meeting went well, thank God, because her head was pounding by that time. At five o'clock she was back at the office, popping ibuprofen and chasing them down with a bottle of water, dealing with emails including a complaint from Ammen about one of their billboards.

That done, she sat back in her chair. The office was quiet, most people having left. Now she knew she had to go talk to Levi. She'd overreacted that morning and once more had been a bitch to him. She needed to apologize. So they'd made the mistake of sleeping together. She needed to clear the air about that too so they could work in the same office.

She pushed up out of her chair and carried her bottle of water down the hall to Levi's office. Which was empty.

Huh. For once, he'd left on time. Which made her feel

like even more of a bitch, because he really did put in long hours. She paused and eyed the huge poster of Justin Bieber on one wall. That was...odd.

"Looking for Levi?"

She turned to see Mason. "I was. Looks like he's gone."

"Yeah, I saw him heading out about five minutes ago."

She smiled and nodded. "No worries. I can catch up with him tomorrow."

"Okay. See you tomorrow."

Back in her office she tried to get a bit more work done, but she was antsy. She wanted to get this conversation with Levi over. Finally at about six thirty, she gave up work.

In her car, instead of heading north toward her condo, she turned onto Illinois. She easily found Levi's building. Parking was another matter, but around the corner she lucked into a spot on the street. Inside, she gave the doorman her name and he called up to Levi's condo.

"Go on up," the doorman said, and she took the elevator to the twenty-first floor. She'd had a few drinks last night, but she remembered the number of his unit.

He opened the door just as she knocked, wearing a wary expression. "Sloane."

"Hi, Levi. Can I come in and talk to you for a few minutes?"

"Are you going to give me shit again? Maybe because I left on time even though I came in late?" Despite his words, he stepped aside to let her in.

Chuck came galloping to greet her. Apparently they were now BFFs since she'd spent the night. She crouched to rub his silky head and he gazed up at her with beautiful big brown eyes that made her chest fill with emotion. Then she rose and faced Levi. He looked more like the guy she'd met in the hotel hall that morning, wearing loose cargo shorts and a well-washed T-shirt. His feet were bare.

"I'm not here to give you shit," she said. "I'm here to apologize."

His eyebrows rose. He wandered over to his kitchen counter and leaned against it. She followed him in.

Last night she hadn't seen much of the condo. It was really lovely. Floor-to-ceiling windows in the living room overlooked a city view. Hardwood floors in a deep taupe color shone in the light from the big windows. The walls were a lighter taupe with white woodwork, and a big red sectional faced a flat screen TV on one wall. The counter Levi leaned against separated the living area from a generous galley kitchen.

"So I'm sorry," she continued after briefly taking in her surroundings. "I was a bitch this morning. I was tired and grouchy and annoyed at myself. I shouldn't have taken that out on you."

He folded his arms across his chest, which she had seen last night to be impressively muscled. She swallowed, remembering that. His face remained neutral. "Thanks," he said quietly. "I appreciate that." He lifted his chin. "Last night you told me it wasn't personal. This morning…it felt personal."

"Yeah. Again, I'm sorry. Look, we made a big mistake last night. That should not have happened. I don't know…" She closed her eyes briefly. "Anyway. I just wanted to clear the air and assure you it won't happen again. It was one night and one night only."

"Huh." He rubbed his chin. "I don't think so."

She blinked. "Pardon me?"

"Did you enjoy it?"

Heat washed up into her face. "Let's not talk about it."

"Did you enjoy it?"

She sighed. "Yes."

"Okay then. Come here."

"Wh-what?" She stared at him.

He straightened and held her gaze. Damn, when he did

that, it was like he put her into a trance. Last night in bed all the heavy eye contact had just melted her brain. She'd never felt so worshipped, with all that sexy attention focused solely on her. Even when guys were good in bed, good at the physical part of it, there was never that intense personal connection.

It sort of scared her.

"Come here," he repeated softly.

Somehow her feet were walking across the floor. She stopped near him. Not close enough for him to touch her. He gestured with his hand to come closer. And she did.

"I was pissed this morning too," he said, voice still low and raspy. "D'you want to know what I wanted to do to you?"

She seemed to have inadvertently swallowed a bowling ball. "No."

"Yes, you do." He shifted closer and traced a fingertip down her nose. "I wanted to spank your ass. And then kiss you. And then bury my cock inside you and fuck you senseless."

Her pussy spasmed. Heat flashed through her veins. She stared at him wide-eyed.

Oh yeah, there was another thing that had been different about him in bed. The dirty talk.

It really did it for her, she had to admit.

His fingertips brushed across her mouth. "I think I should do that now."

She blinked rapidly. "That's not what I came here for."

"I'm not so sure." He spun the chrome stool next to him around so the seat faced away from the counter and sat on it. He circled her wrist and tugged her toward him. She wet her bottom lip, letting him pull her closer. Then suddenly his hands were on her hips and she was face down across his lap. She flailed and caught hold of another stool, but he was steadying her, one hand on her back, the other rubbing her bottom.

"What are you doing?" she cried. Oh for...she knew exactly what he was doing. And her ass tingled in anticipation of it. She closed her eyes.

His warm palm caressed her through her dress. "I love this sweet little ass." He gave her a sharp tap. She blew out a breath. That was just a tease. "Last night I had my mouth here. And my tongue." He popped her again, now a bit harder, but through her dress it wasn't much. She shivered remembering his mouth and his tongue there, between her legs, oh sweet baby geezus, he'd made her come so hard...

He slid his hand up under the skirt of her dress, but it was snug. "Don't rip this one," she warned him. "That skirt was two hundred dollars."

He laughed. His fingers on the back of her thighs made her skin tingle. "I'll buy you a new one."

She didn't give two shits about the skirt. Her warning had just been a feeble attempt to hold on to a smidgen of control.

He spanked her a couple more times and she moaned at the ache in her pussy. Then he lifted her off him and stood her between his widespread thighs. She wobbled on her heels and quivering legs. He held her firmly in place with her wrists behind her back. Her hair had fallen in her face and he let go with one hand to gently stroke it back. His fingers in her hair made her insides heat and tremble.

"You've been spanked," he murmured. "You're about to be kissed." Her face was level with his and he urged her closer, one hand at her lower back holding her wrists, the other cupping her face. Their lips met. His opened against hers in a slow, languid kiss. She'd expected harder, fiercer. Surprise made her open for him and her eyes fell closed at the sensual onslaught. His tongue licked over her bottom lip. "There." He drew back and met her eyes. "You know what's next, right, beautiful girl?"

Spellbound, she just nodded. Her breasts felt full and heavy, and liquid heat was melting down through her, pooling at her core.

"Bedroom." He released her hands, letting his palm linger on her ass. She stepped back.

His bedroom was gorgeous too, another wall of floor-to-ceiling windows looking out over the city. Her feet sank into ivory carpet. The big bed with the thickly padded chocolate leather headboard was centered against a taupe wall. A matching leather armchair sat in one corner next to a dark wood dresser.

Chuck followed them into the bedroom, his nails clicking on the wood floor of the hall then going silent on the carpet. She glanced at the dog. Had he been in the bedroom with them last night? God, she hadn't even noticed. She smiled when Chuck trotted over to a big round cushion in the corner, stepped onto it, circled a few times, pawed at it, circled again, then lay down. Well trained, apparently.

When she looked back at Levi, he was watching her watch his dog, lips quirked. "He won't bother us."

"I suppose he's used to guests in his bedroom."

"Bitchy," he murmured. "That's gonna get you spanked again."

She bit her lip even as her pussy squeezed. It *had* been a bitchy comment, stemming from a twinge of jealousy. And, it pained her to admit it, there might have been a bit of brattiness in the comment too, that shameful secret desire to be spanked motivating her.

"Come on, beautiful girl. Show me that pretty body. Take your clothes off."

She hesitated. Then she gave him her back. "I might need some help with the zipper," she said over her shoulder.

He moved up behind her, the warmth of his body like a caress. He tugged down the zipper, parted the dress, and then his lips touched the nape of her neck. Her eyes closed and a shiver slid down her spine.

His big hands pushed the sleeves of the dress down her arms and the loosened garment fell to the floor. And Levi was kissing his way down her back, soft, open-mouthed kisses along her spine. He went to his knees behind her, hands on her hips. Then he kissed her butt cheeks, first one, then the other.

"Love your underwear," he said gruffly. "These thongs leave you nice and bare." His hand fondled the under curve of one cheek.

She sucked on her bottom lip to keep the moan that rose up her throat from escaping.

"Put your hands on the dresser."

She glanced wide-eyed at him over her shoulder. He jerked his chin toward the dark wood dresser against the wall. She took two steps forward, was going to take more, but he caught her hips, stopped her, so that she had to bend over to reach the dresser. Meaning her ass was pushed back and on display for him. Heat curled low in her belly.

He gave her a little spank on one cheek, then the other, warming her skin. "That's for the bitchy comment," he said softly. "It doesn't matter who's been in this room before. You're here now. Right?"

She moaned her agreement.

He stepped back. "Stand up and turn around," he said, the command in his voice undeniable despite the low tone.

She turned to face him, wearing her bra and panties and heels.

The hot look he gave her damn near singed her hair. "Oh yeah," he said, raking his scorching gaze up and down her body. "That's how I like to see you. In the office you're all businesslike and covered up. Now I know what's under those tidy dresses and skirts—sexy lace. And an exquisite body."

Liquid heat built low inside her, the ache intensifying into a needy throb.

"And those fuck-me shoes," he growled. "I want those shoes on my shoulders when you come."

She swallowed past that bowling ball still lodged in her throat. Heat shimmered over her skin.

"Get on the bed."

She floated over to the bed. Having him tell her exactly what to do took such a huge load off her. She felt lighter. Responding to his commands felt…easy. Right.

Again she questioned her sanity at doing this. Only once before had she ever slept with someone from work. She'd had a brief affair with an art director a few years ago. He'd gotten really serious, really fast, and she'd panicked and ended things. It had been awkward at the office, until he left Huxworth Packard and took a job at another agency. She hated to think that he'd changed jobs because of her, and she'd learned her lesson after that—no office affairs.

But Levi was as much a commitmentphobe as she was, apparently. So maybe a little harmless sex wasn't that dangerous.

Who was she kidding? It was as harmless as a bomb with a lit fuse.

But her body wasn't paying attention to the warnings her voice of reason was trying to give it.

She crawled onto the bed, on her hands and knees, giving him a show. She heard his faint groan. In the middle of the bed, she sat, turning to face him, knees bent to one side. He was rubbing his erection through his shorts.

"Yeah, I'm hard as a spike," he said, his jaw tight. "Tease me with that hot little ass."

She smiled and dropped her gaze to his groin. "Show me how hard you are."

Heat flared in his eyes, then he narrowed them at her.

"Baby." He advanced on the bed. "My bedroom. I'm in charge here. You don't give the orders, you take what I give you. You good with that?"

She dragged her tongue over her bottom lip, met his eyes and whispered, "Yes, sir."

9

Those two words made Levi's dick twitch and thicken even more. Oh yeah.

She was probably being facetious as hell, knowing her, but even so, it was just what he wanted to hear.

"But we need some ground rules," Sloane added.

Levi gave a strangled sound that was both a groan and a laugh. "Of course we do."

She gave him a sly smile. "I'm not trying to take charge."

"Right."

"I just want to make sure…whatever this is…we keep it separate from work."

"Absolutely." That was one of his principal rules. Business and pleasure did not mix.

"Also, I'm not interested in a relationship," she continued.

He frowned. Wait, that was his line.

"I'm not good at them so I don't do them. But…" She tipped her head and gave him a smoky look. "There seems to be some kind of sexual chemistry between us."

Wait a damn minute here. He felt like he was losing control of this. However, he couldn't argue with that. Not a damn bit.

"We're on the same page then, baby," he said smoothly. "Now where were we? Oh yeah, you wanted to see how big my dick is."

She laughed. "I said show me how *hard* it is. I already *know* how big it is."

The appreciation in her voice as she said that made his chest expand.

"Like I said." He strolled closer to the bed. "*I'll* decide when you get to see my dick. First, show me that pretty pussy."

Her eyes darkened.

"You look so sexy sitting there in your lacy underwear. And those shoes. Take the panties off and spread your legs."

She frowned at him. "I'm not sure if I like you telling me what to do."

He laughed. "Babe. You love it. I can see how hot your eyes are. You loved having your ass spanked too. I bet your panties are wet." He moved closer still, his dick throbbing. Christ, he loved it too.

He watched her internal struggle, the battle between hanging on to control and letting herself give it up, which she clearly wanted to do. She swallowed and shifted her legs, her lips tense. She reclined onto her back and lifted her hips to pull off her panties. She did it slowly, torturing him. Then she propped herself on her elbows and spread her legs, high heeled shoes sunk into the puffy duvet.

His breath caught in his throat. That was so fucking hot, and not just the view, but the fact that she'd done what he'd told her to. Adrenaline flashed through his veins at the thought of finding out how far he could go and how much pleasure he could give her. A rush of power surged through him.

He had to stay strong and in control, though. She was no doormat and wasn't going to just lie there. He'd been with pillow queens, who lay there and let him do whatever he wanted. That was no fun. Well, it was fun. Sex was *always* fun. But this...this was *fun*. Taking control of a strong, gorgeous woman? Hell yeah. His lips curved.

"Beautiful girl," he murmured, eyes roving over her slender body. "Now what's going to happen?"

She wet her bottom lip, heavy lidded eyes meeting his. "You're going to fuck me."

"That's right." He tugged his T-shirt off over his head and tossed it aside, then flicked open the button of his shorts, lowered the zipper and let them drop to the floor. He had no underwear beneath them, and his dick bobbed in front of him, stiff and aching. He gave it a stroke and approached the bed. He loved how her gaze was glued to his groin. He stroked again, slow, with a twist of his wrist at the head, then again. Sloane licked her lips.

"See how hard I am for you?"

He walked over to his bedside table for a condom, then knelt on the foot of the bed. "I'm going to bury this cock inside that sweet pussy and fuck you until you scream."

Yeah, his dirty words got to her. He caught the way her eyes flashed, her breathing quickened and that delicate pink flush rose from her chest up into her face.

He donned the condom. As he moved closer on the bed, the delicate scent of her arousal teased him, intoxicating him, making his head spin like he was drunk. It made him even harder.

He moved between her legs, watching her closely. He wouldn't usually just plunge his dick inside a girl without more foreplay, but he knew she was aroused, and this time was about control. That, and making her scream.

Fuck yeah, she was wet, so slick and hot. He eased into her tight body, watching her face. Her teeth sank into her bottom lip as he penetrated her. He clenched his jaw at the sizzle of sensation that burned away his restraint. Okay, it wasn't only about controlling her, it was also about controlling *himself* so he could give her pleasure.

Once he was balls deep inside her, he lowered himself over that pretty body. He clasped her hands in his and held them to the mattress on either side of her head as he rocked his pelvis into her. He kissed her mouth, kept his eyes on her face, loving how her gaze went hazy and out of focus. "Good?" he murmured.

"Y-yes."

He released her hands and rose up onto his knees. He clasped her waist, his hands looking big on her small body, holding her as he drove deeper and harder. Her soft breasts moved on her chest with every thrust. Her gasps and mewls inflamed his senses.

He reached for one ankle and lifted it, setting it on his shoulder. She moved the other one there herself, still wearing those sexy heels. He kissed one calf.

He found her clit and worked it in tight circles, still watching her face, judging her response. That flush grew rosier, her nipples hardened and her pussy tightened in a sublime squeeze.

He took his thumb away and stopped moving.

She gasped and her head lifted off the pillow. "No! I was so close!"

He smiled. "You come when I say, beautiful girl."

Her eyebrow pinched together and her lips parted like she was in pain.

He leaned over her to kiss her and slowly started moving inside her again. She grabbed onto him and her fingernails dug into his back in frustration. That bite of pain excited him and he growled. "Careful, baby. You got me so hot. That tight little pussy squeezing me."

He took her close again, and stopped, eliciting more frustrated whimpers, edging her. Finally let her have her release, satisfaction swelling inside him when she screamed his name as she came. He fell over her and her arms and legs wrapped around him, and he fucked her hard and gave in to his own orgasm. Pleasure ripped through him, stealing his breath, causing stars to burst in front of his vision. He buried his face in her neck and came hard in endless pulses inside her body.

"There you go," he murmured a long time later.

She sighed. "I should be so pissed at you," she said in a breathy voice.

He smiled. "But you're not."

She smacked his shoulder. "Damn, you're cocky."

"Bet your sweet little ass." He shifted up onto his elbows and gazed down at her. For a moment, he couldn't speak. He was cocky, yeah, but holy hell, she was fucking gorgeous and he knew how damn lucky he was to have her there under him.

"I can't stay all night again."

Yeah, he got that. He didn't like it, but he got it. Again, it struck him how weird it was that he was disappointed, when he was usually quick to hustle women out of his place. "That's okay." He kissed her again. "I'll take you home."

"My car's still at the office."

"Then I'll take you there to get it." Though he hated the idea of dropping her off in a parking garage late at night. "Be right back."

He got rid of the condom in the bathroom. When he returned, Sloane stood beside the bed in the bra she'd never taken off and the matching panties. Her gold hair was a tousled halo around her head in the lamplight as she bent to pick up her dress from the floor. He leaned against the doorframe, watching her. "Gorgeous."

She looked up. One corner of her mouth lifted but he saw the hesitancy in the smile and in her eyes. He crossed the room to her and took her chin between his thumb and forefinger. "It's okay, Sloane." He kissed her gently.

She blew out a breath. "I'm not so sure."

"It was good, right?"

She hesitated, then admitted, "Right."

⊙⧓⊙

"Nice poster, dude," Scott said with a smirk, Friday morning.

Levi didn't even glance at the huge picture of Justin Bieber that had appeared on the wall behind his desk earlier that week. "I'm not taking it down."

"Wouldn't have pegged you as a big fan of the Biebs."

Levi grinned and pushed his chair back from his desk to stand. He and Scott were on their way to meet with Mason and Noah with their first round of ideas for one of the Verhoeven craft beer ads. "Say what you want about the kid, he can sing."

Scott shook his head, smiling wryly. Levi hoped this was the end of the hazing.

Mason and Noah were already in the big meeting room. "Okay, let's see what you've got," Mason said.

Levi and Scott arranged their boards.

"Rather than trying to hide the fact that these 'craft' beers are now manufactured by Big Beer, we just come right out and say they are," Levi said, showing him their first idea for the Cedar Springs Brewing Company campaign. "Kind of a cheeky way of poking fun at the push back those other brands got."

Mason nodded, his eyes thoughtful.

They kept talking, showing him their other ideas. Levi was having a hard time getting a read on Mason's reaction, hoping like fuck that his lack of expression didn't mean he hated every single one of their plans.

"Okay," Mason finally said. "There's some decent stuff there. Noah, which ones do you think are most on strategy?"

99

"That first idea would work much better for the Astoria Brewing line," Noah said. "They have a smaller budget and they're a more regional brewery." They had a lengthy discussion and Levi paid close attention, leaving the meeting with direction to move forward on several ideas. He and Scott debriefed in Scott's office.

"That was *great*," Scott said, dropping into his chair.

"Was it? I had no clue. Mason doesn't reveal much, does he?"

"Not if it's good. If he hated them, we'd've known it, believe me. We'd be back to the drawing board so fast our necks would be twisted in knots."

Levi grinned. "Okay, good. So. We've got more work to do. Plus we need to get moving on that television and web commercial for the Cerone brand." of the existing Verhoeven line wanted something big and bold, something that would compete with Heineken and Budweiser. Of course, a client's idea of big and bold wasn't always the same as the creative team's.

"First, let's reward ourselves with a long lunch."

"Hell yeah. We deserve it." But Levi paused. "But let's not take too long."

Scott lifted an eyebrow at him. "Say what?"

Levi was thinking of Sloane and her mandate to get them to clean up their bad boy Brew Crew reputation. Yeah, they totally deserved a long lunch after the hours they'd put in the last couple of weeks. But he didn't want to cause more problems for her. No way in hell was he telling Scott that, though. He shrugged. "We've got a lot of work to do and tight deadlines. But come on. I'm buying."

"Excellent."

Levi and Sloane had seen each other briefly in the office the last few days. He wanted to see more of her. She'd been very clear that whatever was happening between them stayed away from the office, and that was fine with him, but he needed her back in his bed. Like, tonight.

Holy hell, she was his fantasy come to life, a strong, smart woman who didn't easily give up control—but when she did, fuck, the rush... Not only did it make him feel like he could do anything, but he loved giving that to her. Finding out what she liked, what she needed, how to pleasure her hot little body... Goddammit, he'd never been this affected by a woman. He did one-night hookups, occasionally saw a woman more than once if things were good, but he'd never been interested in anything more than that.

With Sloane he was...well, he couldn't say it was an addiction at this point, but he felt like he couldn't get enough of her. It was kind of fucking him up a little, if he was honest, but the sweet way she'd submitted to him, the response he got when he did all the things...yeah, it was like a high.

There was so much more he wanted to do to her. With her. For her. Oh yeah, he was fucked up.

Of course one way to get her attention was to take a long, long lunch.

That was so juvenile. He was better than that. He'd just work late and abduct her when no one else was around. He grinned at the fantasy of tying her up, throwing her over his shoulder and carrying her out of the office.

❦

Sloane sat in Mason's office that evening. As usual, she'd been running all day from meeting to lunch meeting to another meeting while dealing with all kinds of crises. She knew Mason had met with Levi and Scott earlier and was anxious to hear how things had gone.

"Fanfuckingtastic," Mason told her. "Some of their ideas could be huge."

Even as she smiled and her insides squeezed with

excitement, she said, "Bite your tongue. Don't want to jinx it."

"I know, I know." He shrugged. "You never know what's going to hit. The things you think are genius tank, and the ideas you're not so sure of strike some kind of chord with the public and things go viral. I don't know if Levi himself has realized all the possibilities some of their ideas could have."

She bit her lip to keep from grinning hugely, excited for Levi's success. Oh hell. She wasn't excited for *him*. She was excited for the *agency*.

And, she was totally bullshitting herself.

But hey, she did what she had to do to keep herself from freaking out about what she was doing. If that made any sense at all.

"Well, that's great," she said, rising from the chair in Mason's office. She glanced at her watch. Yikes, nearly seven and it was the weekend. "You heading out?"

"I have a few more things to do."

She eyed him. Yes, she and Mason were a lot alike. Many evenings she'd stayed at the office because it was better than going home alone. She knew he felt the same.

Sleeping with Levi had aroused a whole slew of emotions in her—fear, anxiety, resentment. He made her feel so much, and she resented that. Feelings scared her. Made her anxious. She had a hard time trusting people, and yet she'd just turned herself over to him and done whatever he wanted.

She'd loved it.

Which made the fear and anxiety all the more intense.

But the truth was, it had been amazing. He'd given her pleasure beyond anything she'd ever experienced, not to mention a feeling of freedom, freedom to just give in to something and enjoy it.

"Okay," she said to Mason, feeling reluctant to leave him alone. "See you Monday."

He smiled and nodded, and she walked down the quiet hall to her own office.

She'd only been there a few minutes when Levi appeared in her door. Her insides tightened and her belly did a flip. "Hi," she said casually, straightening some papers on her desk.

"I'm here to abduct you."

She smiled at him. "I think you're supposed to sneak in and do that. Not stand there and tell me."

He grinned. "I'm horny. Not psycho."

"Oh. So you're abducting me for sex. I was hoping for dinner."

He laughed. "I can probably manage both. How about dinner in bed?"

"Mmm. Multitasking. I love multitasking."

"That doesn't surprise me."

The smile they shared was warm, and a sweet, sultry hum filled the air.

"Do I need to carry you out of here?" Levi asked, his voice low and raspy.

The idea of that made her pussy squeeze. "Don't be ridiculous. Someone might see."

"That was a joke, Sloane."

She bent her head.

"Although it is a very hot fantasy of mine," he added.

She peeked up at him and saw his lips quirked. She scrunched up her face, then whispered, "Me too."

10

The knock on Levi's door the next afternoon came just after he'd gotten home from his weekend run and he was still wiping sweat off his body while walking around his condo. Sloane had left a couple of hours ago. He opened the door to see Colin, the kid who walked Chuck for him.

"Yo Colin, whassup?"

"Not much." Colin shrugged. "I came to ask a favor."

Chuck hurtled at Colin, his beloved walking buddy, jumping around excitedly. This meant a walk, if Colin was there! Colin smiled and bent to give Chuck a rub.

"Come on in." Levi stepped back from the door and Colin slouched in. "What is it?"

"I'm trying to get more jobs walking dogs. School's nearly over and I want to make more money over the summer."

Levi nodded. At fourteen he wasn't quite old enough for a job, but he had some entrepreneurial spirit, which was good.

"Some people are asking for references," Colin continued. "I was wondering if you'd give me one. You and Mrs. Harper are the ones I've been doing this for the longest."

"I can do that." Levi was happy to help the kid out that way. Colin had been dependable and responsible with Chuck. "You'll still be able to walk Chuck every day though, right?"

"Oh yeah, yeah, for sure."

"So what do you need? You want to give them my number so they can call and ask questions?"

His sister had gone through this when she'd hired a babysitter, for Chrissakes, calling people and interrogating them. But he got that people wanted to make sure their pets were in good hands. He'd kind of taken a chance on Colin when he'd seen the kid's flyer in the store, but even he'd gone along with Colin the first time he'd taken Chuck out to assess how responsible he'd be. Chuck was important to him.

"Maybe you could write something up?"

"Sure. Let's do something up now. Come into my office." He led the way into his second bedroom, which was his home office, and tapped the keyboard of his MacBook Pro. The screen came to life and he sat in the chair while Colin leaned against the custom-built desk that took up one whole wall. "Don't think I've ever written a reference. Guess I'll wing it."

He started tapping on the keyboard, and a few minutes later said, "How does this sound?" He read what he'd written to Colin.

Colin nodded, a small smile on his lips at the words of praise Levi had written. "Awesome."

"Here. I'll print a couple of copies." He added his cell phone number in case anyone wanted to call, and hit print.

"Thanks." A minute later, Colin held the papers but didn't move.

Levi eyed him.

"So, um." Colin looked at the floor. "You're a single dude and you have lots of girlfriends."

Levi blinked. "Uh…" Girlfriends? No way! Girls, hell yeah. Though lately it had all been Sloane…

"There's this girl at school," Colin said, still looking at his skater shoes.

Oh man. How many times had he heard that? *There's this girl…*

"But school's ending…"

"Ah. You want to see her over the summer."

"Yeah. But…I don't know if she likes me."

"You came to the right place for chick advice," Levi began, then paused. He'd given buddies advice about women and dating and sex enough times in the past, but…this was a fourteen-year-old kid. "Hey, you want a Coke?"

"Sure."

They left the office and walked into his kitchen. Levi pulled out a can of Coke for Colin and a bottle of Gatorade for himself. Colin sat on a stool at the counter and Levi leaned against the fridge. "So. What's her name?"

"Ifigenia."

"Huh. Nice name. Okay. What do you two have in common? Besides school."

"We both like gaming. And anime."

"Perfect. You can invite her over to play Xbox."

"I'm afraid my mom won't let me have a girl over during the day when she and Dad are at work."

Levi rubbed his chin. Yeah, he totally got that. Two teenage kids home alone…danger, danger. "Well, see if she'll come over one evening. Or…invite a bunch of friends over and include her."

Colin nodded, considering that. "But what if I want to…you know…"

"Dude. You wouldn't do that the first time you go out with her, no matter what. First you get to know a girl. Treat her with respect." Maybe this wasn't what the kid wanted to hear. "Maybe she'll let you kiss her one day."

"You have different girls here all the time."

Argh. "I'm nearly thirty. It's different. Plus, all the girls I go out with know the deal with me. I'm not looking for a girlfriend."

Christ, he sounded like an asshole talking to Colin about this. His insides cramped a bit.

"And you shouldn't be looking for a girlfriend either, at your age. Just have fun hanging out together."

"What if she doesn't like me? What can I do to make her?"

"Well there's a million dollar question," Levi said with a sigh. He'd never had this problem, but other guys had asked him this. He'd told one buddy to back off because he came across as desperate to women; he'd told another guy he had to have more self-confidence. He didn't know what to tell Colin. "The truth is, you can't make someone like you. Act confident. Not too confident. Don't brag, but don't put yourself down either. Occasionally make a little fun of yourself, if you screw up. Be polite and respectful of her. Show interest in her. And here's the best advice about women you're ever gonna get..." He leaned forward. "Brush your teeth."

Colin's head jerked up and he blinked at him. Then he laughed.

Levi grinned. "I know, I know, it sounds stupid, but honest to God, no girl will ever want to kiss you if you smell bad. Teeth, the whole personal hygiene thing...take a shower, make sure your clothes are clean and brush your teeth. It's huge. Trust me on this."

Colin looked down at himself.

"I'm not saying you smell bad," Levi added hastily. "Just sayin'."

Levi remembered being a fourteen-year-old boy and how personal hygiene had been a huge pain in the ass that his mom and sisters had totally been on him about all the time. And he was eternally grateful to them for that.

Colin nodded. "Okay. Thanks." He finished off his Coke and set the can on the counter. "Thanks for the drink." He jumped off the stool and Levi walked him to the door. Chuck clicked along behind them, tail wagging, clearly hoping for a walk. At the door, Colin held out a fist and Levi bumped it with his own. "Later."

"Later, dude."

Levi headed to his shower, grinning. He'd been giving the kid hygiene advice while he was dripping sweat and probably stank like a locker room.

⦿⟁⦿

Sloane's dad and stepmother were in town for the weekend. They came into the city every once in a while to see a play or a concert and do some shopping. And of course, to see her.

Sloane turned down her stepmother's invitation to go shopping with her Saturday afternoon, as she always did, saying she had too much work to do, ignoring the faint disappointment in Viv's voice. But she did meet them for dinner at Oscar's, a lovely seafood place only a few blocks from the theater where they were all going to see *Jersey Boys*. The maitre d' led Sloane through the bar and a curtained doorway into the restaurant where Dad and Viv already were. They had a small booth and sat together on one side of it. Sitting on the outside, Dad rose to give her a hug.

"Hey, cookie." Dad embraced her. She hugged him back briefly, smiling. "How are you?"

"I'm good."

Viv started to slide out of the booth to also give her a hug, but Sloane quickly slipped into the seat opposite her, giving her a bright smile. "Hi, Viv."

Viv's mouth pursed briefly, but then she smiled too. "Hi, Sloane. You look beautiful."

108

"Thanks. So do you."

"I love that dress. Really brings out your pretty blue eyes."

"Thank you."

"Is it new?"

"No, not really."

Dad and Viv had been married over seven years now. Sloane was happy her father had found someone, but when Viv had come into the picture, it had been hard to accept. Sloane had never given up hope that they were going to find her mom. Then Dad had had her mom declared legally dead because she'd been missing so long, so he could marry Viv.

Sloane was older and more mature now — though really, she'd been mature since that day Mom had disappeared when she'd been fourteen — and she understood that her father had fallen in love with Viv and wanted to marry her. And in some ways, Sloane had been glad of that. Dad had struggled after Mom had left, for many reasons. But even so, it had been hard to accept having her mother declared dead, giving up the hope that one day they'd find her and she'd come home.

Intellectually, Sloane knew that wasn't going to happen. But for so many years there'd been that tiny flicker of hope in her heart. That had extinguished it and it had been difficult not to blame her dad and Viv for that.

"So what are you drinking?" Sloane asked, looking at their drinks.

"Scotch for me," Dad said. "Viv's having wine."

"Wine sounds good."

"Let's order a bottle," Viv said.

"Good idea." They looked over the wine menu and discussed some possibilities. Sloane remembered Levi mentioning the name of that French wine and found herself scanning the menu for it. She couldn't even really remember it but she was curious how much it would be.

Viv and Sloane decided on a bottle of Sauvignon Blanc and ordered it, and Sloane set aside the wine menu to pick up the dinner menu.

"We haven't seen you for so long," Dad said, looking a little wistful. "Wish you'd come visit sometimes, cookie."

"I know." She made a face. "You know how it is." She always told them how busy she was and how demanding her career was, but the truth was, she made excuses not to go home to Oakville.

"How's work going?"

"It's going well." She smiled at Dad. "We're in the middle of working on a bunch of new campaigns for Verhoeven Brewery, and I'm trying to get to know these new craft breweries they just purchased. It's stressful, but I love it."

Her dad liked hearing stories from her work, his pride in her accomplishments evident. That kept them going through dinner. For some reason she found herself telling them about this hotshot new copywriter they'd hired away from another agency and how smart and creative he was. She made them laugh with the stories of his hazing. She did *not* mention that she'd slept with him. Then she heard about how Dad's job at the car dealership where he was now the parts manager was going and how business at Viv's flower shop was doing. She heard about the shopping Viv had done that afternoon. Then they went to see *Jersey Boys*, which she'd seen before but enjoyed again anyway.

After, Dad and Viv insisted on walking her to her car, as if she wasn't used to getting herself around Chicago all the time, then they walked from there to the hotel where they were staying. She'd never invited them to stay with her. She always felt guilty about that even though they never asked to stay with her and neither of them ever said anything to make her feel guilty. But she always sensed their disappointment at how she kept herself distant from them.

The distance wasn't because she was angry at them. She didn't blame them for falling in love and getting married. And they certainly had had nothing to do with why her mom had left. Mom had suffered from bipolar disorder for years. She'd been a good mom who'd held down a full-time job yet still cared for her three children, and her illness had been mostly controlled, but there'd been times that had caused stress in their family. They'd never known if someone had taken her, or if she'd just walked away. There'd been no warning that she wasn't well. The police had never been able to find her. They all assumed she'd probably had a depressive episode and had somehow taken her life.

So it wasn't Dad's fault and it certainly wasn't Viv's fault, but Sloane's life had changed in that time following her mother's disappearance. *She'd* changed. And she preferred keeping her distance.

Which was another reason this thing that was happening with Levi was scaring her. She kept her distance from everybody. But he was making that impossible.

○)〉ૐ(〇

Levi was out with his buddies at Studio V, one of the hottest clubs in town. This was his usual Saturday night—hit a club, have some drinks, hook up with a hot chick, take her back to his place and bang her brains out, then send her on her merry way.

Jacob was doing "family things" with some of Tara's family who'd arrived in town for the wedding next weekend, so it was him, Tucker, Cam and Luke.

Tonight he was weirdly unsettled. Girls kept smiling at him and trying to talk to him and he was just...bored. Yeah, he'd been preoccupied with work all day. After

KELLY JAMIESON

Colin had left, he'd done some work on the pro bono advertising he did for Chicago Anti-Hunger, something he'd done for years, then more work on the Verhoeven accounts.

He'd asked Sloane what she was doing tonight, but she too had some kind of family thing with her dad and stepmother who were in town. She hadn't sounded thrilled about it, but nonetheless he hadn't bothered to try to make any plans with her for Saturday night, although a replay of Friday night would have been excellent.

"Hi." A pretty brunette stopped in front of him. "If I told you I worked for UPS would you let me handle your package?"

He blinked, then burst out laughing. The girl laughed too.

"Too cheesy?" she said.

"The cheesiest."

"I just thought, why should guys get all the funny pick up lines?" She shrugged, holding the straw of her drink between her thumb and two fingers. He studied her big dark eyes, full lips and exotic cheekbones, shiny dark hair falling around her shoulders.

Why not flirt a little? "Like, do you have a map, 'cause I'm getting lost in your eyes?"

"Haha, yeah, like that." She rolled her eyes, smiling. "You need *something* to say when you want to meet someone new. Right?" She give a flirty head tilt.

"Absolutely." He leaned in closer. "I'm Levi."

"I'm Christy."

"Nice to meet you, Christy. You do have nice eyes, by the way."

"Thank you!" She beamed.

"What do you do for a living? I'm guessing you don't really work for UPS."

She laughed. "No. I'm a corporate attorney at Halliwell Delaney."

He spent a while talking to lovely Christy, corporate attorney. She was bright and pretty and everything he usually went for. But goddammit, he couldn't bring himself to offer the invitation she was clearly expecting. Disappointment was evident on her face when he excused himself.

Cam was nowhere to be seen in the dark club, but he found Luke and Tucker deep in conversation, surprisingly not with women but two dudes who turned out to be José Quintana and Scott Carroll. He talked to them for a while, which was cool, then told Tucker and Luke he was leaving.

"Already?" Tucker frowned at him. "Dude, the night is young."

"I know. Just not feeling it tonight." He slapped Tuck's shoulder. "I'll see you guys next week. We have to pick up our tuxes Thursday."

He eschewed a taxi in favor of walking home. It wasn't that far from the West Hubbard club, and it was a nice evening. Sloane was probably home by now. Why did he have this bizarre urge to call her or text her? He actually pulled his phone out of his pocket and looked at it.

Fucked. He was truly fucked. With a sigh, he tapped in a text message.

Immediately he wished he could take it back. It was just after midnight, early for him, but she was probably asleep. She'd see this in the morning and it would be so lame.

But her reply came right away. *What are you doing texting me at this time of the night?*

A slow smile pulled at his lips and he stopped on a corner. *I'm lonely and bored.*

Is this a booty call????????

He grinned. *You do have a sweet booty.*

A kissy face emoticon appeared.

I take that as an invitation to kiss said booty.

You wish.

Yes, I do wish. Where are you?

Home.

Perfect. I want to see you. He hesitated. Ah, why not? *And kiss your sweet little ass.*

This time there was a pause and he pictured her frowning in indecision. Hopefully with maybe a little arousal mixed in. Finally, he got the text with her address. *Yes!* He grinned and did a fist pump. Dearborn. He glanced at the street sign of the corner he was standing on—West Hubbard and Dearborn. It was a sign. Not that he believed in shit like that.

He hailed a cab and jumped in, giving the driver Sloane's address.

11

Sloane closed her eyes, her phone in her hand. Christ on a crutch, what had she just done? A Saturday night booty call because he was alone and horny?

She knew he could have any girl he wanted. She heard the women in the office talking about him all the time. She'd seen flirtatious waitresses slip him their numbers. Why was he alone on a Saturday night?

Her phone buzzed again. *On my way. Not far.*

Welp, he was on his way over, she'd best get dressed. Or something. She'd been in bed reading when her phone had chimed and she'd been curious enough to check who was texting her at that time of the night.

She threw back the covers and jumped out of bed. If he was expecting sex, getting dressed was a waste of time. On the other hand, she wasn't about to greet him at the door naked, and her wardrobe of sexy sleepwear was sorely lacking, since nobody ever saw her sleeping. She looked down at the camisole and panties she had on. Fuck, what was she supposed to wear?

She bit her lip and turned in a circle in her bedroom. The yoga pants she'd had on earlier were draped over the arm of a chair. That would have to do. She slipped them on, and hopped into the bathroom to brush her hair. She was wearing her glasses and no makeup. Nope, she wasn't going to pop in contacts at this time of night and put on makeup. If this freaked him out or turned him off, oh well.

Her doorbell rang a short time later and she peered through the sidelight to make sure it was him on her front doorstep.

"Hey," he said with that sexy smile, walking in. He wore a suit, a dark jacket with narrow lapels and slim-fitting pants over a collared dark shirt but no tie. Apparently he hadn't been sitting at home. He moved into her space, cupped her face in both hands and kissed her.

Damn, that was hot.

He drew back and smiled as he looked into her eyes. "How was your evening with your parents?"

"It was okay. Come in." She closed and locked the door, her senses overloaded with his presence, the scent of his aftershave all citrusy male, how his stubble felt rough against her face, the feel of his mouth on hers, the taste of some kind of liquor on his lips…maybe scotch?

"Nice place. I like it."

"Thanks. I like it too. It's small, but it's good for me."

He shoved his hands into his pockets and walked through the door separating her tiny foyer from the living room. He stood in the middle of it to survey the space, taking in the small leaded windows above the two bigger ones, the fireplace, the door to her kitchen.

"Where were you?" she asked, moving into the room behind him, nerves jumping.

"Studio V."

"Oh."

He turned to face her. "Nice glasses. Very sexy."

"Right." She rolled her eyes.

"This is how you looked that morning at the hotel." He stepped toward her again and her skin tingled. "I thought you were a teenager."

She laughed. "You are so full of it."

"No, seriously. A hot teenager." He rubbed his thumb over her bottom lip.

"That sounds kind of pervy."

"It does, doesn't it?" He pushed some hair off her face. "How old are you?"

"Thirty-one. I don't think I can pass for a teenager."

"Well, I'm glad you're not."

"How old are you?"

"Twenty-nine."

"Ack. Now I'm the perv."

"A cougar." His smile made her insides flutter. His hand lingered on her neck. "Shame on you."

"Um…would you like a drink? Coffee?"

"I've had enough to drink tonight."

She eyed him. "You don't seem drunk."

"Nah. Just had a few at the club."

She wasn't sure what to do. Invite him to sit down? Take him straight to her bedroom? She'd never in her life had a booty call like this.

So when he took charge, once again it was a relief. Dammit.

"Let's sit down." He moved to the couch.

At the office, in the advertising world dealing with colleagues and clients, she was totally in charge. Put her alone in a room with Levi and she was all "yes, sir". She sat beside him, but he tugged her over so her back was against his chest and slid his arms around her. "I didn't wake you up, did I?"

"No. I was reading."

"I figured you were awake since you answered so quickly. If you were asleep I was going to feel like a tool in the morning."

Her heart softened. His body was warm and his arms felt good around her. She leaned into his embrace. He nuzzled her hair and tingles slid down her spine.

"What did you do with your folks?"

"We went for dinner, then to see *Jersey Boys*."

"Nice."

"I've seen it before, but I enjoy it."

His hands moved on her now, stroking her arm, lingering on the sensitive skin inside her elbow, one palm on her stomach. Her head fell back to his shoulder and he cupped her face to turn her toward him and kiss her.

Their mouths met with an instant surge of heat through her body, and she sighed as she opened to him, loving the taste of him, his tongue sliding inside to stroke hers. His thumb rubbed her cheek in front of her ear. Her core tightened.

"Soft skin," he murmured. His fingers slipped under the loose camisole and caressed her belly. "And you taste good."

"So do you."

His hand dropped from her face, stroked down her arm. The other hand slid higher beneath the camisole. Her breasts swelled and ached in anticipation, longing for his touch and then it was there, his big hand covering one breast. His other hand left her arm and slipped between her legs, cupping her pussy. She drew in a long shaky breath, her blood scalding her veins.

"So hot," he whispered in her ear. His lips caught her earlobe and gave a gentle tug. His fingers plucked at her nipple and heat darted straight down to where his hand was between her legs. She parted them to give him more access and he rubbed her through her yoga pants and panties.

He shifted their position on the couch a little more, leaning back into the cushions, spreading his own legs and lifting her onto his lap. Her head fell to the back of the couch beside his and her thighs parted even wider, one leg draped over his. The hand behind her back came up and fisted in her hair, holding her head. He continued to stroke and tease her until her body ached and burned. His hand moved back up to caress her lower belly then slipped inside the yoga pants. He paused to tug at the drawstring tie there, and then he had easy access into the loose, stretchy garment. His fingertips teased the edge of her low-rise panties and her pussy squeezed, aching and empty.

"Do you want to come, beautiful girl?" he breathed. "I can give you that."

She moaned.

"Tell me. Tell me what you want."

"Touch me. Please." She hesitated. "Make me come."

Her face burned, her body trembled and she parted her thighs even more, and then yes, God yes, his fingers slid into her panties. He held her there with a firm touch, his hand big and warm, and her body pulsed. He kissed her ear, the side of her neck, her shoulder, and shivers ran over her skin.

"Soft little pussy," he murmured near her ear.

"More," she moaned. "Please."

"That's it. Tell me what you want. What you need."

"Your fingers…"

He rubbed over her outer lips, then slowly parted them, delving inside to find where she was wet. "Oh yeah, honey, that's sweet. So wet." He pushed the cami strap aside and opened his mouth on her shoulder. When his teeth sank in, so gently, her insides jumped and heated. His fingers continued to explore, dipping and parting flesh, slipping in her arousal, stroking up and down over her pussy. Then he found her clit.

Her body twitched hard, her abdomen tightening. Pleasure zapped through her. His middle finger centered over the knot of nerves, firm and wet, circling.

"Oh God." Her eyes fell closed and she sank back into his embrace, sprawled out on his lap. His hand left her pussy and came up to cup a breast. It swelled into his palm. Roughly, he yanked down the top edge of the camisole, exposing her nipple to him. He sat up and pushed her back a bit. One of her feet came up and planted in the couch cushion and he bent to suck her nipple. She whimpered, sensation rippling from her nipple down through her abdomen to her aching pussy.

His hand tightened in her hair, stinging her scalp, and a moan climbed her throat. She could only imagine what she looked like, splayed out on the couch like that.

His hand returned to her pussy, stimulating her clit with unbearable pleasure as he pressed his nose right in front of her ear. The sound of his harsh breathing mingled with her own panting. The buzz behind her clit grew, sensation twisting up inside her. "Oh there," she cried softly. "Right...there..."

He kept up the pressure, building it, higher. She squeezed her inner muscles and reached for that exquisite peak. Her hips lifted off his thigh and her body twisted and turned in his arms as waves of pleasure pulsed from where his fingers touched her.

"Beautiful," he whispered, kissing her shoulder again. "I love making you come."

She dragged her tongue over her bottom lip. "I, uh, kind of like it too."

She felt his smile against her skin, her entire body still quivering. She sucked in air as he petted her pussy and tugged her camisole back up over her breast. Then he turned her in his arms and she buried her face in the side of his neck, hugging him back around his waist.

"Guess I should go now."

Her head snapped up and she met his eyes. "What?"

His eyes glinted. "Kidding. We're not done yet. Remember...I want to kiss your sweet little ass."

Heat stabbed through her core again. "Right," she breathed.

"And I really need to fuck you," he continued, his voice almost a groan. "I'm in pain here."

"Maybe I can help with that."

He smiled. "Maybe you can. I want to put my cock in your hot little mouth."

Her tongue wet her bottom lip again. She wanted that too.

"Here." He lifted her easily, impressing her with his strength, setting her ass on the couch beside him. He rose and arranged her on her back, her head on the armrest, her body stretched out the length of the couch. Then she watched him take off his jacket, and undo the fly of his pants. He moved to the end of the couch, where her head was, and she looked at him upside down, wide-eyed.

He shoved down his pants and underwear, fixed her position, bringing her head farther over the armrest, then held her head in both hands, gently, and eased forward until his cock brushed her lips.

"Gonna fuck your mouth, baby," he whispered. "That sweet, pretty mouth."

She sighed and opened for him. Her tongue swiped at the intriguing bead of liquid at the tip. His dick twitched.

She watched him as her tongue licked around the ridged crest. He slowly let out a pent-up breath, his eyes hot and hungry. He held her head and gently thrust into her mouth. She blinked rapidly and made a noise of pleasure. The vulnerability of this position made her insides clench, but he was being so gentle and careful with her, reassuring her.

"Damn, that feels good."

She closed her lips around him and continued to watch him. Greedily, she licked and sucked him, taking him even deeper as he carefully fed her his cock. He tasted so good, his skin male and salty and smooth against her tongue. Veins pulsed with life and masculine arousal. She lapped at him again with her tongue, and then he pulled out. He lifted his shaft to present his balls to her.

Oh sweet geezus, that was hot. She blinked at the sight

of his scrotum, which never in her life had she thought of as attractive, but wow, he was big and full, his balls tight against his body. She traced her tongue up the puckered seam, then licked over his balls. A choked noise escaped him. He liked this.

"Oh Christ," he gritted out, pumping his cock as she suckled gently on his tender flesh. Her tongue delved lower, behind his sac, and unbearable excitement built low inside her all over again. She lost herself in the scent of his body in this intimate position, the taste of him on her tongue, the feel of his thin skin between her lips.

He directed his cock back to her mouth and she opened wide to take him. Her eyes drifted closed.

"Yeah, suck me," he groaned. His fingers caressed her hair. "Just like that. Open your eyes and look at me, baby."

She forced her eyes open again.

"Jesus." He stared down at her. "Look at you, enjoying this so much." He used one hand to pull his shaft out of her mouth, traced around her wet lips with the tip, then fed it to her again. She murmured a delighted noise and he groaned. "Oh fuck yeah."

He wet his lips, watching her, controlling the flex of his hips so he didn't hurt her. She wanted more, wanted to take him as deep as she could. The head of his cock bumped the back of her throat and she focused on breathing through her mouth.

"There it is," he muttered. "Gonna come...so close...baby..."

She wasn't sure if he'd pull out, but she wanted him to come in her mouth, wanted to complete this act in that utterly intimate way. So she kept her lips closed around him, still watching him.

"I like it any way," he muttered. "In your mouth, on your tits...you take what you want, baby."

She gave a tiny nod and sucked harder.

His eyes were dark, his face flushed and he wore a look

of such ecstasy it made pleasure swell inside her at giving that to him.

Guttural noises rose from his throat as he came, pulsing in her mouth. He held her head, his head going back, eyes closing. Hot liquid landed on her tongue and she swallowed it down, a tantalizing taste that lingered and made her want more.

He groaned and swiped his tongue over his bottom lip. He dragged his hands through her hair and released her, slowly withdrawing from her mouth. "You love sucking cock, don't you?" he murmured.

Well, she wasn't sure she'd ever loved it that much before, but she'd sure as hell enjoyed *that*. However, his ego didn't need any building. She smiled at him. "That was okay."

He choked on a laugh and staggered around to sink to the floor beside her, kicking aside the pants around his ankles. He rested his head on the couch. "Babe. That was epic."

⟳⟲

Sloan lay on her stomach on her bed, head on her arms. Levi lay crosswise. He kissed the small of her back, his hand curving over one butt cheek. Lovely. So lovely.

"Come to the wedding with me next weekend."

Her head jerked up, the muscles that had been so relaxed from several amazing orgasms tightening. "What?"

"You need to have some fun outside the office or the bedroom."

"I have fun," she snapped.

"You really don't."

"I went out tonight, didn't I?"

"With your parents."

"My dad and stepmother," she corrected in a low mutter.

"Whatever. Also, it didn't sound like you really enjoyed it."

She sighed and lowered her head back down to the mattress. "I'm not coming to the wedding."

"Why not? I need a date."

"I won't know anyone there."

"You'll know me. Come on. We'll drink some champagne, dance a little, make out in a corner somewhere... It'll be fun."

"I do like champagne."

He traced a finger up the crack of her ass. A shiver worked over her skin. "I'd like to lick champagne off your gorgeous body." He touched the hollow at the base of her spine. "Right here."

Another shiver.

"I booked a room at the hotel for that night," he continued, idly running his index finger up her spine. "We can stay there."

Tingles slid over her skin at his touch. "You and me in a hotel room again," she murmured. "Déjà vu."

He laughed. "Not the same at all. This time we'll be in the same room. And *we'll* be the ones making all the noise."

She smiled, eyes closed. "What hotel?"

"The Drake."

"Nice." She paused. "What about Chuck?"

"Colin's going to look after him."

She really didn't want to go to a wedding with him. That would involve meeting his friends, and apparently his family. They'd been having hot, kinky sex together. They were *not* dating. Going to a wedding together was like a date.

But he'd got her all mellow and submissive, as he did every time, and she found herself agreeing to this proposition.

"Tell me why you didn't enjoy your evening with your

parents. I mean, dad and stepmom. Is she a wicked stepmother?"

"No. She's not wicked at all. She's a very nice lady who owns a flower shop."

"So what's the problem?"

"It's a long story."

"Tell me."

His hands continued to play over her butt and the backs of her thighs. Her insides quivered and since her brain was basically mush, she started talking. "My mom went missing when I was fourteen."

His hand stilled on her thigh and his body tensed.

"They never found her," she continued. "We still don't know what happened to her."

"Christ. That's fucking awful."

"It is. I mean, it was a long time ago now. But it *was* pretty awful." That was downplaying it admirably. It had been hell. "She'd struggled with mental illness in the past, but she'd seemed to be doing well when that happened. We didn't know if someone abducted her, or…killed her." She swallowed. "Of if she took her own life. They never found her body. The police investigated for months afterward to find a trace of her and came up with nothing."

He made a sympathetic noise. "I can't even imagine, Sloane," he said slowly. "That must've been so hard." He stroked her hair in a lingering, comforting caress.

She left out the part about them investigating her dad, focusing on him as a person of interest in his wife's disappearance, along with the details of the pain she'd felt, the burning emptiness, hoping and wishing for her mom to be found alive and okay.

"After that, everything changed. My dad couldn't afford the house we lived in on only his income so we had to move to an apartment. I had to give up my figure skating because we couldn't afford it. I had to change schools and leave all my friends behind, and we couldn't take our dog with us."

"You had a dog?"

"Yeah. A cockapoo. Teddy."

"Ah, Sloane." He pressed his mouth to her back.

"Starting over in a brand new middle school where I knew nobody was hard. And I had to look after my little brother and sister."

"How old were they?"

"They were eleven. They're twins." She let out a short puff of air, remembering. "I basically was like a mom to them after that. My dad wasn't much help...he was messed up. I stayed at home to go to Calhoun College until Becca and Eric went away to school. Anyway, we survived. Then my dad started seeing Viv. It was...good. It was nice for him to have someone. But then, they wanted to get married. So my dad had to have my mom declared legally dead."

"Ugh." He rolled away from her now, turned on the bed and snuggled up to her back, pulling her into his arms. His heat and weight pressed her down and the tenseness that had crept into her body eased. "That's terrible."

"Yeah. I know it was crazy, but I'd always hoped that one day they'd find her. That somehow she was still alive somewhere. I knew there was no rational explanation for how that could happen...how she could just have disappeared that long but still be alive. But...growing up, I always had that little hope."

"That's understandable." He kissed her shoulder.

"I guess I kind of resented it when Dad did that, so he could marry another woman. At that point Mom had been gone for about eight years. It's not that I hate Viv. She's very nice. It's just...I don't even know how to explain it."

"I think I get it. Even though your mom was most likely

dead, having to do it that way, to actually make that call, seems...cold."

"Yes!" She turned her head toward him. "That's it."

"Like you all were turning your back on her."

"Exactly! Giving up hope felt like...giving up on her. Anyway. I've just never been able to feel close to Viv. Or to my dad, actually. He's better now, but he checked out and put everything on me, and that affected our relationship. Now, he wants me to go home and visit, and he wants us to all be a family. But it's weird."

"Where are your brother and sister?"

"Eric lives here. He's an investment banker. Becca lives in New York. She's an editor for *Sparkle* magazine."

"They feel the same about your dad and Viv?"

"Mmm. Not exactly. Eric and I haven't really talked about it that much, but Becca and I have. For them, they don't feel close to Dad because they never really got any love or affection from him. He was just not there for us. They're not angry or resentful, it's just that he's almost a...stranger to them."

"That's really sad."

The way he said that made something hot swell up in her chest. He wasn't judging how she'd felt. He wasn't pitying her. He was just saying something that was very, very true. And for some reason she found herself turning into his embrace, pressing her face to his neck, and holding on tight.

12

"That's a stupid idea."

"No it's not." Levi chucked a crumpled-up Post-it at Scott across their desks Tuesday morning.

"It is and you know it."

"Okay. How about this: 'It's what your right hand is for'?"

Scott burst out laughing. "Okay, that's good."

"'I don't always drink beer. But when I do, I drink a lot of it.'" Levi deepened his voice.

"I'm not writing that down."

"Fine. Be like that." He paused. "'If you tap it, they will come.'"

"That only works for draft beer. And why are so many of your ideas about sex?"

Levi grinned. "Thanks."

"That wasn't a compliment."

"I'm taking it as one. Come on, man. Sex sells. We all know it."

"Hey, you know what I learned the other day?"

"I'm afraid to ask."

"Apparently hops have aphrodisiac qualities for women. Something about estrogen."

"Shut the fuck up. Drinking beer makes women horny?"

128

Scott shrugged. "Maybe we should do some research on that."

Levi grinned. "Get some girls drunk and get laid. Whoa." He rubbed his chin and stared into space while ideas percolated. "Can we use that?"

"Nope, no, no. Forget that."

Levi sighed. "Let's go have lunch."

"Can't. I'm having lunch with Dash."

"What?" Levi frowned. "You're cheating on me with another copywriter?"

"Just keeping you on your toes. See you later."

Levi watched Scott leave with a reluctant smile. The guy was growing on him and Scott seemed to be warming up to him. He tapped his fingers on his desk. He needed someone to have lunch with. What was Sloane doing? Nah, she'd never agree to have lunch with him. Whatever was going on between them was going on outside the office, she'd made that very clear.

He hadn't seen his sisters in a while, and Essie worked not far from here. Maybe she was free for lunch. He sent off a quick text message and got a reply agreeing to meet him at Biryani House two blocks away.

◯◖◗◯

Sloane was striding along Madison after a quick trip to the bank when she passed a small patio restaurant. She glanced at it, then took a second look after seeing Levi sitting at a table for two. With a woman. Not someone she knew, so no one from the office.

At that moment Levi looked up and saw her. His smile for her was instant and he lifted a hand to wave. She shaped her mouth into a smile also, waved and kept going.

A bad burning feeling inside her made her realize she hadn't eaten lunch. Hungry. She was hungry. She'd planned to pick up a salad on her way back. She walked blindly down the street, her mind consumed with who that woman was with Levi.

He didn't have a girlfriend, she knew that, but she did know he liked to date a lot.

Beh. It didn't matter who she was. Why was she even thinking about it? They weren't in a relationship and she had no right to care about who else he was seeing, whether it was for lunch or dinner or hot sex.

That burning feeling in her gut intensified.

She paused in front of the Lachman Building. She hadn't stopped to get that salad. She sighed. Maybe she wasn't hungry after all. She pushed through the revolving doors into the lobby and tapped across the marble tiled floor to the bank of elevators. She'd just go back to her office and work. She probably had a granola bar in her desk.

She should not be going to that wedding this weekend with Levi. That would be a mistake. She'd find him later — when he was back from lunch — and tell him that.

Her afternoon was crazy with meetings with various account managers reviewing projects and dealing with several minor crises, including a call from Cody at the Steel brand about an ad that was supposed to be on a website. It hadn't been seen all day and they wanted to know why. She made a phone call and fixed that. Then Joe called her into his office. Somehow she had a feeling it wasn't to congratulate her on solving all those problems or to tell her the new suit she was wearing was very nice.

She sank onto the chair in his office and crossed her legs, smoothing her skirt.

"All day long, all the stalls in the men's room were occupied."

She looked sideways, then down, then up. "Uh." Was Joe losing his mind? He wasn't that old. Surely he could not be experiencing early onset dementia? She'd heard stories from back in his early days when he'd been able to drink anyone under the table…was he drunk? "I'm sorry to hear that," she said lamely.

He frowned. "They weren't really occupied. Someone went into every stall and put a pair of stuffed pants and shoes in there as if they were sitting on the toilet. They must have locked the doors from the inside and crawled under."

She bit her lip. "Oh."

"As much as I admire the effort and ingenuity that went into that, it was a little awkward when Tom and Jack were here." The CEO and chief marketing officer from Verhoeven.

She swallowed and closed her eyes briefly. "It might not have been the Brew Crew guys."

"Of course it was them! They're the bad boys of advertising." Joe's face flushed. He waved a wild hand. "We've talked about this before, Sloane. This has to stop."

She tried not to visibly wince. *Shit!* "I'm sorry, Joe. I'll have another talk with them. They're bright guys, I'm sure they'll understand the consequences of something like that when a client is here."

"I know I can count on you."

But the way he said the words made her worry that maybe he wasn't so sure about that.

She walked into her own office, kicked the wastebasket with a pointy-toed shoe and sank into her chair. Had her Brew Crew done that? Had Levi been a part of it? She dropped her head into her hands for a few minutes, imagining guys going into the men's room, finding the stalls all occupied, waiting, giving up… A choked snort of laughter erupted from between her lips, but she clamped down on the humor. Even Joe had known it was funny. But he didn't want that stuff going on any more.

What could you do with a bunch of creative, talented people who were smart and confident? But this was a business. That was a cold, hard fact. And she needed to be cold and hard.

It was too late today to do anything about it. That would be something to look forward to tomorrow. But she still needed to talk to Levi.

She walked down to his cubicle.

"What do a blonde and a beer bottle have in common?" she heard Scott ask Levi as she approached.

Levi snorted. "What?"

"They're both empty from the neck up."

Sloane's eyebrows lifted.

The two guys noticed her standing there. Levi gave her a weak grin and held his hands up. "I didn't say that. *He* said it."

She gave Scott a long, cool look.

"It's a joke," he said. "Not about anyone in particular. Certainly not about you. Definitely not."

"Did you need something, Sloane?" Levi asked.

Dammit. She didn't want to have this conversation in front of Scott. "Um, no. Did you have a nice lunch?"

"Hey, I only took a little over an hour." He raised his hands.

She blinked. "Ooookay. I have no idea how long you were gone."

"Oh." He grinned, that sexy, boyish, nipple-tingling grin. "In that case, it was more like forty-five minutes."

Scott snorted and Sloane felt her lips twitch. She needed to get this over with. "Can I talk to you in my office?"

"Sure." Levi rose from his chair and followed her down the hall.

With the door closed, she turned to him. "I can't go to that wedding with you this weekend."

"Uh...why not?"

"I just can't."

He gave her a narrow-eyed look. "That's not a good enough reason."

"It's the only reason you're going to get," she snapped.

He moved closer and she took a step back. Something

about his demeanor made her feel...uncertain. He was confident. In control. Her pulse fluttered.

"You're coming to the wedding," he said firmly.

"Levi, no. It would be a mistake. You and I should not be doing...this...whatever." She waved a hand.

He stepped closer and again she tried to move back, but found herself against the wall. He crowded her, pressing his big body against hers.

"Not here," she whispered.

"I'm not going to fuck you here in your office up against the wall," he growled. "Although maybe I should. Maybe you'd like that."

She moaned.

"I just want you to be honest with me. What's going on?" His lips nipped at her jaw.

"Nothing!" God, he smelled so good, and his big muscles made her pussy quiver. She turned her face away from him.

"That was my sister."

She went very still. His sister. She swallowed. She mentally sorted through how she wanted to respond to this news. Heat swept down through her. There was no good way. She was an idiot. She'd made a fool of herself. Anger at herself made her push at Levi. "Move away."

"Fine." To her surprise he stepped back. But then he further shocked her by lifting a hand to her face, cupping her cheek and turning her head to meet his eyes. "You're coming to the wedding."

She held his gaze, her chest going hot and tight at the undeniable command in his tone. "Fine," she said shortly.

⌒◯◌✳◌◯⌒

They'd arranged to try on and pick up their tuxedoes for the wedding Thursday at noon. All five guys—the groom, Jacob, best man, Levi, and the three groomsmen, Tucker, Luke and Jacob's brother Daniel—were there. Levi, Daniel and Tucker were on their lunch break. Luke was an ER doctor and had a day off. Jacob had taken vacation time because Tara had him running all kinds of errands and driving visiting family members around all week.

"I'm not saying she's Bridezilla," Jacob said as one of the sales associates in the store checked the fit of his trousers. "But she's got this wedding app on her phone and she's keeping track of everything. Including RSVPs. By the way Levi, she wants to know who you're bringing to the wedding. She doesn't believe you're actually bringing a date."

"I am." Levi frowned at the rental tux jacket as he put it on. He owned a perfectly good tuxedo, but had to rent this one because Tara had to have all the guys in matching suits, vests and ties.

"Who is it?"

"Sloane Granderson."

"What?" Jacob's head whipped around. "Seriously?"

"Yeah, seriously." Levi had mentioned her a couple of times to Jacob, once when they were working out at the gym, another day when they'd had beers after work.

He was still confused about what had gone down Tuesday when she'd tried to get out of coming with him. Intuition told him that it had something to do with her seeing him with Essie, and probably jumping to the conclusion that he was screwing around with another woman. But if that was the case, why hadn't she just said that?

Because she was jealous. And either she didn't want to admit it, or she didn't even recognize it as jealousy.

The last time a chick had been jealous of him, he'd run...fast. Because that meant she was way too serious and no woman had any claim on him or right to be jealous, and he'd see whomever he wanted to see. Those were his rules. But now, the idea that Sloane was jealous at seeing him with another woman, even though it was his bossy older sister, made his masculine pride puff up. That was the confusing part.

"I thought she was a ball breaker," Jacob said.

He frowned. "She's a strong, assertive woman."

"Ball breaker."

"Shut the fuck up."

Jacob narrowed his eyes at him. "Why do I have the feeling you're keeping shit from me?"

"Because I am." Levi grinned. Yeah, they talked about women and sex and any kinky things they'd been able to get away with—their first blow jobs, first bondage, first butt sex. But he'd noticed that when things got serious with Tara, Jacob had stopped spilling details. And now he found himself in the same weird boat. Talking about the things he did with Sloane just seemed…wrong.

"So you two are dating?"

"I wouldn't call it that." He adjusted the tie in the mirror. "Are we done here? I have to get back to work."

"The tux is perfect," another associate told him. "You were an easy fit." He looked at Tucker. "You, on the other hand, were a challenge." Tuck was six foot three and over two hundred pounds, with massive shoulders. "You can take it off," he said to Levi. "I'll get it bagged up for you."

Levi bolted into the spacious changing room and began to disrobe. This had already taken more than an hour.

He handed the garments out to the sales associate who took them. Levi emerged in dress pants and shirt and tapped his fingers on the counter as the guy took his time hanging the tux in a garment bag.

"You all look fabulous," the sales guy told them. "It's going to be a beautiful wedding."

"I'm going for a manicure after this," Jacob said.

Levi gave him a look. "A manicure?"

"Tara wants my hands to look good. The photographer is gonna take pictures of our hands with our rings on."

"Tell her to stop stepping on your dick," Luke advised him.

"I'm afraid to talk to her. She's wound super tight right now."

Christ, was this all worth it? Levi shook his head. Finally he was done. He grabbed the garment bag. "I'll see you guys tomorrow night," he said. "Six o'clock, right?"

"Right. First the rehearsal, then dinner right after."

"Great."

He legged it out of the shop just off Michigan Avenue, nearly sprinting the ten blocks to the office in the heat. He had a meeting at one thirty he didn't want to be late for.

He kept thinking about the story Sloane had told him about her mom. And how she'd had to take over looking after her brother and sister. That was a lot for a fourteen-year-old kid. That was the age Colin was, who was slouching around saying, "There's this girl..." and walking dogs to make a little money. He imagined Sloane as a fourteen-year-old, all serious and responsible. Imagined her moving to a new school where she knew no one at that age. She'd probably needed a mom then, but she was the one looking after everyone else. Probably devastated and hurt by her mom's disappearance. Whether something had happened to her or she'd chosen to leave her family — which really fucking sucked — whatever the reason, having your mother desert you would be pretty painful. And giving up a dog — fuck! That *really* sucked.

Thinking about it gave him a weird ache in his gut.

He carried his garment bag into the building, sweating like a cold beer bottle in the sun, and headed to his office. Crap, he was about to be late.

He ran into Sloane coming down the hall, on her way to

a meeting room. Man, just seeing her made him happy. She looked, as usual, gorgeous, wearing a sleeveless blue dress and a pair of strappy sandals.

She eyed the bag. "Shopping?"

"No. This is my tux for the wedding. Had to have a last fitting and pick it up today."

"Ah."

"Don't worry," he said in a low voice near her ear. "You'll get to see me wearing it on Saturday."

"I'm so excited," she said in a dry voice.

"And you get to take it *off* me on Saturday." He winked as he continued down the hall while she walked the other way, enjoying her little huff of shocked laughter.

He was the last one to arrive at the meeting, although he was only two minutes late, and for once nobody busted his balls about it. He slid into a chair as Mason started talking to the communications guys from Wolfgang Black Brewery, one of Verhoeven's new craft breweries, about some of the ideas they'd been working on.

Levi quickly took in their doubtful expressions.

"I don't know," Jeff said. "That's not what our competitors are doing."

"Well, sure," Mason said. "That's the idea. You want to stand out from the competition."

As the discussion moved along, Levi felt uncomfortable with some of the comments Jeff and Rudy made about Verhoeven. Criticizing their "big beer" mentality. He and Mason exchanged glances.

"Maybe we could combine those two ideas," Jeff said.

Fuck, if Levi had a dollar for every time he'd heard that, he'd be retired and living on the Riviera. Okay, slight exaggeration, but still. He resisted the urge to roll his eyes as he and Scott explained why that wouldn't work.

Levi started asking questions. When he wasn't sure why the client was rejecting everything, he found a sense of curiosity usually helped. He eventually teased out of them a better feel for what they were looking for, but by the time the meeting was over, he still felt uneasy.

Mason showed the client out and Noah stood. "Hang on, guys," he said. "I'm going to see if Sloane's around."

He returned with Sloane at the same time Mason came back. "What's up?" Sloane asked, slipping into a chair.

"Those two dudes are going to sabotage this campaign," Levi said.

She blinked at him. "Oh come on, Levi."

"He's right." Noah sat at the table again. "They've got issues with Verhoeven." He filled Sloane in on some of the things they'd said.

She listened intently as they all shared various pieces of the meeting. Damn that was hot.

No, no, focus.

Finally, Sloane rubbed her forehead. "I'll talk to Derek," she said, naming the VP of communications at Verhoeven. "Maybe even Tom." Tom Verhoeven. CEO. Big cheese. Head honcho. "He needs to know about that."

"Yeah," Mason agreed. "They might want to replace them with a management team they've picked themselves, someone who's on board with their strategic plan for the brand. Because those guys are *not* on board."

"That's going to be a fun discussion." Sloane sighed. "Okay, leave it with me."

Levi wanted to follow her down the hall to her office where he could massage that frown off her forehead and make her feel so much better...

Giving himself a mental shake, he returned his attention to business.

"Okay," Mason said. "While you guys are here, what's the status of the Cerone campaign?"

13

"Who is that woman crying?" Sloane whispered to Levi.

"That's Tara's grandmother. Apparently they're very Catholic and she's upset that they didn't get married in a church."

"Oh dear." Sloane eyed the elderly woman sitting on a chair against the wall, family members huddled around her offering tissues.

"She'll survive. I'll dance with her later. Old ladies like me."

"*All* ladies like you," she said with an eye roll.

Levi grinned. "Including you, right, beautiful?" He leaned in and rubbed his nose against hers. She couldn't help but smile.

"Including me. Although I'm not sure why I let you talk me into coming to this wedding. It's not much fun being the best man's date. I've barely seen you."

They were standing in the Gold Coast Ballroom at the Drake Hotel. Tara and Jacob had said their vows a short time ago in a lovely ceremony. Then the bridal party had disappeared to get photos taken and had only recently reappeared—minus the bride and groom—to begin the reception. Waiters circulated with trays of champagne and finger foods as guests mingled before dinner.

"I know. I'm sorry." He frowned. "I should have realized."

He'd introduced her to his family and had apparently asked them to take her under their wing since she didn't know anyone else there. Jacob and Levi had grown up together and their families were good friends too, so they'd all been invited to the wedding.

"Your sisters are hilarious, though."

"My sisters are a pain in my ass," he muttered. "But not as much as they were growing up. One day they might actually acknowledge I'm an adult now."

She grinned. She could tell they loved their baby brother, despite the teasing insults and advice with which they inundated him.

A little excitement when one of the guests had broken her ankle coming up the stairs at the front entrance had also passed the time. Sucked for the girl, who was now at the hospital. She'd been wearing sky-high platform shoes and had fallen off them and snapped her ankle. This made Sloane wince and vow to be more careful in her heels.

"You look amazing," he said in a low, husky voice. "Love that dress."

Her skin heated. "Thank you."

"Uncle Levi!" Two small bodies flew across the carpeted floor and jumped up and down in front of him. Sloane had earlier met his niece Emily and nephew Elijah, the children of his oldest sister Madeleine. "I saw you in the wedding, Uncle Levi!"

Everyone in the ballroom had known that because five-year-old Emily had jumped up on her chair and yelled, "Hi, Uncle Levi!" waving frantically when he'd appeared with the other guys. Just another girl who loved him.

Sloane smiled at the little girl in her pretty pink party dress. Her younger brother was equally adorable in black pants, a pale blue dress shirt and patterned vest. Their mother Madeleine appeared and smiled at Sloane.

Levi bent and picked up Emily. "Hi, princess. You look beautiful."

"So do you!" She squeezed his neck in a hug.

Levi turned his attention to Elijah and gave him a fist bump. "Hey, dude."

Elijah beamed adoringly at his uncle. "Hey, Uncalevi."

Emily turned her big blue eyes just like her uncle's on Sloane. "Can I sit beside you at dinner? Mommy says I can't sit beside Uncle Levi 'cause he's gonna be um...getting head—"

"Sitting at the head table," Madeleine interjected.

Sloane exchanged a quick look with Levi, both of them suppressing smiles.

"I'd rather sit with you, princess," Levi said.

"I'm not sure if we're sitting at the same table," Sloane said to Emily with a smile. "But if we are, you can for sure sit beside me. That would be fun."

The bride and groom appeared in the doorway then, beaming and glowing. Tara was a beautiful bride, her dark hair cascading down her back in loose curls, a veil pinned to the back, her wedding dress a frothy white confection that left slender shoulders and arms bare and showed off some impressive cleavage. Sexy yet classy.

"I wanna go see the bride! She looks like a for real princess!" Emily wriggled out of Levi's arms and dashed off. "Come on, Elijah!"

The little guy obediently followed his sister.

"She's so bossy," Levi said. "I wonder where she gets that from." He rolled his eyes at his sister, who punched his shoulder before following her children.

When Sloane had first seen Levi standing up at the front for the ceremony in his black tuxedo, she'd been swamped with a rush of emotion. She wasn't sure what that emotion was and didn't want to try too hard to name it. Weddings. They always did that to people, right?

He'd winked at her as he'd passed by escorting the maid of honor out following the exchange of vows. She found herself...jealous of that maid of honor, a pretty redhead looking gorgeous in a green dress, holding on to Levi's arm.

Who picked green for their bridesmaids' dresses? But Tara had, a satiny moss green, each bridesmaid's style a little different—two strapless, one V-neck and another with spaghetti straps. With white rose bouquets accented with greenery, they looked stunning, and the guys in black tuxedos with moss green pocket squares and white rosebud and green leaf boutonnieres complemented them perfectly.

Now, with their champagne glasses in hand, Levi took her around and introduced her to his buddies Luke, Tucker and Cam, some other friends, members of Jacob's family who apparently were like his own, and finally the bride and groom.

"So, this is Sloane." Jacob shook her hand and gave her an appraising look. He was almost as good looking as Levi, with dark blond hair in a very short cut, standing about an inch shorter than Levi and a little heavier. "Happy to meet you."

"Likewise." She respected his assessment of whether she was a good enough date for his best friend. "I appreciate you having me here on your special day. Congratulations to both of you."

"I didn't believe he'd actually bring a date," Tara said, dark eyes gleaming. "And he even introduced you to his family. Whoa, Levi."

Sloane gave Levi a sidelong glance. "Should I feel honored?"

Tara laughed and Levi rolled his eyes. "Moving on." He took Sloane's hand. "Don't forget, Tara, I'm making a speech tonight. You don't want to piss me off."

"Gah!" Tara actually looked nervous. "Levi..."

He gave her an evil grin and tugged Sloane on to introduce her to more people.

"I've been tormenting her for weeks with what my speech is going to be about," Levi said.

"Please tell me I'm not the only woman you've ever introduced to your family."

He shrugged. "Okay."

She frowned. What the hell did that mean?

Eventually people were directed to take their seats for dinner. Sloane was at a round table with Levi's single sister Essie, his other sister Heather and her husband, Nick, his parents, Michael and Linda, and a cousin of Jacob's and his date. Levi's other sister Madeleine was at a table beside them with her husband, Bryan, and Emily and Elijah.

"Sloane, Sloane, sit here!" Emily said.

"She can't sit with us, honey." Madeleine smiled at Sloane. The pretty place cards indicated where each guest was to sit. "See...what does this say?" She got Emily to read the place cards, sounding out the names. Pretty good for a five-year-old.

"But hey, my seat is right here." Sloane pulled out the chair right behind Emily's. "It's pretty close."

This seemed to satisfy Emily, who for some reason seemed to have taken a liking to her.

The dinner was amazing, filet mignon with caramelized onions, goat cheese crusts and truffle butter. The entire wedding was incredible. The head table sat in front of tall windows draped in velvet, city lights visible beyond the glass panes. White and pale peach roses and glowing candles adorned every table, along with gilt chairs and snowy tablecloths. Sloane could only imagine how much it had cost. Who was paying for this shindig? She knew Levi's family was wealthy, so it made sense that Jacob's family was also probably well off since he and Levi had grown up in the same neighborhood, but was Tara's family rich also? Although these days it wasn't necessarily the bride's family who paid for the wedding. Lots of couples paid for it themselves.

Levi came to visit a few times during dinner, pausing with a hand on the back of Sloane's chair to exchange some banter with his family. He was so freakin' gorgeous in that tux he took her breath away every time she saw him. She just wished he wasn't sitting so far away.

As if knowing what she was thinking, he bent down and murmured in her ear, "Duty's almost done. Once the dinner's over, we make a few speeches, cut the cake and I have the obligatory dance with the maid of honor." His hand rubbed over her back, the skin bared by her dress. Tingles slid down her spine.

"That cute redhead?"

He gave her a slow, heated smile. "What? She's cute? I hadn't noticed. It's just Tara's friend Brynn. Anyhoo. Soon I'll be done and you and I can do those things we talked about."

"Um, what things?"

"Slow dancing. Making out in a corner. Licking champagne off your sexy body."

Heat flared low inside her. "Oh, right. Those things." She reached for her wineglass and took a big gulp, then whispered, "Your parents are sitting right *there*."

He gave her a wicked grin as he moved away.

Sloane had to admit she enjoyed the dinner. Levi's family made sure to include her in conversation, although there were a few times she felt a little lost. She loved that they all had a sense of humor, which shouldn't have been surprising given Levi's wit. She did sense Linda and Michael's interest in her, though they kept things very casual and light.

Then it was time for the speeches. Tara's father made a lovely toast to the bride and groom, and Jacob replied to that and toasted the bridesmaids. And then it was Levi's turn. He took the microphone with an ease that again shouldn't have surprised her.

After thanking Jacob on behalf of the bridesmaids, Levi began. "I'm told the best man's speech should last as long as the groom can last in the bedroom." He paused. "So thanks and have a great night everyone!" He began to walk away from the mic and after a beat, a roar of laughter filled the ballroom. Sloane watched Jacob cover his face with his hand, shaking his head but grinning.

Levi, also grinning, returned to the mic. "Seriously, Jacob, you're a great guy and I'm honored to have you as my friend and sometimes partner in crime. We won't get into all the crimes with this mixed audience." He paused, smiling as people laughed. "I've been his partner in crime on a few wild nights, but also a friend he can tell anything. And I do mean anything — which gave me a lot of material for this speech tonight." As people laughed again, he shot Tara a wry smile. "Don't worry, Tara, what happens in Vegas stays in Vegas. And Los Angeles." He paused. "And Bangkok."

Tara shook her head and lifted her glass at him.

"Jacob and I have known each other since elementary school. You're like the brother I never had, Jacob, only better because you didn't actually live with me." More laughter rippled through the crowd. "We walked our dogs together, raced our bikes, had our first big make out session together." Shocked titters greeted this statement. "No, no, not like that!" He waved his hands to more laughter. "Jacob was in the closet while *I* had *my* first make out session." The guests laughed again. "No, no, not 'in the closet'...I mean literally, he was hiding in the closet." He grinned.

"This is the guy I accidentally gave a black eye, played Pokemon with and got drunk with...but enough about the bachelor party."

More laughs. Sloane smiled, elbows on the table, wineglass in hand. She had to give a little eye roll at mention of the bachelor party. Yeah, that hadn't been Pokemon they'd been playing.

"Saturday night has always been our night to hit the clubs and some of you may not know it, but Jacob is a great dancer. He often charms the girls with his amazing moves. Er, I should make that past tense. He *used to* charm the girls with his amazing dance moves. In fact, at one of those clubs not so far from here, he met Tara and I'm sure it was his dancing that attracted her. Right, Tara? Right?" He turned and looked at her. She laughed and shook her head. "Okay, maybe not." He paused. "Tara, you are an amazing woman, and you totally deserve someone special. Jacob, good thing you married her first."

Another burst of laughter filled the room. Sloane's heart shifted in her chest.

"Jacob, when you met Tara, I'd like to say I knew immediately that she was the perfect woman for you. However, that would be a lie because at first I thought she was way too good for you." He paused again for the laughter. "Tara is beautiful and smart and funny and kind. But it turns out you two *are* perfect for each other. Since you've been with her, Jacob, I've seen you relax and loosen up and not take life so seriously, something I apparently failed to teach you. She brings out the good side in you— which is pretty damn difficult."

He grinned at the audience he had in the palm of his hand.

"For a long time, Jacob swore he wasn't falling in love with Tara, but I knew it was true love the day he actually *talked to her on the phone.* Yep. Not just texting, folks. They *talked* to each other. That's how I knew it was serious." He paused to take a sip of water as more chuckles filled the room.

"Now I think I'm supposed to pass on some kind of

profound advice about marriage. But I'm the last guy in the world who should give advice about love or marriage." His self-deprecating eye roll and smile made Sloane's heart quiver. "However, not knowing anything about a particular topic has never stopped me from talking about it." The laughs this time obviously came from those in the crowd who knew him. "So I decided to do some research and get advice from the experts. First of all, I went to Emily, my five-year-old niece." More laughter rippled through the room and behind Sloane, Emily bounced on her chair and clapped at mention of her name. "Here's Emily's advice for Jacob—be a good kisser. If you're a good kisser, Tara might not remember that you never do the dishes."

He took another sip of water. "Then I went to our buddy Trent. You might not think a guy who's been divorced twice would have good advice about marriage, but hey, he swears he's learned some things. Trent says the most important thing is to learn how to fight. Now..." Levi settled his hands on the podium, "...telling newlyweds to fight might not sound like the best advice. But Trent says there's a right way and a wrong way to fight, and you should learn how to fight the right way." He smiled at Tara and Jacob. "And then I went to Jacob's grandparents, who've been married fifty-three years. That's right, folks." Someone started clapping. "Yeah, let's give them a round of applause." Levi applauded too. "So here's the advice from Trudy and Gill Leech. They say that there will be times you'll hate each other and you might fall out of love. But the key to a successful marriage is letting yourself fall in love with each other *again*. And again." He paused. "And again."

Levi picked up his wine glass. "Now, as a man who will drink to pretty much anything, it gives me great pleasure to invite you all to raise your glasses and join me in a toast to Tara and Jacob."

Sloane smiled, her heart full of emotion once again, and lifted her wineglass to clink against the others at the table. She watched Levi walk over to Tara and hug her, then give his best friend a big, masculine hug and back slap that was clearly heartfelt. She took in the beaming smiles of Levi's family, full of pride and amusement, and she knew exactly how they felt.

Dammit. This was so bad.

The bride and groom cut the cake, the music started and Tara and Jacob danced to Ben Howard singing "Only Love". Sloane's heart took another dive.

She watched Levi join in with that maid of honor—Brenna...no, Brynn—for a short dance, and then he was done with the formalities and was making his way through the tables toward her. His tux fit his big shoulders perfectly, and he was so beautiful as he walked toward her she was mesmerized.

Florence + the Machine started singing "Never Let Me Go" and Sloane's eyes held Levi's as he stopped in front of her chair and held out a hand. "Dance, beautiful girl?"

She let him pull her out of her chair and lead her onto the dance floor. Something weird was happening. She was all tingling and shaky, her chest full and tight, the room spinning a little around them even though she hadn't had that much to drink.

He was a good dancer. Of course. He rested one hand on her waist, though it quickly drifted lower to her hip, then her lower back. His other hand held hers tucked between them as they moved to the music. He gazed into her eyes, the corners of his mouth lifted.

"That was an amazing toast," she said, her lips feeling stiff. "Everyone loved it."

His lips curved more. "Thanks. I'm glad it's over. Biggest stress of the whole fucking wedding."

"You didn't look stressed."

"Don't put your hands inside my jacket," he said. "My pits are super sweaty."

She choked on a laugh and leaned her forehead against his shoulder. "Oh my God. Oh my God." She was saying that about more than just his joke. She felt like she was falling...spiraling down a tunnel helplessly, out of control, feeling all the things she didn't want to feel.

14

Somehow, later that evening Sloane found herself seated next to Levi's mother, telling her the whole sad story about her own mom and her disappearance. Linda's gentle manner and interested questions had sucked her in, and now Linda's sympathy was threatening to make her cry. Sloane never cried.

Maybe it was the champagne.

Wasn't bubbly supposed to make you happy?

Linda patted her shoulder. "You must be so strong. And it sounds like your younger brother and sister turned out just fine."

"They're great," she agreed. "I'm so proud of them. Even though Becca lives in New York, we're always in touch on Facebook and email, and we visit. And even though Eric's busy, he keeps in touch too. He calls to ask how to get a mustard stain off his new shirt or how to hardboil eggs, and we have lunch every couple of weeks. He let me stay with him while my bathroom was being renovated."

She talked more to Levi's sisters, who had no compunction in telling her all kinds of tales about young Levi.

"Levi is spoiled rotten," Essie said. "But it's our fault."

Heather and Madeleine nodded their agreement. "Mom and Dad were supposed to be done having kids after Essie," Madeleine, the eldest, said. "They kept trying for a boy and ended up with three girls."

"That's always the way," Sloane agreed. "I know someone who was trying for a girl and ended up with four boys."

"Yep. Then along came Levi, a surprise baby, but the boy they'd always wanted. Of course they were prepared to give him anything and everything he ever wanted."

"And there were Essie and Heather and me...how old?" Madeleine looked at Essie.

"I was five when he was born," Essie said. "He was my very own real life baby doll."

"Yeah, me too." Heather grinned. "I was seven. We actually fought over who was going to change his diapers." She rolled her eyes. "Then who was going to push the stroller and...well, you get the picture. Little Levi was pampered and spoiled rotten."

"Remember that stuffed dog he had?"

"Squidgy."

"Yeah. He slept with that dog until he was twelve."

"No, I think it was more like fifteen." They all laughed.

"Remember that time we went to Disneyland?" Madeleine said. "And he left Squidgy in the hotel bed and when we got back to the hotel that night we couldn't find it anywhere." She smiled at Sloane. "He was devastated, crying his eyes out. We were all running around the hotel trying frantically to find the damn thing for him. The maids had changed the bed and accidentally taken it with the laundry. Hotel staff hunted it down and found it in the laundry room and brought it back."

Sloane grinned. "Lucky."

"Actually, he might *still* sleep with that dog." Heather tapped her chin. "It's entirely possible."

Sloane smiled. "If that's an attempt to get me to tell you

whether I've slept with him…what the hell, I'll bite. I can confirm he does not sleep with that dog anymore."

All three of his sisters grinned at Sloane's directness. "I like you," Essie said.

"What are you telling her about me?" Levi appeared beside her and handed her another glass of champagne. "Never mind, I don't want to know."

"Squidgy," Sloane murmured as she lifted the flute to her lips.

Levi laughed. "I loved that dog."

Then it was on to getting to know his friends, Cam, Tucker and Luke. "Er, do they know I was in the room next door to your bachelor party?" she asked Levi as they approached the group.

"Yep." He made a face. "I had to share that astonishing coincidence the day I started at Huxworth Packard. I'd already told them I'd run into you in the hall the next morning and gave them hell again for making so much noise. Just wanted to make sure they knew the extent of my humiliation thanks to them."

"Well, this could be awkward."

"Ah, they're good guys."

He was right. They were good guys. Luke Chen was a handsome Asian man with chiseled cheekbones, short black hair and a lean build. Tucker Dempsey was huge and built, a firefighter, and Cam McFarlane was allegedly a police officer but in Sloane's opinion looked more like one of the guys from *Duck Dynasty* with his long hair and full beard.

"He's a cop?" she whispered to Levi in an aside.

"He's working some undercover case."

"Ah."

Tucker and Luke wore tuxes identical to Levi's, but Cam wasn't a member of the wedding party and wore a suit.

"Dude." Cam slapped Levi's shoulder. "Best speech ever."

"You killed it," Tucker agreed.

"Thanks."

"Tara was worried about what you were going to say."

"I know." Levi grinned. "I had even better jokes about Jacob's sexual prowess and the wedding night but I held back out of respect for Tara."

"And her parents," Tucker said. "The last thing the bride's father wants to hear is how his new son-in-law is going to bang his baby girl tonight."

"True."

"So, Sloane," Cam said. "Did you really catch Levi watching porn at work?"

Sloane choked on a sip of champagne, but recovered quickly. "Why yes, as a matter of fact I did."

"Only you could get away with that and not be fired," Tucker said.

"I wasn't really watching porn," Levi said mildly. "I told you it was a setup."

"So you say." Tucker shrugged but Sloane saw the way the corners of his mouth lifted.

She was having fun. At first when she'd arrived at the hotel not knowing anyone, she'd considered making a run for it, telling Levi she got sick or something, and even for a while after that she'd wondered why Levi had bothered inviting her since he was busy with the bridal party. But now…she was having so much fun.

She danced with Levi's friends and watched Levi dance with Emily and then, yes, with Tara's grandmother, who was no longer sobbing about her granddaughter's mortal sin. Sloane and Levi danced again, slow and sexy. When it was time for the bride to toss the bouquet and for the groom to sling that garter, she and Levi tacitly agreed to make their way to the farthest corner of the ballroom so there was no danger that either of them would catch anything.

"Almost ready to call it a night?" Levi murmured.

"Whenever you are. You're the one with obligations."

"I've done all my official best man duties. Tara and Jacob are staying here tonight, and I've already arranged for champagne and candles and rose petals in their room."

"Aw. That's so romantic."

"There's a bottle of champagne chilling in our room too." He lifted her hand to his mouth and kissed it. "And I can't wait to get you up there and get your delectable body naked and do dirty things to you."

Lust did a slow, happy roll in her belly. "Let's go."

"Much as I want to bolt, we should say good night."

Many older guests had already left. Levi's sister Madeleine and her husband had taken the kids home. Apparently Levi's friends had plans to stay either as long as the bar was open or as long as the bridesmaids stayed. All of them were currently busting moves on the dance floor and laughing their asses off.

"I hope we'll see you again," Levi's mom said to her as they hugged.

Sloane murmured something noncommittal and hugged Levi's dad too, and they finally walked out of the ballroom.

"Your family is very nice," she said.

"Yeah, sorry my mom was all up in your business. She's just, you know...a mom."

Sloane didn't have a mom who was all up in her business and she thought it was kind of nice. "It was fine. She's lovely."

Levi held Sloane's hand as she maneuvered down the short flight of carpeted steps in her spiky heels. Maybe he was just being extra careful after the guest who'd been carried out on a stretcher earlier. Or maybe he was a gentleman.

They'd met in the lobby earlier and he'd given her a key card so she could take her overnight bag up and leave it in the room, so her things were already there.

"Did I tell you how gorgeous you look?" He shifted closer to her.

"Um, a couple of times. But I don't get tired of hearing it."

"Love the dress."

"Thanks." She swept a hand down her rib cage, over the metallic gold fabric that was ruched and wrapped around her body, then over her waist and hip. She liked the dress too, and the metallic gold, pointy-toed heels that went with it.

"Golden girl," he murmured, lips near her ear. "All shiny and sexy."

Her breathing hitched just as a ding announced the arrival of an elevator car. They stepped inside and were whisked to the ninth floor. They weren't alone, so they rode in silence.

She was pretty sure she wasn't drunk, but she felt…dizzy. She was all full of feelings she wasn't used to having and didn't know what to do with.

He followed her into the room and the door closed with a thunk behind them. A lamp illuminated the room. The king bed was centered beneath heavily draped windows, and a small love seat, a chair and a couple of tables were arranged at the other end of the room. A champagne bucket with a bottle in it sat on the coffee table, along with two fluted glasses. She smiled.

She set her beaded purse on the desk and moved into the room. Levi walked up behind her and slid his arms around her. She sighed and covered his arms with hers. He nuzzled the side of her neck. His body was big and warm at her back, hugging her from behind, and her eyes drifted closed at all the sensations bombarding her.

"Been waiting for this all damn day," he groaned, sliding one hand up to cup her breast. "Watching you in this sexy dress. Those fuck-me shoes."

Warmth spread through her. "I kind of felt the same about you in your tux. Very sexy."

"Gonna get you out of this dress now." He kissed her where her neck met her shoulder. Her head tipped to the side to give him access, and he ran his tongue over her shoulder. Shivers cascaded down her spine. Then he took a step back and found the tiny hidden zipper tab beneath the V in the back of the dress. He tugged it down and pushed the dress off her shoulders, then slid it down over her hips. She wore a strapless bra and thong panties, both in a nude color, which was kind of boring, but oh well. He kissed the center of her back as he flicked open the bra and let it fall.

She looked over her shoulder and started to turn toward him as he untied the bow tie around his neck and pulled it out from beneath the collar of the pintucked shirt. He set his hands on her shoulders, keeping her in place. "Stay like that a minute," he murmured.

She waited, her skin tingling everywhere, sensing him as he moved behind her. He tossed his jacket aside. Then, still behind her, he reached for her hands and gently drew them behind her back. She felt fabric at her wrists and her belly did a flip of excitement as she realized he'd tied her up with his bow tie.

"What are you doing?" She turned her head.

He touched her cheek, bringing her face closer and leaning in to kiss her. "Tying you up."

"I got that." She tested the strength of the binding. Yep, she was tied. "Why?"

"Holy fuck, that's hot," he murmured, apparently looking at her nearly naked body and bound wrists. He brushed her hair aside and opened his mouth on the back of her neck, grazing her with his teeth. "And you're asking me why? Come on, baby."

Yes, she knew why he was tying her up, and geezus, it excited her. She loved it when he took charge, not that she'd admit it to him. Then again, she was fairly certain he knew exactly how much she liked it. Being bound made her even more helpless. Mingled with the excitement was a tiny edge of fear. She was alone in a hotel room with a man...just like she'd overheard a couple of weeks ago.

But it was Levi.

He moved around in front of her. Her eyelashes fluttered as she blinked rapidly, her lips parted. "Shh," he murmured. "It's okay. Do you trust me?"

Her tongue swiped over her bottom lip. She swallowed.

"Be honest, Sloane." He held her gaze.

"What are you going to do to me?"

He smiled. "Oh, baby. I'd love to list everything I want to do to you, starting with sucking on those pretty nipples. Licking your sweet pussy until you come on my face. Fucking you until you come again on my cock. Paddling that little ass until you're so wet and aching you beg me to fuck you again. Maybe even—"

"Okay, okay," she cut in breathlessly. "I get the picture." His words alone made her wet and aching.

He smiled. "I'm going to make you feel so good. I just want you to let go. Just feel."

Oh sweet baby deity. So tempting. Liquid heat was sliding down inside her. She felt breathless. Edgy. Excited.

He rubbed his thumb along her bottom lip. She parted her lips and he slid his thumb inside, over the edge of her bottom teeth then brushing her tongue. Some kind of instinct made her close her lips around his thumb and suck. She closed her teeth gently on his thumb as he slowly drew it out, watching her intently.

"Damn, that's hot."

It was.

"Do you trust me?" he asked again. He held her gaze steadily. "I promise you it will be good. And if I do anything—*anything*—you don't like, you just have to tell me to stop."

The idea of just giving in to it and letting him take over made her knees wobble with yearning. Oh God, she wanted that, so much. But it terrified her at the same time.

"What are you afraid of?" he murmured, stroking her cheek.

She knew exactly what she was afraid of. Admitting it out loud made her vulnerable. But she already knew that Levi was trustworthy. "I'm afraid of losing control."

It was more than losing control of her body. Much more. It was losing control of her feelings. Today had stirred up all kinds of emotions inside her. *Levi* stirred up all kinds of emotions inside her. Those things scared her. And letting him take control and do things to her that she desperately wanted...made her afraid she was going to feel even more.

It was all a jumbled mess of confusion in her head, and anxiety twisted in her gut.

"Stop thinking about it," Levi said. "I can see your mind working. Let's just let go of everything and enjoy tonight, okay?"

She pulled in a long slow breath. She wanted it. She thought about how she felt...yes, the idea of surrendering made her stomach twist with anxiety, but it also made her pussy clench hard. Yes, there was risk and danger...and yet with Levi, more than anything she felt desired. Safe. Secure.

Could she do that? Could she let go of everything and enjoy? Or should she just tell him no right now and make her escape?

15

"Okay," she whispered. "I trust you."

Her words hit him like a fist to the chest. Because all of a sudden, this wasn't just sex. Her trusting him to tie her up, letting herself be that vulnerable, was a huge fucking gift. He recognized that and for a moment it gave him pause. It was also a huge responsibility. He had to take care of her, make sure it was good for her, make sure he didn't hurt her.

Sex had always been easy and fun for him. Hookups and sometimes a few dates. He'd never felt responsible for a woman before. He liked giving women pleasure, and he'd been told he was pretty damn good at it. But he'd never felt like a woman had put herself into his hands and trusted him with everything she had.

But he didn't want to freak the fuck out and make this all heavy and serious. This was still supposed to be fun. His dick was still telling him to get on with it, hard and throbbing.

The air around them had become hot and pulsing as they looked into each other's eyes. "Thank you," he murmured. "Now get your pretty ass over onto the bed."

Her mouth pursed, the corners tipped up, a sultry half smile that made his chest expand. And made his palm tingle with the desire to feel that ass smack against it. She pivoted on one of those metallic spiky heels and walked to the bed, hands at the base of her spine. All she wore was a nearly invisible pair of beige thong panties and gold shoes. And that fucking sexy black tie around her wrists.

She sat on the edge of the bed.

He grabbed the bottle of champagne and carried it and the two glasses to the table beside the bed, along with the thoughtfully provided towel.

"How can I drink champagne with my hands tied behind my back?"

He smiled. "You're not going to drink it. Not yet, anyway. Lie down." He pulled the dripping bottle out and opened it with a soft pop of the cork, then carefully filled one flute.

She toed off her shoes and complied. He sat beside her on the bed and sipped the bubbly wine, watching her, taking in the excitement flaring in her eyes. Then he tipped the glass and poured champagne onto her chest, just a small trickle that ran down between her breasts to her stomach.

She gasped. "That's cold!"

"Mmm. And your body is hot. This exquisite body deserves champagne." He leaned down and gave her a long slow lick from her belly up over the groove of her abdomen to her breasts. He poured more right on her tits, some of it spilling down her sides to the bed. Again, he licked it off her, circling a tightly puckered nipple, the champagne fizzing on his tongue.

Her body quivered and a soft moan escaped her lips. "Your tongue is hot."

"Want to lick you everywhere," he murmured. He sucked her nipple, then moved to the other one. More champagne. More licking. He traced the contours of her breasts with his tongue, lapped wine from the small hollow at her throat where her pulse fluttered crazily.

"You're getting the bed all wet."

"Who cares? Roll over."

She bent one leg and planted a foot into the mattress. "I can't."

He smiled. "Here." He set the wineglass down, reached for her and flipped her over.

"I love how you can do that," she gasped, now facedown on the puffy white duvet.

He held the glass above her back and poured a thin stream of champagne. It landed between her shoulder blades and ran down to the base of her spine.

"That bow tie might be toast," he mused as the champagne wet it. "Oh well." He commenced more licking and tasting of her delectable soft skin, including the curves of her ass and the backs of her thighs.

Sighs and moans filled the air. Sloane's body twitched and trembled.

"I might be getting drunk," he said long moments later. "Need you on your back again, gorgeous. I want to taste that sweet pussy. You and champagne. There's an intoxicating combination."

He helped her return to her back, made sure her hands were okay beneath her, then poured champagne all over her panties, soaking them.

"Oh my God," she cried.

"Yeah." The wet fabric outlined pouty lips. He kissed her there on that triangle of wet silk, then pulled the panties lower with his teeth. She lifted her hips to help him, and when he got them down to her knees he lost patience and used his hand to tug them all the way off. "Spread your legs, beautiful girl," he murmured. "So I can sip champagne from you here."

She obeyed so sweetly and he drizzled wine onto her pussy. She sucked in a sharp breath.

"Still cold?"

"Y-yes."

"Let's see." He lapped at her. Her flesh was so hot it was a wonder the wine didn't sizzle when it landed there. He stroked her with his tongue and she gave a throaty purr.

He lifted one foot to his shoulder as he took his time tasting her, drizzling champagne and making her shiver. "You're making me drunk." He licked her again. "Champagne and your sweet pussy." He rubbed his tongue over her clit and her hips lifted to his mouth. "There you go. Come for me, pretty girl." He sucked her clit and felt her body convulse, her soft cries the sweetest music. "Yeah. Just like that. Beautiful."

With a lingering kiss on the inside of one thigh, he pushed back and rose from the bed. He set the wineglass on the table and stripped off his clothes, then grabbed a condom from the drawer where he'd stashed them earlier. He joined her on the bed, kneeling between her spread thighs.

"Probably time to untie you," he said. "Let's do that." He rolled her to her side and plucked at the sodden tie. Christ. The knot was tight and now that the fabric was wet, it wasn't going to come undone. He scraped with his short fingernails and swore.

"What's wrong?"

"Can't get the knot undone. No worries, beautiful." He kissed her shoulder. "Be right back."

He hadn't planned this, but luckily he had a small pair of scissors in his shaving kit. He retrieved them from the bathroom and snipped the fabric, freeing her hands.

"Lucky you had those." She stretched her arms.

For a moment, that sense of responsibility weighed on him and he felt a kick of guilt that he'd put Sloane at risk. He reached for her hands and clasped her wrists, rubbing over her skin. "No shit." He'd experimented with a little bondage in the past, and even though he'd never had any problems, he knew he needed to have some kind of scissors or shears nearby just in case. But the bow tie had been a spur of the moment thing. "Are you okay?" He stroked up and down her arms

"I'm fine. Other than I need you inside me."

"Oh yeah. Hell yeah."

He grabbed the condom and suited up, then stroked the head of his dick up and down through her pussy. "Nice and wet," he murmured. "I like that."

She licked her lips, watching him, first his face, then his cock where he was entering her. "Do it," she whispered. "Please. Fuck me."

Her words aroused him, his blood scalding through his veins. He slid in deeper. "Fuck, that feels good," he gasped. He held her legs, pushing them back and open. "Take all of me, beautiful. Just...like...that."

He paused once he was fully seated inside her, his balls pulsing with the need to come. He swallowed hard. Fire licked up his spine, every nerve ending hot and tingling. He looked down at Sloane and once again amazement at her trust in him swelled inside him.

"You feel so good inside me," she whispered to him. "So big."

That was always good to hear.

He began to move, holding her thighs, rocking his hips into her. The sweet pull of her body on his dick had his blood surging, pleasure pouring through him in waves. "Touch yourself," he ordered. "Make yourself come again."

"You're making me come." She complied though, her slender fingers going to her clit. Damn, that was hot. Her eyes fell closed and her back arched, pushing those gorgeous tits up higher. "Your cock inside me makes me come so much harder."

Damn, his little suit was picking up on the dirty talk. He liked that. A lot.

"You like my cock inside you."

"Yes."

"Fucking you." He thrust harder.

163

"Yes."

"Christ." He couldn't stop. He pounded into her as her fingers worked.

"Yes," she cried. "Oh God. Yes!"

She gasped and wailed and came around him as he exploded inside her, both of them straining for each other, fuck yeah, perfect. When her hand dropped limply to the bed, he fell down over her and held himself deep inside her, his mouth on the side of her neck, his cock jerking with each hard pulse of semen.

"Sloane."

"Mmm."

He didn't know what he'd started to say. He just had to say her name. *Mine. You're mine.* Those were the shocking words that popped into his head. He'd never felt that before — possessive. Claiming. He'd never met a woman or fucked a woman he'd wanted to keep forever.

And there was another fucking scary word. Forever.

Like the vows Jacob and Tara had said earlier. He swallowed through a tight throat, and slowly pulled out and moved off Sloane, holding the condom on his semihard cock. He rolled over and reached for a tissue and got rid of the condom. Still breathing hard, they lay side by side. He set a hand on her thigh.

"This bed is a mess," she finally said.

"I know." He turned his head and met her eyes. They smiled.

"Well, we might as well go to town."

And his eyes widened as Sloane reached for the bottle of champagne, picked it up and poured some onto his chest.

Licking champagne off Levi's body had been fun, but

by the time they'd both had another orgasm — wow — the bed was truly a disaster. And so were they. When she'd sucked Levi, instead of coming in her mouth, he'd pulled out and come on her breasts. Watching that was so erotic she almost came from that alone. Then, sticky and messy from sweat, champagne and semen, they'd staggered into the bathroom to shower together.

That had been fun too.

After that, she'd pulled out the new nightie she'd gone shopping for earlier today.

The look in Levi's eyes was gratifyingly hot when she sauntered out of the bathroom in the mauve silk slip dress edged with pale pink lace above her breasts and at her thighs.

"Whoa," he breathed, reclining on the pillows on the bed. They'd tossed the wrecked duvet into the corner and he'd pulled back the top sheet. "Very sexy."

"Thank you."

She curled into his arms and he tugged the sheet up over them. He'd poured the last of the champagne into the glasses and they sipped it. His fingers played with her damp hair.

"Okay, admit it," he said. "When you saw me having lunch with Essie, you were jealous."

Her body tensed, then relaxed again as she pushed out a breath. "Okay. Yes. I was jealous. But don't think that means anything."

He chuckled. "What would I think it means?"

"I know what's happening between us is just...this. And you have every right to have lunch with other women, or date them or screw them, or whatever."

He was silent. "Good to know," he finally said. He took another mouthful of champagne. "So. How long have you worked at Huxworth Packard?"

"Just over five years."

"Before that?"

"Lawry's. I started there after college, working in traffic. That was a great way to learn how the agency worked. Worked my way up to account manager, then made the move to HuxPack."

"You love your job." He stated this, and she smiled.

"Yeah."

"What do you like about it?"

"Mmm. I like the client interaction. I like getting to know their business and helping them develop their strategies. Building a relationship with them."

"You like working with Verhoeven?"

"I do. It was a challenge at first. The beer industry is male-dominated—as is the advertising biz, still—so I had to prove that I knew what I was doing. It's been interesting to get to know the beer business, and their challenges, and help them solve those problems."

"I was so stoked to be working on the beer account." She smiled. "The Brew Crew."

"Yeah."

"I also like working with smart, creative people every day," she continued.

"Like me."

She grinned. "Yes, people like you."

"That's what I like too." He rubbed her hair between his fingers. "I love the challenge of it. Finding the balance between risk and payoff. I like solving problems too, and I like how there are no wrong or right answers. But there's a bigger picture too."

"Like what?"

"The influence advertising can have is huge. We have the power to influence how people see things and think about things, maybe change how they think about things."

She lifted an eyebrow. "By advertising beer?"

He smiled. "Well, yeah. Maybe. I just meant, critics claim advertising is bad because it makes false claims, tricks people into wanting things they don't need, creates a consumer culture that's focused on objects and having more."

She nodded. Sure, she'd heard those things.

"But it's a way of informing people too," he continued. "Giving them information, letting them consider the information, evaluate it and interpret the message."

"Yes. Absolutely. Although there are a lot of commercials that don't give any information whatsoever about the product."

"Okay, true. Some advertising is just to develop a liking for a product or brand, by showing them how the product will make them feel. Fun. Sexy. Whatever. Informational versus transformational."

She smiled. "It's also entertainment."

"Yes! For sure. The best ads are entertaining. To craft a compelling message and get that across in a few seconds and have the consumer enjoy it, maybe even laugh...that's really amazing when you think about it."

She loved the passion in his voice.

"Yeah, I wanted to work on the beer account," he continued. "It's fun and different. But I'm really proud of the work I did at AdMix for Faramond Pharmaceuticals, and I'm just as proud of the pro bono work I do for Chicago Anti-Hunger."

Faramond was a pharmaceutical company that had developed an incredible medication for treating autoimmune diseases a few years ago. "I didn't know you worked on that campaign for Faramond. And what do you do for Chicago Anti-Hunger?"

"Mostly print advertising, fundraising materials, web stuff."

"Pro bono."

"Yeah."

"That's awesome."

He shrugged. "It's how I was brought up. We had a lot,

and my parents always taught us we had to give back and help others. That's one way I do it."

She swallowed, her throat strangely tight. "Do you like it at Huxworth Packard? I know it was a rough start."

"I've had my days wondering if I did the right thing, not gonna lie. Still not a hundred percent sure. I thought I was good at my job and now…nobody seems that impressed."

Her smiled slipped off her face. "You *are* good at your job. I told you that before."

"You haven't even seen much of my work yet." He squeezed her shoulders.

She turned her head to look up at him. "Is it because of me that you feel like that?"

"No." His quick frown assured her that he spoke the truth. "I just need to find my place. Everything was easy at AdMix. Well, not everything. There were crazy demanding clients there too." He hitched one shoulder. "But I had a great AD and we just clicked."

"Yeah." *Find his place.* "Are things not working with you and Scott?"

"Yeah, yeah. He's good too. It's just…different."

She shifted again and looked him in the eye. "Not everything is easy, Levi."

He blinked. "What does that mean?"

"I mean, you're a prince, right? If I didn't know that before, I know it now after meeting your family. Everything comes easy for you."

"That's not true." He narrowed his eyes at her.

"Sure it is." She patted his chest. "It's not your fault. I'm just saying…sometimes you have to work for what you want. And sometimes, the things you have to work the hardest for mean the most."

"I do work hard. When it comes to my career, I bust my ass."

"I know you do! I've seen you there at seven at night

still working. Never mind. Mason's impressed with you."

"Yeah?"

"Yes." She finished her champagne and reached across Levi to try to set it on the table. She couldn't reach, but he took the glass and set his empty one down too. "I think I'm falling asleep."

"Yeah. It's late." He flicked out the light and they settled into place, curled together.

She wasn't used to sleeping with a man and it felt...wonderful. Safe and warm. As she drifted between awake and asleep, she reflected on the day. And the night. She thought about how much fun she'd had at the wedding. How much fun she'd had with Levi. How he made her feel, whether they were laughing together or dancing, or having sex. He made her feel good. He made her feel desired. Cared for. Handing over control to him as she had let her truly, utterly relax. It was something she wasn't sure she'd ever felt in her life, and for sure hadn't since her mom had left.

She'd taken on so much responsibility, had been the one they all relied on. In her job, she was business-focused, solving problems and keeping clients happy. It was pretty heady stuff to be the focus of someone else's care and attention, especially when that focus was on making her feel so good.

16

Levi closed the door of Sloane's office Monday morning and leaned against it. "Did you really mean that?"

She looked up from her computer and frowned at him. "Mean what?"

"That you wouldn't care if I went out with other women."

Yes, this had been bugging the hell out of him the rest of the weekend. She'd confessed she'd been jealous when she saw him with Essie. Which therefore meant she did in fact care if he went out with other women. Which he strangely had no desire to do *and* the idea of *her* seeing other men made him want to punch someone.

He'd managed to ignore that when they'd woken up together Sunday morning and enjoyed a slow, lazy sixty-nine, another shower together and a room service breakfast before checking out of the hotel and going their separate ways. After that, even while he was picking up Chuck from Colin's place, working out at the gym and then doing his effing laundry, he couldn't stop thinking about this. It was stupid.

Her eyebrows rose. "Why are you asking me that?"

"That's not an answer." He stepped toward her desk. "Do you want to go out with other guys?"

Her forehead creased. "Um. I don't know."

"Oh. Great."

"No other guys are asking me out," she said.

"Well, if they do, you're going to say no."

The eyebrows shot up again. "I beg your pardon?"

He set his hands on her desk and leaned toward her. "I don't want you going out with any other guys. I don't want to go out with any other women. Yes, the sex is off-the-hinge hot, but there's more to us than that."

She stared at him. "What are you saying?"

"I'm saying, we're…we're dating. In a relationship."

She tilted her head to one side. "I told you, I'm not good at relationships."

"Well, neither am I." He paused. "Not sure I've ever had one, actually."

Sloane's lips twitched. "I'm not sure it's a good idea to be involved with someone from work."

"Too late."

She pursed her lips. "I don't want people here to know about it."

"Why not?"

She blinked. "I just think it's better to keep work and personal stuff separate."

"Well, yeah, sure, but why can't people know…" He almost said *you're mine.* Good God. What was happening to him? "…we're seeing each other? Is there some company rule I don't know about?"

"No."

"'Cause I'm pretty sure Renzo is banging that media girl, Phoebe."

"Really?"

"Oh yeah. Also, I walked in on one of the other media girls giving that AD who works on cereal a blow job in the men's room."

She choked.

"And how about those rumors about you and Mason?"

"You know those aren't true."

"I know. But still." He sighed. "Okay. Nobody knows about us." He straightened. "So I'll take you out for dinner tonight."

"I can't." One corner of her mouth lifted. "I'm having dinner with Mason and Tom Verhoeven."

Shit. "Tomorrow night?"

"Dinner with the head of digital sales and advertising from *Around Chicago* magazine."

"Oh." He paused, then blurted, "You like me, right?"

She looked at him for a long moment while his words hung in the air between them. Christ. Then she closed her eyes and he saw that her hands were gripping the armrests of her chair. "Yes," she whispered. "I like you, Levi." She opened her eyes. "I'll come to your place after I'm done with dinner tonight."

"Okay." He grinned. Good. There. "See you later. Gotta get back to work."

He left her office, enjoying the slightly dazed expression on Sloane's face. She was always so poised and in control, but he loved that flustered look, like when he'd just fucked her breathless or licked her to orgasm. He was getting to know her better and she needed to let go a little more.

Okay, not in the office. He got that. He whistled as he strolled back to Scott's office, where he was doing something crazy with Photoshop, working on the ideas they'd come up with. "Check it out."

Levi peered at his monitor. A big hairy dude reclined in a bathtub full of bubbles reading a book, his feet hanging over the edge, a glass of wine sitting on the side of the tub. With no copy, the only words were on the label of the beer bottle in the bottom right corner—Flying Pigs Pale Ale.

Levi grinned. "Yeah! Perfect." Just what they'd talked about.

"And this one." Scott clicked his mouse. Another image appeared, this one two men holding hands.

Levi shook his head and sighed. "Nah. That one doesn't work. Too homophobic."

"I thought so too. One more."

Another dude in a pink tank top and tiny athletic shorts appeared, again with the Flying Pigs Pale Ale bottle.

"Awesome."

"Last one."

Back to the hairy dude in the bathtub who had one leg out of the water covered with shaving foam and a shaver in his hand. Levi snorted with laughter. "I fucking love that one."

Scott grinned. "Okay." He turned away from his computer. "We need to get to work on the Natural Belgian Blonde. You know where we're going with that one."

"Pamela Anderson."

"Dude. *Natural* blonde."

"Can we make some kind of joke about the curtains matching the carpet?"

"Fuck no!" Scott paused. "Besides, these days there isn't as much carpet."

"Ahaha!" Levi laughed so hard he just about split a gut.

Scott laughed too.

Then… "I know!" Levi just about blew up. "There's no actual blonde woman in the ad. Just a picture of carpet and drapes. That don't match. No, no…they *do* match. Perfectly. With some kind of crazy pattern."

"Ah!" They leaped up and high-fived each other. "Hang on, hang on." Scott clicked his mouse a few times and Pharrell William's "Happy" blasted from his computer. They both started dancing. Levi had his arms in the air and was thrusting his pelvis when Joseph Huxworth walked by. Joseph paused and eyed them. And he wasn't alone. Presumably that was a client. Crap.

Levi dropped his arms and jerked his head at Scott, who lunged for his computer mouse and cut the music.

"Uh, hey, Mr. Huxworth." Levi smiled. "Just celebrating our incredible creative genius."

"Uh-huh."

Sloane appeared with a cute crease between her eyebrows. "What's going on? We heard music blasting."

"The boys were celebrating," The Hux said.

Sloane's expression clouded and she shot him an exasperated glance, bugging her eyes out at him. He spread his hands wide, bugging his eyes out back at her.

Joseph and the client continued down the corridor.

"What were you doing?" Sloane hissed.

"We were dancing," Levi said. "For fuck's sake. Dancing for about thirty seconds."

"Dancing? Seriously?"

"You should try it. It's fun."

"I know how to dance!"

His eyes met Scott's. They shared an evil grin. Scott reached for the mouse and the music started again, that happy, infectious beat. Levi grabbed Sloane's hands and pulled her into the open space of the office.

"Ack!" She tried to pull her hands away but he held on tight and spun her into a dance move.

He grinned when heads popped up over cubicle walls and others started to appear. Bailey and Phoebe both started dancing, then Dash and Hunter and Renzo joined them in what appeared to be a choreographed routine. He'd seen people do this at a club one night. "Flash mob," he said to Sloane, who was apparently trying not to laugh as more people joined in.

When they song ended, laughter filled the office in place of the music, everyone smiling and breathing a little faster.

Joseph Huxworth reappeared, this time sans client. "Sloane," he said. "I'll see you in my office."

Sloane's smile slipped off her face and she tugged her dress down.

Shit.

Apparently Sloane wasn't exaggerating The Hux's request to tame down the Brew Crew's antics.

Shit fuck shit.

"Okay, that was fun," Sloane said calmly. "Back to work, everyone."

Their eyes met and her mouth twisted.

"Fuck," Levi said in a low voice. "I'm sorry."

She lifted a shoulder and gave him a fake smile. "No worries."

She disappeared, everyone went back to work, and even though he and Scott were still high from their brilliance, something gnawed at his gut. Worry. Concern for Sloane. Fear that he'd been the one to get her in trouble.

They were just dancing. Resentment bubbled inside him. Was this the kind of place he wanted to work? Did The Hux want to stifle all the creativity out of them because of how things looked to the client? He muttered curses under his breath as he tried to get his head back into a place where he could work on another Verhoeven brand.

He resisted the temptation to run to Sloane's office every five minutes to see if she was back and make sure she was okay. He'd see her tonight. Right now they had jobs to do. She wanted to keep things on the down low there at work. He could do that.

Patience had never been one of his strengths but he made it through the day. He watched Sloane leave with Mason through narrowed eyes. Yeah, yeah, he knew they were just friends. He believed her. But Mason was having dinner with Sloane and he wasn't.

Deadlines were creeping up on a couple of the campaigns. But hell, lots of time yet. He worked better under pressure so he wasn't worried. He left the office at a decent hour, met up with Luke and Tucker for a beer and discussed what Jacob and Tara were probably doing on their honeymoon in London.

"Fucking," Tucker said glumly. "Which I am not."

"What happened to the bridesmaid you left with on Saturday night?" Luke said. "She was fucksome."

"She was so drunk she passed out."

"I hate it when that happens," Levi said.

Luke and Tucker's attention turned to him. "So what's the deal with you and the sexy blonde?"

At that point, Levi realized that Sloane's carpet—what little there was of it; maybe a rug?—definitely matched her drapes. Because...blonde.

What a dick he was.

No, he'd be a dick if he shared his thoughts out loud with his buddies.

"We're dating," he said.

"Yeah, we got that. She's hot. She doesn't *look* like a ball breaker."

He rolled his eyes. "Because she's not."

"She's into you big time."

Levi perked up. "Really? Why do you say that?"

Tucker shrugged. "The way she looked at you. But then again, every chick looks at you that way."

Levi raised his middle finger at his friend. "No, seriously. You think she is?"

They both gaped at him. "Dude," Luke said slowly. "Are you...doubting yourself?"

Levi laughed. "Hahaha. No."

It was Sloane he was doubting. She'd admitted she liked him. He liked her. A lot. They had fun together even when they weren't in bed. Although most of their time together had been between the sheets. That was going to change. Only, not tonight. Or tomorrow night. But dammit, he was going to take her out on a date.

Tucker snapped his fingers in front of his face. "You still with us, man?"

Levi blinked. "Yeah."

They both smirked at him. "Jesus. You got it bad for her, don't you?"

Levi just shrugged and lifted his beer.

She arrived at his place shortly before nine that evening, still in the dress and heels she'd worn to work. He'd been sitting on the couch playing Xbox and the music from the game filled the condo. She joined him on the couch and he turned the volume down so it was background noise.

"How was dinner?"

"Good. We had a good discussion about where they're going with some of these new craft beer lines. And possibly changing some of the management people that came with them when they acquired them."

"What happened with The Hux earlier?"

She blinked. "The Hux?" Then she laughed. "Oh my God. Is that what you call him?"

"Only to you. Were you in trouble?"

She shook her head then sighed. "No. Not really. He just reminded me again about keeping behavior appropriate when there are clients around."

"We didn't know there was a client with him."

"I know."

"He hates my guts, doesn't he?"

"No, he doesn't. Of course not. Just...tone it down."

"I know what the solution is."

"What?"

"We just don't allow clients in our office."

She burst out laughing. "Like that'll work. We kind of need clients, Levi."

He grinned.

"Maybe just keep the crazy fun stuff confined to the

staff lounge," she suggested. "That's what it's for."

"Got it." He pushed her hair back from her face with both hands. Her eyes flickered. His gaze dropped to her mouth and her lips parted. He could tell she thought he was going to kiss her. And he was. But that was it. After brushing his mouth over hers, he moved back and pulled her next to him, his arm around her shoulders. He picked up the remote. "So. Wanna play Xbox with me? Or watch TV?"

"Uh..."

He smiled. "Okay, we'll watch TV." He found an episode of *Two and a Half Men* just starting.

He knew she was off balance when he didn't try to do anything more. After the TV show he kissed her and they made out until they were both melting down and she was begging him to fuck her and he said, "No."

"What?"

"Not tonight." He kissed her again. "I'm not your Monday night booty call."

She gave a strangled laugh. "Oh my God."

"You can come over tomorrow night after your dinner too, if you want. We can watch back-to-back episodes of *Two and a Half Men*. I love that show."

"You're serious."

"Yeah." It was fun torturing her a little, keeping her on the edge.

⚬⟩⟨⚬

Friday night he got Sloane to confirm she had no business dinners or other engagements planned. He told her to come to his place dressed casually and prepared to stay over. She arrived at six thirty, wearing jeans rolled at the ankle, flip-flops and a loose pink tank top. Once again she looked like a teenager. He grinned as Chuck went crazy for her, and she crouched to pet him and rub his belly when he rolled to his back on the floor.

"You're so cute," she crooned to Chuck. "Aren't you? You're such a good boy."

When she stood, Levi set his hands on her hips and touched his mouth to hers. "You look great. So different than professional Sloane."

She smiled. "I'm not always in business mode."

"Good. Okay. Let's go. Here, I'll put your bag in the bedroom." He took the tote bag she carried along with her purse.

"Where are we going?"

"Navy Pier."

"What?"

"Yeah. We're going to be tourists. Go have dinner, go for a boat cruise, ride the Ferris wheel."

"You're kidding me."

"Nope. We can walk there from here, it's not far."

They strolled along the sidewalk toward the lake, hand in hand, lots of other people around on a warm Friday evening in June. They talked a little shop, and that was okay because they both loved their jobs. He liked hearing her insights from the client end of things. He wouldn't tell her the ideas that he and Scott had been dancing about on Monday. He wanted to wow her when she saw them more developed.

He hoped he wowed her. He really wanted to wow her.

They did all the things he'd said and more. Sloane was reluctant to go on the Ferris wheel, revealing an endearing fear of heights, but he promised her he'd hold on to her the whole time.

"Face your fears, baby," he said. "That makes them so much smaller."

"Phht." She frowned at him. "I'm not that afraid. Let's go."

But she did clutch his hand the whole time.

179

They had margaritas and nachos on a patio. They went on a boat cruise. They even stopped at the beer garden to listen to some music and drink beer, sadly not Verhoeven beer, but oh well.

"Verhoeven is going to do a brew cruise," Sloane told him. "Beer tasting and you can meet some of the brewmasters from Cedar Springs."

"That's a cool idea."

They talked about all kinds of things—music, people at work, stories from their childhoods. Like how Levi's sisters used to dress him in their outgrown girls' clothes and put him in the stroller and take him for walks in the neighborhood. Sloane choked with laughter. He liked making her laugh. He liked watching her too, the way her eyes sparkled as she took in the view from the top of the Ferris wheel, the way she smiled and her cheeks got pink from the lake breeze on the boat, the way her silky gold hair blew into her face and tangled in her long eyelashes.

She had funny stories too, but he sensed that she had to go way back to find them. She alluded to her mom's illness and how sometimes things felt out of control when her mom was sick. It sounded like Sloane had been the one taking care of their family even before their mom had disappeared.

They talked about favorite movies and TV shows. She wasn't as much of a fan of *Two and a Half Men* as he was, although she'd laughed through a couple of episodes with him the other night. "Charlie Harper is my role model," he told her with a straight face.

"Shut up. He's an alcoholic womanizer with mommy issues!"

He grinned. "He's a successful chick magnet who makes his living writing ad jingles." Levi held his arms out.

"Oh my God! You are unbelievable."

He laughed and leaned over to smooch her mouth. "I'm yanking your chain. Sort of. Yeah, he's a commitmentphobic lush, but come on, he has a helluva lot of fun. I like to have fun."

"I know." She rolled her eyes.

"What's wrong with having fun?"

Her lips twitched. "There's a time and a place for it."

"Are you having fun right now?"

The smile struggled to break free. "Yes."

"Good."

It was nearly midnight when they left the pier, strolling leisurely back to his condo in the still-warm darkness.

"Why wouldn't you have sex with me this week?" she asked as they neared his building.

He wasn't sure if she'd appreciate the real reason, so he said, "Absence makes the snatch grow fonder."

After a few seconds of shocked silence, she punched him in the shoulder. "I can't believe you just said that." But she was laughing and he had to laugh too.

"Sure, be annoyed," he said. "But it's true." His hand slipped to her ass and gave a squeeze. "By the way, your ass looks great in these jeans. Can't wait to tap that."

"You're a pig."

"But you like me. Don't you? You said you did." His arm slid around her waist and pulled her against him in a hug.

She was shaking her head but laughing as they entered the lobby of his building. After a quick ascent, the elevator discharged them onto the twenty-first floor and then they were in his condo.

"Is the sex ban still in effect?" she asked. "Because if it is, I'll take my stuff and go home. I can get my orgasms another way."

"That's a *great* idea."

Her eyebrows pulled down. "What is? Going home?"

"No. Watching you give yourself an orgasm." He took her hand and tugged her toward the bedroom.

17

It was hot as hell.

Sloane touched her tongue to her top lip, watching Levi from beneath heavy eyelids. He sat in the armchair in his bedroom. Watching her. Propped up on a pile of pillows, naked, knees bent and spread wide, she touched herself.

Her fingers slicked up her natural lubricant and rubbed over her clit. Nerve endings jumped and buzzed. Her nipples ached.

His dark, steady gaze mesmerized her. Everything else shrank away into the shadows, an electrical current running between them. She rubbed over her breast with her left hand, pressing the soft flesh then squeezing it. His groan reached her ears.

He'd directed this entire show, from which article of clothing to remove first, to how the pillows were arranged and where she should touch herself. He'd moved the chair so she could see him between her knees and he was looking right at her pussy.

First, he'd had her running her hands all over her body, her thighs, her stomach, her breasts. Pinching her own nipples. Then parting her thighs and touching herself.

He reached behind his neck and pulled his T-shirt off,

baring that beautiful chest to her. It was so far away, though. She watched with avid eyes as he lifted his ass off the chair and pushed his jeans and underwear off. His cock lay huge and stiff on his belly. So beautiful.

Now he was naked too, and that was even hotter. He parted his muscular, hairy thighs and she could see his balls all round and full. He gave his cock a slow stroke, looking down at himself, then back at her.

"You like my dick."

"Yes."

"You want it inside you."

"Yes."

"Did you miss fucking me this week?"

She whimpered. "Yes."

"Me too, baby. But you were still here nearly every night."

"Y-yes."

He smiled. "Roll over."

She swallowed and complied.

"Hands and knees," he instructed. "With that sweet ass up in the air. Arch your back...like that, yeah...Christ." He groaned again. "So fucking sweet, those plump, pink lips. And your pretty asshole."

Her inner muscles were clenching and unclenching with lust, and when he said that last bit, fire burst in her belly.

"I wanna fuck your ass," he murmured. "What do you think of that, baby?"

She bit her lip and lowered her face to the bed, on her elbows. "N-not sure. It sounds hot."

"It could be. Very hot. I'd be careful with you. Take it slow and easy. Now turn onto your back again and spread those legs."

She rolled over and settled into position, her pussy pulsing with need. *Oh my God.* Anal sex. He was so dirty. And she frickin' loved it.

Her skin burned everywhere as her fingers found her clit again. She watched Levi again between her knees, relaxed in the chair, jacking off with slow strokes, his body so beautiful, big, lean enough to show off carved muscles in his legs and abs and shoulders.

"That's it. Play with that little clit. Make yourself come."

Sensation built, that buzz of pleasure. She'd been so close, all along. Her ass tightened, inner muscles clenched, and she let it build, higher. Her eyes fell closed and her head pushed back into the pillows. It ripped over her, fire burning over her clit as it swelled and pulsed beneath her fingertip.

"Beautiful," Levi said. "So goddamn hot."

She dragged air into her lungs. Limp and quivering, she opened her eyes. What was going to happen next? Would he fuck her? Or...

His hand moved faster on his shaft, his wrist circling as he stroked up over the head and back down, and that was so sexy.

"Watch me," he directed her.

"I am." She couldn't look away. It was dirty. And hot.

He cupped his balls with his other hand, the tempo of his strokes increasing again. His thighs clenched and unclenched, his hips moving as he fucked his hand. His breathing went choppy and harsh noises escaped his lips. His eyelids fell closed and she watched in fascination as he came, thick white semen spilling over his hand, onto his belly, his palm squeezing out more in slow, tight pulls.

She quivered everywhere at the carnal beauty of it. She sighed. "Oh, Levi."

For a few moments, he didn't move. Eyes closed, he gave a slow smile, head resting on the back of the chair. His chest rose and fell with rapid respirations. "Hell," he muttered. "Gonna have to shower." He didn't move for a few minutes, then slowly straightened. "Come on. Shower with me."

"I don't need a shower."

"No, you don't. But I'm gonna wash you up and get you all clean for what I want to do to you next."

More heat flashed through her veins. She rolled off the bed and followed him into the bathroom. Glass doors enclosed the bath/shower and he turned on the water, stepped in then held out a hand to help her step over the side of the tub. She slid the door closed and steam rose around them.

He faced the water and rinsed off, then turned and pulled her up against him. He looked down at her. "That was fucking hot, Sloane."

She nodded.

He kissed her, long and sweet, licking and sucking at her mouth. Then he grabbed a bottle of body wash and squeezed some into his hand. He ran his hands over her, getting her all sudsy, her front, her pussy, then he turned her and his soapy fingers slipped between her butt cheeks and rubbed there. Her glutes clenched at that foreign touch, sensation spreading in waves through her body. One finger circled her back entrance, probed lightly, just barely entering her, then slipped back out. She groaned.

He kissed her bare shoulder then stepped back and reached for the bottle again. When he'd washed himself, he cranked off the water and pulled the glass door open. He grabbed a thick towel, and the careful, attentive way he dried her off made her heart flutter. Then he gave her a tap on the ass and said, "Go get into bed."

"I need to brush my hair." It had gotten damp, mostly the ends.

"Where's your brush? In your bag?"

"Mmm."

"I'll get it. You get in bed."

She slid between his sheets as he walked naked to her small bag near the door, rummaged and found her brush. His sheets were lovely, pure white and a high thread count. "Did your mother or your sisters help you decorate?" she asked, sitting with the covers up over her breasts.

He grinned. "How'd you know?"

"Most guys aren't that into high thread count sheets and color-coordinated plush bath towels."

He sat on the side of the bed and started to brush her hair. Oh God. Her eyes closed, shivery sensations running over her skin. That felt so amazing.

"I like nice things," he said unapologetically. "But yeah, I'm not much into shopping."

The brush pulled down through her hair, over and over, and lethargy swept over her. "That's so nice," she mumbled.

"There." He set the brush aside then joined her in the bed. He slid down and pulled her on top of him. She rested her hands on his chest, set her chin on top of them and looked at him while he filtered his hands through her hair. "Love your hair."

I love you.

Her eyes widened when those words popped into her head and for a moment, panic flared as she thought she'd said them out loud.

What the fuck?

"What's wrong?" He frowned at her.

"N-nothing." She turned her head so her cheek rested on her hands. "I'm good. Um, tired."

"Yeah. We did a lot of walking in the fresh air." He stroked a palm over her hair. "Wanna sleep, baby?"

"Mmm. Maybe. Yeah."

She rolled off him and faced away from him on her side, tugging the duvet up to her chin. The bed moved as Levi repositioned his pillows and settled. Over on his doggy bed in the corner, Chuck groaned in his sleep. Silence descended.

City lights glittered outside the big window and she

stared at them. Not sleepy. Nope. She was wide-awake and terrified.

"You're tense as hell," Levi finally said. "Not sleeping."

He was not wrong. She sighed.

"Talk to me, Sloane." His hand on her shoulder was gentle as he pulled her to her back. He propped himself up on an elbow to look at her. "What just happened? You seemed all into it earlier. Is it because I said I want to fuck your ass?"

Her breasts tingled despite her stomach being in knots, and every muscle contracted. "No," she whispered, though she could have used that as an excuse for her freak out. She sure as hell wasn't about to tell him the truth.

She cared. She felt something for him.

This was so bad.

"It's okay, Sloane. You like me. It's okay."

Fuck, fuck, fuck. He got her. So damn much. That scared her even more. She resisted the urge to slap her hands over her face.

"Sure I do." She smiled. Traced a finger down the middle of his chest. Okay, she could totally distract him from this uncomfortable conversation. "And I want you to fuck my ass."

He gave her a squinty look but she could see the heat flare in his eyes. And she felt his cock harden against her thigh. He wanted that. And truthfully…it excited her too. Okay, she was deflecting an awkward conversation about emotions. No, she was distracting her own mind from an awkward conversation about her emotions. She didn't have feelings. She *couldn't* have feelings.

Something huge and black inside her yawned wide. If she cared…it would be taken away from her. She'd experienced that over and over. Her mom. Her dad. Her dog Teddy. Her skating. Her friends and teachers and everything that was familiar to her. Her first coworkers and friends when she'd started into the business world, who hadn't really been friends after all. And now Levi. She couldn't care about him.

But she could let him fuck her and make her come so hard she didn't remember any of that shit.

He actually gave her a suspicious look, then groaned. "As if I can resist that." He pulled her up against his body and the sensation of being skin to skin the entire length of their bodies was unbelievably voluptuous. She sank into it, his hand holding her face as he kissed her. Their mouths opened to each other, his thumb brushing the corner of her mouth. As the kiss slowly ended, she turned her head and took his thumb into her mouth and sucked it.

His hot gaze met hers. "Oh baby," he moaned. "You are so getting fucked. But first I want to suck those sweet little nipples." He urged her flat onto her back and ran his tongue down the side of her neck, over her collarbone and then the top of one breast. She inhaled sharply and a shiver worked down over her body.

He licked around her nipple, licking her breasts, rubbing his stubble there, then sucking gently on her skin. Her nipples tightened into aching peaks, the skin pulling up to the center with delicious tautness. Then he traced his tongue over one puckered tip. Her breath whooshed out of her.

He took one nipple into his mouth and sucked. Her womb tightened and liquid heat settled between her thighs. Her abdominal muscles shuddered.

He played with her breasts for a long time, cupping them gently, sucking and biting her nipples until she was burning up and writhing on the bed. "Need you," she gasped. "Please. Inside me."

"Oh yeah. You got it, beautiful girl."

He shifted away, lifted her and flipped her onto her stomach. He bent and opened his mouth on the small of her back in a slow, sensuous kiss that melted her even more. Then he stretched across her and yanked open the drawer of the bedside table. He straightened with a condom and a small bottle in his hand. She bit her lip, her pussy quivering.

He swept a hand down her spine, curving his palm over her butt. He gave a gentle squeeze and her body throbbed with lust. "Gonna play here a bit," he murmured, now with both hands on her cheeks, petting and squeezing. He moved between her legs, kneeing them apart. He kissed her lower back, then her butt, then his hands gripped her hips and lifted her up onto her knees. As she'd been earlier when he'd admired the view.

"Up on your knees, beautiful. Show me that pretty pussy again."

Heat suffused her body from her hairline to her toes. With her ass in the air, her elbows on the mattress, his tongue stroked over one cheek, then the other. His mouth opened on her skin in long lush kisses, across her buttocks and lower back and thighs. His lips closed on her skin and gently sucked, then moved on.

He ran the tips of his fingers up and down her outer pussy lips, rubbing over them, then used his tongue there too, licking slowly up and down. Then his tongue delved deeper. A moan climbed up her throat. She cupped one of her own breasts and squeezed.

His mouth sucked her flesh inside, so gently, and then he paused and she lifted and turned her head to see him studying her, his mouth wet, his eyes hot and carnal. With his hand on her back, he pushed her back down and then his face was buried in her pussy. He nipped with teeth, gave her slurpy suckling kisses, and licked everywhere, including her back entrance.

Her heart pounded and her blood heated her veins. She lowered her body to the mattress, gasping and groaning as he played there in that wicked erotic way. Elbows bent, palms flat on the mattress, she let him eat at her. His hands squeezed her ass cheeks, thumbs parting them for his mouth and tongue.

When she pushed back up onto her elbows, unable to stay still with all the sensations coursing through her, he reached beneath her and cupped a breast, his tongue continuing to lick her everywhere.

Oh God, that was so incredible and so unfamiliar to her. Her heartbeat hammered in her throat and she struggled to breathe. Heat burned over her skin.

Now his hand slid up her back, slowly and tenderly, fisted her hair for a moment, then released it and stroked back down. She stretched her arms out above her head, face to the mattress, her lungs on fire.

As he licked around her back entrance, his thumb slipped inside her vagina where she was so wet, then dragged down to her clit. Her body jolted at the contact on that sensitive bud that was aching to be touched. His thumb rubbed there as he licked and sucked. Sensation swelled and swirled inside her, an urgent need to come.

"Not yet, baby," he murmured. "Wanna be inside you when you come. It's gonna be so good."

She wet her bottom lip, quivering in anticipation. She heard the bottle of lube open and close and then coolness drizzled over her heated flesh. Levi massaged it around with his fingertips, rubbed over the entrance of her ass, and then shockingly, a finger pushed inside her. Slow and careful, but still a sensation unknown to her. Excitement shimmered through her even as her body tightened at the intrusion.

"Easy," he murmured, a hand on her low back. "Slow and easy. Relax."

She willed her aroused muscles to relax, sucking in air.

"That's it." His finger slid in and out, the sensations radiating from his touch through her body in electric tingles. "First I'm gonna fuck your pussy. Keep playing here. Get you all ready. Then I'm gonna fuck your ass."

As usual, his dirty words amped up her stimulation. Heat flowed through her veins.

He paused to put on the condom and push into her pussy. The heavy penetration burned and stretched her. She loved it. She moaned into the mattress.

"Yeah. That's it. So hot, Sloane." He reached over and gathered her hair up again, tightening his grip, pulling her head back. "Is that good?"

"Yes. God yes. So good."

"I like to know. You can tell me how you're feeling."

A smile tugged her lips. He was giving her commentary; she supposed it was only fair that he got to hear back from her. "I love your cock inside me," she said breathlessly. "Filling me like that."

"Yeah." He gave another long slide out and then back in. His finger continued to slide in and out of her ass with the same rhythm. Slow. Easy. Exciting. "Okay, baby." He pulled out, squeezed more lube and rubbed it over his latex-covered cock and her ass, and then the head was there, pressing against her. His hand on her hip was firm and reassuring. Then he was in, fire rippling there as he penetrated her.

"Ah, God!" she cried out, fingers gathering up the bedsheet. Dark, edgy pleasure swept through her, sensations she'd never experienced — intense and sizzling.

"There, that's it. Take me…" Levi groaned, both hands now gripping her hips, his voice deep and thick. "Yeah, just like that. Fuck, that's hot. So tight."

He slid in deeper still. Her body tightened and her entire pelvis filled with heat. He leaned over her, planting his fists into the mattress on either side of her, and kissed her neck, just in front of her ear, her shoulder, then dragged his mouth along her upper back to the other shoulder. His hips continued to move against her.

"Deeper," he murmured in her ear. "Take me deeper. Push that sweet little ass back against me."

His words inflamed her even more. She did as he bid, taking him deeper. She sobbed at the fiery ecstasy whipping through her.

He rose back up onto his knees. His hand slipped around to find her clit, pinching it. She cried out, unable to stop herself, a barrage of sensations tearing through her. It took so little to make her come, all that pleasure almost unbearable, and she rocketed up, lights exploding in front of her eyes, pleasure ripping through her in nearly painful waves.

"Ah yeah, that's it," he groaned. "Gonna come too...soon..." He slid in and out faster, then withdrew completely. Still with her eyes squeezed closed, heart thundering, she was only vaguely aware of what he was doing, until she felt the hot liquid of his ejaculation on her lower back. He must have whipped off the condom so he could come on her.

She collapsed flat on the bed. Her bones had turned to liquid. She was unable to move. Levi stretched alongside her, half on her, his arm around her, one heavy thigh over hers. "Good, baby?"

"Better than good. Oh my God. I can't even..."

He kissed her shoulder. "Gonna take care of you. Clean us both up. Be right back."

He was dirty and wicked, and sweet and tender. And he was completely screwing with her head, and her heart—never mind her body.

18

"Sloane." Levi's lips were tired but he managed to eke out her name.

"Mmm?"

After cleaning them both up following the most amazing sex he'd ever had in his life with the most amazing woman he'd ever met, he was in his bed, Sloane's sweet ass pressed into his groin, his arm around her and one of her tits filling his palm. He was nearly asleep and she might be too.

"You do like me, right?"

After a short pause, she said, "I do, Levi. I've told you twice. I like you…a lot."

"I like you too." He hesitated, rubbing his face against her hair. "What is that perfume you wear?"

He heard a surprised huff in the dark. "It's Givenchy."

"Oh. I fucking love it."

Her body vibrated against his as if she was amused. "I'm so glad."

"Don't ever stop wearing it."

"Okay."

"When is your birthday?"

She shifted in his arms. "What? Why?"

"I'm gonna buy you a gallon of that stuff for your birthday. When is it?"

Amusement shaded her voice. "Not until January."

"And you'll be thirty-two?"

"Yes."

"My birthday is next Friday."

"Oh."

"It's my big three-oh. I'm catching up to you."

Her giggle escaped this time. "You obviously weren't a math major."

He smiled against her hair. "Come on. You're thirty-one. I'll be thirty. Only a year apart now."

He felt her silent laughter again.

"You don't have to get me a present," he added.

"Okay."

"But you know when someone says that, it really means, if you don't get me a present I'll be hurt."

She laughed out loud. "Ooookay."

"My friends all want to go out that night," he said. "Will you come with us?"

He sensed her hesitation, but then she said, "I'd love to."

Warmth spread through his chest. "Okay. Good."

He snuggled her even closer against him. Goddamn, she felt so good in his arms. In his bed. In his life.

Jesus. He'd never thought that about any woman. A few dates and women started talking relationship and he was done and moving on. But the idea of not having Sloane in his life made him want to hurl. He should be terrified. Running. He waited for that urge to come.

Nope.

Not only was she the hottest thing ever in bed, she entertained him and made him laugh out of bed too. He liked women a lot, but he'd never had so much fun with anyone. She also made him feel weirdly all protective, like when she'd been afraid of the Ferris wheel. Not like that was particularly dangerous, not like he'd had to beat off a herd of ferocious attacking wild beasts to defend her, but still, it made him feel all big and strong to reassure her and tell her she was safe with him.

And she was. Always. He wanted to look after her and make her happy. Usually for him, making a woman happy equated to making her come. Done. He could do that, easy. This was so much more than that.

He fell asleep with a smile on his face and Sloane in his arms.

◯◐◍◑◯

They spent most of the weekend together. He was determined to show her that what they had was more than sex. They took Chuck for a long walk by the lake on Saturday, then she went home to change. He picked her up and took her to his favorite blues club, Indigo, where they ate hamburgers and onion rings and listened to some fantastic music. Then they had sex.

He'd gone nearly a week without sex to prove his point to her. No need to belabor the point. Heh. And he fucking loved how sweet she was, how she let him take the lead, take control and feel like a fucking sex god, but she was an amazing sex goddess who gave him so much back in return. The way she responded and trusted him made him feel...honored. Respected. Grateful.

Christ only knew he hadn't been feeling very respected at work. Which only made him appreciate her even more.

They talked about so many things, discovering little oddities about each other, like that when she ate Bits & Bites, she only ate the pretzels and the cheese bits. "What's wrong with the other bits?"

She shrugged. "I don't know. I just don't like them as much."

They had a mutual love of Garrett's Chicago Mix popcorn and brownies, a mutual hate of cucumbers. And he revealed to her his utter disgust for yogurt, which made her laugh so hard. "And tofu," he added. "I fucking hate tofu."

"I'm going to make you a tofu stir-fry and you're going to love it."

"I didn't know you could cook."

"Please." She gave him a look over her glasses, which made her appear so cute and smart. "We would have starved after my mom disappeared if I hadn't figured out how to cook."

"True." As always, being reminded of how she'd stepped up and looked after her family made his heart shift in his chest.

When they watched TV and a commercial came on, Levi said, "When I watch TV with the guys, they get up and leave when a commercial comes on. Or if it's DVRed, they fast forward through the commercials."

She gave him a wide-eyed look. "No!"

"Yes."

"They're the best part of some shows!"

"I know, right?"

And then they critiqued the commercials, praising them for their brilliance or snorting at how lame they were.

"Way too vanilla," Levi stated.

"Vanilla?"

"Yeah. Safe."

She bit her bottom lip. "I like vanilla."

"Babe. You are so not vanilla."

"I thought we were talking about advertisements."

He grinned. "Everyone likes vanilla. But it's not memorable. Nobody gets *passionate* about vanilla. It's playing safe, and that's no fun."

Their eyes met with a sizzle and he knew she got what he was saying. Yeah, they were talking about advertising, but she totally got the metaphor. He grinned.

"Now, that Coke Zero is pretty smart," Levi continued. "Men won't drink Diet Coke. Put it in a black can and call it Coke Zero and boom! Men buy it." Sloane was looking at him funny. "What?"

She turned her gaze back to the big screen TV on his wall. "Nothing. I just think you're...smart."

"Of course I'm smart." He tried to sound offended.

She smirked. "And modest."

"I think we established some time ago that modesty is for pussies."

"True."

"Anyway, I think you're smart too." He leaned over and smooched her pretty lips.

And that led to more sex, this time on his couch.

It was a great weekend.

⸎

It had been a terrifying weekend.

Monday morning Sloane pushed through the revolving door into the Lachman Building after a quick run to Starbucks.

How many times had she come so close to saying the L word? It was crazy! It just kept rising to her lips and hovering dangerously there. She'd admitted she liked him. That was okay. But she couldn't *love* him.

After the weekend, when he'd taken her to Navy Pier and then Saturday taken her to that blues club, she'd questioned herself a million times about what she was doing with him. That Friday night when those terrifying words had popped into her mind, she'd nearly had a heart attack.

Spending that much time with Levi was obviously a mistake, if she was going to start having ridiculous thoughts like that.

She was *not* in love with the man. It was just all the...the...sex. And the fun. The laughing. The sweetness of watching him with Chuck. It was making her all soft.

She lifted her chin as she strode down the hall to her office. She was back in her preferred environment now. The office. Back to business. As she passed Levi's office, where he was not yet at work, she once more noticed that ridiculous Justin Bieber poster. Still there.

That made her smile and shake her head. What a goof he was to leave it there.

Stop! Stop with all the...mushy girly feelings. Gah!

She dove into work, her tall Starbucks cup close at hand. An email from Derek at Verhoeven saying they wanted to work on an entirely new approach for their branded point-of-sales materials for Herstal. Something cool and different to have in liquor stores and restaurants. Hmmm. They quickly arranged a meeting with Brent and Hoyt, Herstal's brand managers, to discuss it further.

She, Noah, Mason and Alia, one of Huxworth Packard's print producers, were meeting with one of the photographers who'd submitted a bid on the shoot for the Steel brand. Sloane knew Mason and Alia had wanted to go with Josselin Ames, but her bid had come in the highest. They wanted to meet with her and get more details about her proposal and how it would fit with what they and the Steel brand managers were looking for, see if there was any room for adjustments in her bid. Steel wanted a print and online campaign with a fun, social ambience separate from their television commercials.

They reviewed model headshots, layouts and location needs, and determined that Josselin was the only photographer who'd included travel expenses in her bid. Because the shoot would be in Chicago and travel would be minimal, Josselin was flexible and willing to negotiate.

They went back and forth on a few points until Sloane was satisfied with the numbers.

"I typically have a crew in mind when I'm doing the estimate," Josselin told them. "They're on hold until you actually book me, but I've already reviewed rates, expenses and layouts with them, as we've discussed."

By the end of the meeting, Sloane had her mind made up. Josselin understood what they and the client were looking for. She and Mason exchanged glances and she knew he'd decided too. She'd gotten to know him pretty well. Alia was very neutral. Naturally, they didn't want to commit to anything until they'd had a chance to discuss it, or give Josselin false hopes if they ended up going with someone else. But ultimately, Sloane and Mason would make the decision. Over the years they'd worked together, Sloane had learned to trust Mason's judgment about creative aspects while she kept an eagle eye on budgets and deliverables.

After Alia showed Josselin out, they continued their discussion. They'd all liked what they heard so agreed that they would offer Josselin the job.

"I'll get in touch with her this afternoon," Alia said. "I'll try to set up a creative call between me, Josselin, Cory from Steel, and Julie Erikson, who I want to use as stylist, as soon as I can. I'll arrange for her advance so she can book the location and cover her upfront expenses."

"Excellent."

A productive morning. Then it was off to lunch with the marketing head of Chalmers Outdoor Advertising, with whom they placed a lot of billboard ads, and his assistant. Lang was about her age, an attractive man she enjoyed talking with. After a lovely lunch and some good discussion about pricing and turnaround times, his assistant excused herself to go to the ladies' room.

Lang smiled at her. "I always enjoy having lunch with you, Sloane."

The tiny hairs on the back of her neck prickled. Something about his tone of voice had changed. She smiled back at him. "Likewise."

"I'd love to continue our discussion some other time. Maybe over dinner?"

She gave a light laugh. "I thought we just covered everything we wanted to discuss."

"Actually, I was thinking our dinner would be less business and more...personal."

She met his eyes. His mouth tipped up into a hopeful smile.

"As in, a date," he prompted when she said nothing.

Shit.

She'd fended off unwanted invitations from clients in the past, although most clients knew it wasn't a good idea for them to have a personal relationship. But she'd occasionally accepted date invitations from other business partners, like Lang. Not much ever came of them, as most men seemed to lose interest in her pretty quickly, but she'd dated.

But Levi had told her—she wasn't dating anyone but him.

Amusement that she was actually taking that seriously curled inside her. Who did he think he was, telling her what to do like that? He wasn't in charge of her life.

Truthfully...she had no desire to date Lang. Or anyone really. As that sank in, she realized how truly fucked she was. Not only was she having feelings for Levi that she shouldn't, he'd made her lose interest in anyone else.

For that reason alone, she almost accepted Lang's invitation. But that wasn't fair to him. She wasn't interested in him. That would just be using him to...to...well, she wasn't sure what she'd be doing. Showing Levi who the boss was? Ha. Trying to convince herself that her feelings for Levi weren't really all that intense? Right.

"I'm sorry," she said finally, her voice soft. "I'm kind of...seeing someone."

"Ah." He made a face, an adorable face of brave disappointment. "I didn't know that."

"It's fairly recent."

He smiled. "Lucky guy."

She shook her head, smiling, and dropped her eyes as Lang's assistant returned. Lang bought lunch, which was very nice, and they shook hands on the sidewalk in front of the restaurant.

Dark clouds had amassed in the sky. She cast glances toward them as she hurried back to the office, hoping the rain would hold off until she was there, as she didn't have an umbrella. No such luck. A few drops hit her just as she rounded the corner but before she could reach the door of the Lachman Building the clouds burst. Rain pelted down. *Shit!*

People started sprinting, some whipping out umbrellas. In her spiky heels, she started to run.

"Sloane!"

She paused at her name called behind her, looking over her shoulder. Levi jogged up, a big black umbrella in his hand. Her steps slowed and then he was there, protecting her from the rain.

"Hey, sexy girl," he murmured, smiling. "You're getting all...wet."

They stood on the sidewalk, the huge umbrella sheltering both of them as rain pounded down around them. She moved closer, bringing her Kate Spade purse under the umbrella too. Now close enough to see Levi's glinting blue eyes and smell his warm, citrusy scent. His free arm went around her waist, pulling her up against him.

"I have to say I'm impressed by your ability to run in those shoes."

She smiled. And then he kissed her, right on the street in front of the office.

His lips were warm and firm as they brushed over hers. They shouldn't be doing this.

She looked up at him and as usual, melted inside.

"I just turned down a date," she said.

His eyebrows snapped together above his nose. "What?"

"A date. I got invited on a date."

The smell of the rain on the city pavement rose around them, warm and earthy. A car horn blared as someone darted across the street against the lights.

He studied her, obviously thinking over what she'd just told him. "Was he a seventy-year-old man with no hair?"

She choked on a laugh. "No."

"Was he young and good-looking?"

"Define young."

"Under forty."

"Then yes. And very attractive."

His eyes narrowed, then a grin spread across his face. "Go, me."

Her eyebrows rose. "What?"

"If you turned down a seventy-year-old man, well…I'd expect that. But you turned down some handsome dude…for me." He smooched her lips again.

"Your ego is so big it's a wonder there's room for me here under this umbrella."

His smile went crooked. "Babe. It's huge."

"That's what she said."

He burst out laughing, his arm around her lower back tightening into a hug.

"Where did you get an umbrella this big?"

"It's for golfing."

"You golf?"

"Of course." He rolled his eyes. "My parents made me go to golf camp every summer at the country club."

"Of course." She loaded tone into her voice. "The country club."

They smiled as they gazed into each other's eyes.

"Come on. I can't be late, or I'll be in trouble with the boss."

She grinned and fell into step with him. "I'm not your boss."

"What? Wait, what did you say? Speak into this microphone." He held his hand up to her face, and she laughed again and pushed it away.

How did he suck her into these feelings, every single damn time?

19

Sloane dried off in the ladies' room after she and Levi got back to the office, getting her head back into business mode. She brushed out her damp hair and wiped off her shoes with paper towels. Walking down the corridor toward her office she ran into Kaleb.

"Hey, Sloane."

She smiled at Kaleb. "Hi. How are things going?"

"Good. In fact, pretty damn amazing."

She lifted one eyebrow. "Great to hear. How so?"

"Remember I told you about the buying program Bailey was working on?"

She nodded. Where media buyers used to negotiate price on the phone and enter media buys into an Excel spreadsheet, now they were using data-driven, real-time, platform-based buying, and Bailey had developed her own buying program. "Yes, although I have to admit I don't totally understand it."

He grinned. "I hear ya. Anyhoo, it's working great. Saving us tons of time and giving us way better information."

"Good to hear."

"Who would've thought cute little Bailey had such a technological mind."

Sloane frowned. Bailey frequently got underestimated. The younger woman was bright and hardworking, although she did disappear every day right at five o'clock. Not that that was a problem, but in this business, leaving on time every day could lead people to question your commitment to the job. But Sloane knew that Bailey busted her butt every day to get her work done and had never failed to meet a deadline, and she was always aware of budget constraints. She was a smooth negotiator and had made a number of great deals with various media outlets. Her research was always thorough and her follow-up meticulous.

She was also young and into technology, savvy about using modern tools to place ads. And yet so many at Huxworth Packard looked down on Bailey because she was little and cute and blonde and had big boobs.

"You shouldn't judge a book by its cover," she said. Then she rolled her eyes. "Cliché alert."

"Ha. Clichés are clichés because they're true." He shrugged. "You're right." He continued down the hall toward his own office.

Sloane paused, thinking about what she'd just heard. Then she changed direction and instead of returning to her office she went to find Bailey. She found her and Phoebe in the coffee bar, stirring lattes.

"I think they should call moustaches mouthbrows." Phoebe touched her fingertips to her upper lip. "Like eyebrows. Only here."

Sloane blinked at Phoebe. She turned to meet Bailey's eyes.

Bailey's lips twitched. "That's a good idea, hon."

Sloane repressed a sigh.

"Did you need something, Sloane?" Bailey turned to her.

"I just wanted to talk to you for a minute. Can you come to my office?"

"Sure."

"Kaleb was just telling me about the buying program you developed." Sloane led the way across the open space and then down the corridor to her office. She noticed Levi and Scott sitting on the couches in the corner of the staff lounge, throwing a tiny football back and forth. "He's very impressed."

"Oh yay! That's so great."

Sloane gestured for Bailey to have a seat, taking her suit jacket off. She hung it on the back of her chair and sat. "I know you don't want to be a media buyer forever."

Bailey nodded slowly. "That's right."

Sloane tipped her head. "I think you should join me for lunch tomorrow. I'm meeting with Derek from Verhoeven, and Brent and Hoyt from Herstal."

Bailey's eyes widened. "Really?"

"Yes. We're going to talk about their branded point-of-sales materials. I know that's not media stuff, but it would be good for you to hear that discussion. Get more of a sense of the bigger picture. Other facets of the business."

"That would be awesome."

Sloane nodded. "Good."

"Thank you so much, Sloane." Bailey jumped up and hastened back to her cubicle.

"What would be so awesome?"

She looked up to see Levi leaning against her doorframe. Her heart bumped and warmth spread through her chest at seeing him. Dammit.

She could not fall in love with this man.

This gorgeous, funny, creative man who made her laugh and made her hot. The deeper she got into this, the more it was going to kill when it ended. She needed to protect herself.

"I'm taking Bailey with me when I have lunch with Derek, Brent and Hoyt."

"Ah. Cool. She seemed really stoked about it."

Sloane shrugged. "It'll be a good learning and networking experience for her."

"Why would you do that for her?"

She blinked. "Um. I just said."

He smiled at her. "You like her."

Sloane frowned. "Of course I do."

"You're not such a hard-ass as you seem."

"Yes, I am. Get back to work."

He grinned. "Come to my place tonight. I'm going to make you dinner. And then I'm going to make you come."

"Shhh!" She bugged her eyes out at him and he laughed. "I can't tonight. I'm having dinner with Kirk and Alex. It'll be late." She didn't know that, but she was nervous about seeing too much of him. It was risky.

"Damn." Disappointment tugged the corners of his mouth down. "Oh well. Maybe tomorrow." He pushed away from the door and left.

Hard-ass. She wasn't exactly a hard-ass. Clearly she had some kind of soft spot for Levi Wolcott. And possibly little Bailey. And Chuck. Chuck had definitely wriggled his warm puppy body and big brown puppy eyes into her affections. Maybe she should get a dog of her own.

She'd always wanted another dog. As a kid, she'd had the idea that once she was an adult and on her own, she'd be able to get a dog, but now it was impractical with the long hours she worked. Although, Levi did it. The truth was, she was afraid. She'd loved Teddy so much, giving him up had shattered her heart into even smaller pieces. She could never do that again.

But maybe if she had a dog, she would lavish love and affection on him. He would love her back unconditionally, expecting nothing more from her than food, water and an occasional belly rub. Then she wouldn't be stupid enough to have feelings for a person who would leave her and hurt her.

She had one more task before she went to her next

meeting. She had a birthday present to buy. She turned to her computer and went online. A Google search brought up some ideas, and there…exactly what she was looking for. She loved Google. Within a few moments, she'd tapped her credit card number in and placed an order, shelling out big bucks for next day delivery.

⌒⌇⌐

Levi and Scott met with Mason to review progress on the commercials for the Cerone brand. Levi wasn't completely happy with what they'd come up with, but it still pissed him off when Mason rejected every single concept. "Back to the drawing board," Mason said. "But remember your deadline."

Yeah, yeah. Deadlines. Whatever.

He threw himself into his chair, linked his hands behind his head and frowned at Scott.

"What did they say when it was back to the drawing board, before there were drawing boards?" Scott mused.

"Back to the stone tablet, I guess. Shit."

"I know." Scott sighed. "We got this, dude. Don't be discouraged."

"I'm not."

He was. This shouldn't be so hard.

"I feel like getting drunk," Scott said.

"Right now?" Levi perked up.

"Hell yeah."

Levi was so on board with that idea. But damn. That would *not* play well with Sloane. Or The Hux. "Let's see what we can get done. Then go for drinks. I'm thinking tonight I'm in the mood for…tequila."

"Yeah. Patrón. Excellent. Now. Let's talk about beer."

They kept at it for the rest of the afternoon and Levi felt they'd made some good progress. So he didn't feel guilty leaving at five thirty and heading to Bon Vivant. On the way out they ran into Bailey, Phoebe and Carly, and Scott invited them to come too. What the heck. Sloane was out wining and dining clients.

Bailey had to decline and rushed off, but Carly and Phoebe came along. They sat at a high-top table for four. The girls ordered lemon drops, and Scott and Levi ordered their tequila shots.

"Line 'em up," Scott instructed the waitress.

"No beer?" Phoebe asked.

"Not tonight. Lately my desire for beer has waned," Levi said. "I'm sure it's just temporary, though."

"Hey ladies," Scott said. "Have you ever noticed that after you drink beer you're horny?"

Carly and Phoebe exchanged glances. "I don't drink beer," Carly said.

"Me either," Phoebe added.

"Maybe you should try it," Scott said seriously.

"I don't get it," Phoebe said. "Why would beer make you horny?"

"It's the hops," Scott explained. "For some reason it has some kind of effect on women. I've heard."

"Hops?" Phoebe blinked.

"Honey, you work on the beer account," Carly said. "You don't know what hops are?"

Phoebe grinned. "I know the bunny hop."

Levi swallowed his groan. She had a smokin' hot body and a pretty face, but she was as sharp as a bowling ball. How the hell did she manage to find places for ads?

He remembered how pleased Bailey had looked leaving Sloane's office. Bailey was super cute too, little and blonde with a great rack, but somehow he had a feeling she was more than just a looker. Sloane wouldn't be helping her out if she were just a dumb blonde.

He should be ashamed of himself for stereotyping, but that totally didn't count because Sloane was blonde and she was *so* not dumb. So it wasn't like he considered *all* blondes dumb. Far from it.

On the other hand, he was pretty sure Phoebe wasn't actually blonde. Heh. Then he remembered the fucking awesome ad he and Scott had come up with for the Natural Belgian Blonde Ale.

"What's so funny?" Phoebe was looking at him curiously.

"Nothing. Just thinking about one of the ads we're working on."

"You guys are so smart." Phoebe leaned her elbow on the table, chin on her hand, her admiring eyes fixed on him.

"Uh. Thanks."

"But you know how smart guys can be kind of geeky?"

He just blinked.

"You are totally not geeky," she continued. "Do you work out? Because you're in great shape."

He shifted in his chair and cast Scott a glance. "Yeah, I work out a few times a week."

"I could tell." Her gaze swept up and down his body. The top half of his body that she could see above the table.

"Totally," Carly agreed.

Scott rolled his eyes. "More tequila shots here!" he called to the waitress.

The girl hustled over to the table. "You bet," she said.

"I'll have a beer," Phoebe said.

"What kind of beer, hon?" the waitress asked, planting a hand on her hip. She reeled off the long list of available brews. Phoebe looked at Levi with big eyes.

"She'll have a Rockslide Red," he said.

The waitress smiled at him. "More tequila for you, sugar?"

Levi smiled. "Nah, I'm good. Thanks, babe."

Scott did another eye roll. "Why the fuck am I here?" he muttered.

"Dude," Levi said. "Don't even think of leaving."

If Scott left him with these two, he was gonna need a *lot* more tequila.

"I saw this thing on YouTube today," Carly said. "Did you know that the human penis is the largest of any primate's?"

Scott choked on his tequila.

Levi grinned. "Size does matter."

Phoebe eyed him with a flirty look. "You don't seem too worried about that."

"Nope."

Christ. This was the kind of conversation he could have some fun with. Only, he wished it were Sloane here looking at him like that and talking about his size. This was kind of creeping him out, though he didn't want to let on.

"What were you doing on YouTube at work?" he asked Carly.

"Research." She winked at him.

"Ah. Of course."

"Everything is supersized these days," Phoebe said.

"Are you saying size *doesn't* matter?" Scott asked her.

She laughed. "Sure it does."

"You know what?" Carly said. "Guys are so insecure about their size and worried about what women think, but most women aren't that picky. I mean, as long as you're more or less in proportion to your body, it's all good." She eyed Levi. "I bet you're well proportioned."

Jesus.

"So are you saying humans having bigger dicks than monkeys?" Phoebe asked.

It took a while for that original statement to get through, apparently.

Carly blinked. "Um. Yeah."

"What about gorillas?"

"I don't know about gorilla penises," Carly admitted. She looked at Levi.

He held his hands up. "Me neither."

After a few more rounds, the conversation was getting raunchier, the sexual innuendoes were getting more obvious, and Carly and Phoebe apparently wanted to go to someone's place and have sex. All four of them.

He had to get out of there. Now. Alone.

⌒◯⧉◯⌒

"Thank you again for inviting me," Bailey said to Sloane on their way back to the office after their lunch meeting the next day. "That was fascinating."

"It was a good discussion." Herstal wanted to do a holiday promotion and get some special displays into retail outlets. "It's a tight time frame, though." They chatted a bit more about the meeting, then Sloane said, "Phoebe didn't seem to be feeling well this morning."

Bailey snorted. "She's hungover."

"Ah."

"She and Carly went out for drinks with Scott and Levi last night. And apparently it was quite the crazy and late evening."

Sloane kept her face neutral as they walked along North Wells Street. "Really."

"They invited me, but I couldn't go. Maybe just as well. I'm not sure if doing crazy sex things with coworkers is the best idea."

Geezus. "I'm sure it's not," Sloane said evenly. "Especially if you value your career."

"They're all crazy over Levi," Bailey continued. "But nobody's been able to actually get him out on a date."

Sloane's stomach tightened. "Does that include you?" she asked casually. "Are you crazy about Levi?"

Bailey gave a huff of laughter. "Um. No."

"Do you have a boyfriend?"

"No. I don't have time for a boyfriend."

Huh. Sloane knew Bailey wasn't working long hours. So why was she too busy for a boyfriend?

At that moment, Sloane's cell phone chimed. She reached into her purse and found it, still walking. Dad. Huh. She tapped the screen to answer.

"Hi, Dad."

"Sloane."

Silence.

"Dad? Is everything okay?"

"Are you...where are you?"

"I'm on my way back to the office." A shiver ran down her spine. "Why? What's wrong?"

After a brief silence, he said, "I got a call from the police this morning."

She stopped. Bailey kept going a few steps before noticing that she wasn't with her any more, then paused and turned. Sloane held up a finger and turned a half turn away. "The police?"

"Yeah." He sighed. "They found your mom."

20

"What?" Sloane's skin went cold despite the June heat and her stomach knotted. "They found Mom? Is she...?" She swallowed. "Is she alive? Where is she?"

"Yeah." His voice was thin. "She's alive. She's in jail. In California."

Sloane's face froze. Her lungs constricted. "Oh my God."

"I don't know all the details yet. The police are coming to see us tonight."

"Oh. Do you want me to come?"

He cleared his throat. "Yeah. You should be here, cookie."

She nodded, though he couldn't see. "Okay. I'll clear my schedule for this afternoon and be there..." She closed her eyes briefly, picturing her calendar and how long the drive would be to Oakville. "By five. Do you want me to see if Eric can come?" Obviously there was no way Becca could get there from New York.

"Okay. Thanks, cookie. See you soon."

She ended the call, and paused with her head bent. Bailey turned and came back to her. "Are you okay, Sloane?"

214

She looked up at the younger woman and saw the concern etched on her forehead and in her eyes. "Yeah." She forced a smile. "I'm okay. A little family issue has come up. Let's get back to the office."

"Okay, sure."

They were only half a block away so they were soon there. Sloane headed straight to her office and pulled up her schedule on the computer. She narrowed her focus to this, one thing at a time, shutting out all the other swirling crap. She was going to have to cancel one meeting, but luckily that was it for today. She made the call and rescheduled, then phoned Eric.

"Hey, Sloane." He sounded surprised to hear from her. "Whassup?"

"I have some news." For a heartbeat she resented her father for making her do this. "Where are you? Are you alone?"

"Yeah, in my office."

She took a deep breath. "The police called Dad today. They found Mom."

Silence. Pretty much her reaction too. "Seriously?"

"Well, unless it's some mix-up. They're going to Dad's place tonight to give them more details. I'm driving out there this afternoon. Do you want to come with me?"

"Shit. I can't." He paused. "I have an important client meeting this afternoon, I just can't miss it."

"I understand. It's okay. I'll call you and Becca once I know more."

She debated calling Becca then decided she'd just make one call once she knew more. Then she headed to Mason's office to let him know she was going to be out for the rest of the day.

He too showed concern. "Anything I can do?" he asked, when she told him a family emergency had called her out of town.

She shook her head. "No. But thanks. I'll just go deal

with this and see you tomorrow." She paused. "Please don't say anything to anyone else. This is…" She hesitated. How did she tell Mason that her mother was in jail? But it could totally be a mistake. "This is awkward. Please just say I'm out of the office on business if anyone needs to know."

"Sure. I can do that." Once again, she sensed an understanding on his part that went deeper than most, a shared sense of loss and tragedy. Maybe one day Mason would talk to her about what had caused that sadness that always lurked beneath the surface.

She hesitated before she left. Should she talk to Levi? She felt a strong tug of need to tell him what had happened. To maybe get a hug from him, for him to tell her it would all be okay. She squeezed her eyes closed briefly. No. He didn't need to be involved in this. This was her issue to deal with.

As she rode the elevator down to the parking garage, she debated whether it was worth it to go home to change. She had time. A quick trip into her condo and she was back out wearing shorts, a tank top and flip-flops. That would be more comfortable for the two-hour drive to Oakville.

She was there well before the promised five o'clock and pulled into Dad and Viv's driveway behind Dad's car. She'd had lots of time to think on the way there, imagining what she was about to hear, why her mother was in jail, what the hell was going on. In fact, her mind was so consumed by it she didn't even remember the drive there. Had she run any red lights? Cut someone off while changing lanes? Her stomach was in knots and her palms were sweaty as she pulled the keys from the ignition, grabbed her purse and headed to the front door.

After Dad had met Viv, after Sloane had moved to Chicago to pursue her career, he'd moved in with Viv at her home, a house in a new development on the edge of town, much nicer than the low-income apartment they'd lived in after Mom had disappeared. Sloane had never spent much time at Viv's home, other than obligatory family holidays.

She rang the doorbell and her dad opened it immediately. "Hi, cookie." His eyes warmed. "So glad you're here. Come on in." He held the door for her and she stepped inside. When he closed the door, she eyed him then moved into his hug without a thought. He was her dad. They didn't show a lot of physical affection, but at that moment, hugging each other felt like the only thing to do.

They held on to each other for long moments, and she sensed her father's distress.

"This is so effed up," he finally murmured as he released her.

"Yeah." Sloane turned to see Viv in the living room watching them. She'd never seen Viv look like that...her face in pale, tight lines, her mouth thin, eyes shadowed. Yet she gave a tentative smile to Sloane and lifted her arms.

Sloane hesitated. She wasn't a huggy kind of person and in the past, she'd resisted Viv's attempts to be physically affectionate. She didn't know Viv that well, and while she liked her, she certainly didn't love her.

But at that moment, it came crashing down on her what this meant to Viv. The man she'd married was in fact married to someone else. Someone who was supposed to be dead. But wasn't. Putting herself in Viv's shoes, imagining how she'd feel if that happened to her, made Sloane walk up to Viv and encircle her with her arms. Viv's relief was palpable. She made a soft noise that might almost have been a sob.

This wasn't Viv's fault. None of it. Not that Sloane had ever really blamed her, but maybe she'd never really thought about how Viv felt all this time. And Sloane felt herself whispering, "It'll be okay."

"Thank you," Viv choked out, squeezing Sloane tighter. They drew apart.

Viv swept her fingertips beneath her eyes. "Would you like something to drink? Coffee? Iced tea?"

"Sure. Iced tea would be great."

They all walked into the kitchen, all blue and white and pretty with a big vase of fresh flowers on the kitchen table. A cell phone rang and Viv picked it up from the counter. "It's the store," she said. "Excuse me. I rushed out of there."

Dad poured a glass of iced tea for Sloane while Viv left to take the call, and they sat at the table.

"So tell me what you know," Sloane said.

"Not much more than what I already told you on the phone." Dad's face too had drawn into a taut mask. He shoved a hand into thinning gray hair. "Cynthia's in jail in Long Beach, California. They arrested her last night for drug trafficking and earlier today she told them her real name. She's apparently been living under a different name all this time."

Sloane's eyes widened. A sharp knife twisted in her heart, hot, piercing pain. "How could that be?"

He shrugged, his eyes reddening. "I don't know, cookie. I don't understand it. Any of it. Detective Thurman will be here at six thirty. Do you remember him?"

"Yes." She nodded, her insides clenching tightly. She'd hated that detective. She'd been convinced he believed Dad had murdered Mom and hid the body, with all the questions they'd asked of Dad at the time. She'd been furious at him, and one memorable day had actually yelled at him to leave them alone and try harder to find the person who'd really hurt her mom. And he never had been able to. Just hearing his name made her stomach roll.

"He wanted to talk to us in person," Dad continued.

Viv returned to the kitchen. "Sorry about that. Just had to take care of a small problem. Some missing roses." She tried to smile.

"Have a seat," Dad said, standing. "I'll get you some iced tea too."

"Thank you, dear." Viv blinked and looked around the kitchen. "I guess it's a little early for dinner. Maybe after the detective comes, we can order pizza or something."

Sloane nodded, though eating was the last thing she felt like doing, her stomach jumping with nerves.

They spent the next hour talking, imagining possibilities and explanations for what could possibly have happened. Finally Detective Thurman arrived. His hair had grayed a lot more since the last time she'd seen him, and his waistline was a little thicker, but she remembered his face. Although now, the sadness and kindness in his eyes took her aback. He wore a suit, not a uniform, and accepted a glass of iced tea and joined them at the kitchen table.

Detective Thurman showed them the mug shot that had been taken last night and Sloane stared at it. Her mother's eyes looked back at her, but the rest of her looked nothing like she remembered. Her mom's shoulder length light brown hair was bleached to straw, her face was thin and tough looking, with lines around her eyes and mouth. Hints of her prettiness remained, but Sloane had to swallow as nausea rose up her throat, bitter and choking.

"That's her," Dad confirmed in a low voice. "Jesus."

Detective Thurman nodded and put the photo away.

The story he told them was…terrible. Hurtful. And so bewildering. Apparently Mom had talked more to the police officers in California. She'd admitted that she'd walked away from their home all those years ago and had never intended to come back. She'd confessed that some of her memories from that time were a blur, like she'd been in a fog. Likely a severe depression. She'd met up with some bikers at a bar who'd offered her drugs, then invited her to ride along with them. And she'd gone.

She'd been living as the old lady of some biker guy for

the last few years, using a different name. She had no children and told everyone she didn't want any.

At that, Sloane lowered her head and focused her burning eyes on the pale blue tablecloth. A hand rubbed the middle of her back. It was Viv's. Then Viv reached for Sloane's other hand and gripped it. For once, Sloane held on.

"What does this mean for us?" Dad asked quietly. He looked at Viv.

"I don't believe Cynthia's reappearance can disrupt your marriage," Detective Thurman said. "But you should probably talk to a lawyer. If there were any death benefits paid or life insurance policies, you may be liable to repay those."

Dad squinted, but shook his head. "There wasn't any life insurance. But yeah, I'll talk to Bill."

Sloane saw the look of relief cross Viv's face and again her heart squeezed in sympathy.

"It wouldn't matter, Viv," she said softly. "You and Dad love each other. *You're married.*"

Viv gazed back at her, and her eyes flooded again. "Thank you, Sloane. It means so much to hear that from you."

"I never gave up on this case," Detective Thurman said, surprising all of them. "It haunted me. I know you all blamed me for the investigation I had to do. But we cleared you, Mr. Granderson. I wasn't out to get you. I just wanted the truth."

Dad nodded, his mouth a grim line. "I understand. That didn't stop the neighbors from believing I had something to do with it. People I thought were friends turned their backs on me."

Sloane's eyes widened and her hand went to her throat. At fourteen, she'd been devastated about all the losses she'd suffered. She hadn't even realized that was something Dad had endured. And yet…she did remember now, little things that had happened, like when her friend Olivia's mom wouldn't let Olivia come over to play…but then they'd moved away.

"I'm sorry you all went through that," the detective said quietly. "We'll keep you apprised of any new developments. Unfortunately, this probably isn't going to give you the kind of closure you need."

They showed the detective out, and then all returned to the kitchen. They sat silently for a long time.

"Do you want to see her, Sloane?" Dad asked.

She swallowed past the thickness in her throat. "No."

Viv spoke up. "Maybe you should."

Sloane's head jerked around to look at her stepmother. "What? Really?"

Viv nodded somberly. "Maybe that would be the closure that you need. To see her face-to-face. To finally ask her why. How she could leave her children and never come back."

Sloane's face got tight, pressure building behind her eyes. "I don't think I could do that."

Viv nodded. "I understand. It's not something you need to decide right now. This has all been a huge shock. As time goes on, you may find yourself wondering. Hurt. Or angry. I can't even imagine."

Sloane nodded.

Then Viv looked at Dad. "Do *you* want to see her, Art?"

Sloane's breath caught. She saw the look in Viv's eyes…the apprehension. The fear.

Viv was afraid Dad still loved Mom.

God. Sloane squeezed her eyes shut and curled her fingers into her palms. It had been so hard when Viv came into the picture, not replacing her mom as a mother, but certainly replacing her as Dad's wife. He'd moved on. And that had been difficult to accept. But now…the idea that Viv thought Dad might still care, that he might even want to go back to Mom, made Sloane want to vomit.

"No," Dad said immediately. He reached for Viv's hand and looked into her eyes. "I do not ever want to see her again." His tone was firm and clear. "I love you, Viv. I'm sorry this happened. You didn't sign on for this."

"It's not your fault," she whispered, lifting Dad's hand to kiss it. "It's okay. We'll get through this."

"Yes, we will. This changes nothing for us. Nothing that matters."

Their love for each other was the brightest spot in this dark fucking nightmare. And at that moment, Sloane missed Levi so much it was like a physical pain shafting through her core. She needed him there, his big broad shoulder to cry on, his strong arms to hold her and his caring to soothe her.

Oh sweet loving Lord. She should never have gotten involved with him. Now she thought she *needed* him.

Viv ordered pizza, even though nobody was hungry. They made tearful calls to Becca and Eric. Becca wanted to be with them, so they planned that she would come home this weekend and they could all get together.

And Sloane drove back to Chicago with another couple of hours alone to think about things. She couldn't make sense of much of it. Long ago she'd come to terms with her mother's mental illness. She knew it could make people do things they normally wouldn't. Her mom could have wanted to leave—what mother with three kids *didn't* have days when she felt overwhelmed?—but to start a whole new life for all these years? Didn't she care at all about the lives she'd brought into the world?

Viv was right. Sloane was pissed. Pissed way the fuck off.

She walked into her condo, dropped her purse and headed out the back door into her courtyard. She swallowed hard as she took in all the beautiful plants and flowers she'd nurtured and tended, thinking this was some kind of spiritual connection with her mother. Even in the dark they were lovely, the big white hydrangeas glowing in the moonlight, the shrubs all textured shadows.

She stomped over to a fountain of lilies, grabbed hold near the base with both hands and ripped it out of the ground. Dirt hit her in the face and she fell on her ass. She let out a choked sound as she hurled the clump of soil and roots and bruised leaves across the patch of lawn, lily petals scattering. Then she wrapped her arms around her bent knees and sat there and cried, like she hadn't since the day her mom had left.

21

Levi hadn't seen Sloane pretty much all day Tuesday, but that wasn't unusual. He'd had meetings and he assumed she had too, but at six o'clock when she hadn't come back to the office he frowned.

He saw Mason leaving and almost asked him if he knew where Sloane was, but stopped himself. Instead he sent her a text message.

Hey sexy girl. Want to get some dinner?

He didn't get a reply immediately, so he did some work. An hour had passed before he realized he still hadn't heard back from her.

He studied his phone. He made a face. Obviously, she was busy. Ah well. He texted his buddies using the group he'd created. Jacob was home from his honeymoon and he hadn't seen him yet.

Hey Jacob, ball and chain too heavy for you to leave the house for brews?

Haha asshole. Where we going?

Cam and I are already at Don Pedro's, Luke texted. *Meet us here.*

Sounds like a plan.

Levi shut down his computer and grabbed his sport jacket from the back of his chair. As he drove to Don

Pedro's, he again wondered what was up with Sloane.

Remembering last night with Scott and Carly and Phoebe, and the looks they'd all shared that morning, he became uneasy. Had Sloane heard that he'd been out with them last night? She wouldn't be pissed about that, would she?

Nah. He was the one who'd insisted they were in a relationship. She knew he wouldn't screw around.

Over drinks, they heard about Jacob's honeymoon, the things they'd done in London, Tara's jet lag that had made her fall asleep every afternoon and then be awake all night.

"The perfect honeymoon," Luke joked.

"I did manage to keep her entertained during the night," Jacob said modestly. "But she was pissed because she wanted to do more shopping and kept falling asleep over lunch."

Levi went home early, took Chuck for another walk, screwed around on Twitter and Instagram for a while, then went to bed. Still no word from Sloane.

In the morning, they were both in the same meeting to review the status of the Cedar Springs and Cerone brands. She walked in, her usual put-together sexy self, wearing a fitted bright red dress and, of course, heels — today shiny nude-colored pumps. He caught her eye and winked as they took their seats at the long table in the meeting room. Then his forehead tightened. Even though she gave him a little uptick of the lips in response to his wink, her eyes drooped a bit at the corners and on closer inspection were pink and puffy. She'd done a great job with the blush and eye shadow, hiding pale cheeks and puffy eyes, but still...although he was probably the only one noticing.

Because he noticed everything about her. How she tossed back three cups of coffee during a one-hour meeting. How her mouth kept sliding into a sad curve. How she doodled endlessly on her pad of paper and actually missed a question Mason asked her, blinking at him in response.

Something was wrong.

Fuck this bullshit that they couldn't be a couple in public. Right then and there he wanted to demand to know what was bothering her so he could punch whatever motherfucker had put that sad and worried look on her face.

Was it The Hux? Was he on her back again about their bad behavior? Had there *been* bad behavior?

Now *he* was the distracted one. *Focus.* This was business. He'd get her alone after the meeting.

Deadlines were zooming closer. Faster than a speeding love train. Ha. Scott was freaking out. Levi, on the other hand, was calm. He loved deadlines. Deadlines made him get shit done.

Scott wasn't the only one who seemed tense in the room, so Levi tried to lighten the vibe with a little joke. "I meet all my deadlines directly in proportion to the amount of bodily injury I expect to receive from missing them." He looked around the table at blank stares. "Not funny, huh?"

Sloane's lips twitched and everyone else groaned.

"I see you've set aside this special time to humiliate yourself," Scott said.

Levi showed him his middle finger behind his raised pad of paper.

"Enough, boys and girls," Mason said. "We'll meet again Monday morning. Have something to show us."

When he went by Sloane's office a short time later, she wasn't there. He saw her speeding off to a meeting later, but it wasn't until after five o'clock he finally managed to corral her in her office alone. He shut the door and walked behind her desk where she sat, propping his ass against the desk, nudging her chair with his knee so she faced him. "Hey, beautiful girl. Are you okay?" He reached out and brushed a strand of hair off her face.

"Of course." She smiled at him.

She was lying.

"Why didn't you answer my text last night?"

"God, I didn't even see it until this morning. Sorry. My phone was off."

He frowned. Her phone was never off. He knew that because one time she'd tried to get out of bed to answer it when they'd just had sex. He'd put a stop to that pretty goddamn quick. There was more than one reason for the restraints fastened to his headboard.

"What were you doing last night?"

"I just, um, went to visit my dad and stepmom."

"On a weeknight? You drove all that way there and back?"

"Uh-huh." She smiled and looked at her computer screen.

"Are *they* okay?"

"Yeah, of course."

He paused. Something was up. But she seemed okay. Mostly. "So. Dinner tonight instead?"

"Yeah, I don't know…I have so much work to do."

"Me too, actually." He grimaced. "How about we work a couple hours more, grab a pizza and take it back to my place. We can…unwind…together." He winked at her.

She smiled. "That sounds great. But I just had pizza last night."

He shook his head. "Fine. We'll get sushi. Whatever. I'll swing by in a while."

She pressed her lips together, then nodded.

A couple of hours later, they drove in separate vehicles to his place. He picked up the sushi on the way and she was waiting in his lobby when he got there. "I have to get you a key," he murmured as he kissed her, then moved past her to the elevators. "You could be up there waiting for me. Naked."

She laughed.

He was relieved that she seemed okay now. Maybe she'd just had some kind of disagreement with her folks or something.

They ate edamame and dynamite rolls and spicy tuna rolls while watching *Two and a Half Men* and laughing. Warm affection rolled through him as she fed Chuck little pieces of shrimp, even though she knew Chuck wasn't supposed to get people food. Then she picked up his dog and snuggled him against her chest. He loved that she loved Chuck. He loved…having her there.

CHAPTER BREAK

Friday morning, Sloane looked up from an email from Derek at Verhoeven to see Bailey in her office door, her eyebrows pinched together and her mouth tight.

"Good morning," Sloane said.

"Do you have a minute?"

"Sure. Come on in. What's up?"

Bailey pressed her lips together. "I have a problem. I have a revision to a billboard campaign that's supposed to be at the printer Monday and it isn't ready yet. A hundred billboards, across the country."

Sloane frowned. "Which one?"

"The one for Steel."

"Shit."

"Yeah."

"Who's the printer?"

"Bowes. They're waiting for it. If we don't get it to them by Monday, there's going to be a rush job penalty."

"Why isn't it ready? Where's the hold up?"

"Isaiah. Hunter got the copy written and it's been approved, but Isaiah hasn't finished the layout."

"Did you talk to him?"

Bailey sighed. "Yes. He blew me off."

"Shit."

This wasn't the first time one of the guys had dismissed Bailey and it pissed Sloane off.

"Yeah. A rush job penalty will put us over budget on this job." Bailey's face tightened with anxiety. "I'll get the blame for that."

"No, you won't. I'll go talk to them."

"Should I come with you?"

"Yes. You should." *Watch and learn, little girl.* Sloane smiled as she rose from her chair. "Come on."

They hiked through the office to Isaiah and Hunter's cubicle. "Hey guys. The billboard ad for Steel. Where's it at?"

"We don't have time to get it done." Isaiah frowned, looking up from his computer screen. "We have too much other shit to do. We don't have time to spend all day dicking around with a billboard. Push it back."

"We can't push it back. It's already been revised once and it's due at the printer Monday morning."

"There's no way we can get it done by then." Hunter leaned back in his chair and crossed his arms.

"Look, this'll take probably four hours of your time. Not a big deal. But to Bailey and to the client, this is hugely important."

"Isaiah has to draw storyboards all day today for our commercial presentation Monday." Hunter straightened. "He can't lose four hours today to a billboard. We're already behind trying to get this commercial figured out."

"Billboard takes priority. There's a deadline we can't miss with the printer. A rush job penalty is not going to make anybody happy. This has to be at the printer Monday. If your other stuff also needs to be done Monday, come in on the weekend. Understood?"

They both nodded. "Got it," Isaiah mumbled.

"You guys always come through." She softened her tone. "Is there anything we can help you with?"

"Uh. No."

"Well, let us know if there is. Anything. I'm counting on you and I know you can deliver." She paused. "Also, when one of the media buyers reminds you of a deadline that she is going to be held accountable for and have to deal with, you don't just ignore her."

"Right. Sorry."

Sloane led the way to Noah's office. She filled him in on the problem and what had just occurred. "Did you give them enough time to do the job?" she asked directly.

Noah rubbed his chin. "Yeah. I think I did. Maybe. Khadim was pushing hard."

"Maybe you need to monitor their work a little more closely. Remind them of their deadlines. Isaiah didn't seem to think this was a priority. He basically ignored Bailey when she tried to talk to him about it. Bailey will be checking with them Monday morning."

"You know billboards aren't a priority to them."

"They are to the media people. And the client." She lifted one eyebrow at him.

He sighed. "Yeah, I know. They just get busy with other shit and put the billboards off and end up scrambling. I'll be on them."

She led Bailey back to her own office.

"Thank you, Sloane." Admiration shone in Bailey's brown eyes. "I want to be you when I grow up."

Sloane laughed and took a seat. "Okay, Monday morning, let me know what happens."

"I will." Bailey hesitated. "Why wouldn't they listen to me?"

Sloane huffed out a breath. "This is a tough business for women, not gonna lie. It takes time to earn their respect. You're doing the right things, Bailey. You work hard and do a great job."

"Thank you." Bailey's gratitude was clearly heartfelt.

"Be patient, Bailey. You're young. You need experience."

Bailey smiled and nodded. "Thanks again."

Sloane wished she'd had someone who'd helped her out when she started her career. Bailey was a smart girl but it never hurt to have a little assistance along the way.

❦

Friday was Levi's birthday. Nobody at Huxworth Packard knew that. But there was a bunch of red balloons tied to his chair when he got to his office, one of them a Mylar balloon that said *Happy Birthday!* He paused, studying them.

It had to have been Sloane.

"What the hell are those for?" Scott walked into his office. "Is it your birthday?"

"Yeah."

"Hey, happy birthday, man."

"Thanks."

"Got big plans for tonight?"

"Yeah." Levi sat. "Going out with friends." And Sloane. "To Studio V."

It didn't take long for others to notice the balloons and come over to wish him a happy birthday, and the other creatives even took him out for lunch. Over the weeks he'd been there they'd finally stopped tormenting him and seemed to accept him. Maybe even...like him.

He hadn't seen much of Sloane the last couple of days. She'd been super busy dealing with a major PR crisis. Drew Burney, NFL quarterback and star of one of Verhoeven's big advertising campaigns including TV, print and web, had been arrested Wednesday night for driving under the influence.

Needless to say, this was not great for a beer spokesperson.

Levi'd been busy too, with that looming deadline for

the Cerone campaign. He was going to take Friday night off, since it was his birthday, but he and Scott were going to be working this weekend.

Yesterday afternoon, the breakthrough he'd been waiting for happened. His mind had gone back to the first brainstorming session he and Scott had had, the things they'd talked about, and the idea that had been hovering at the edges of his mind suddenly materialized. Fuck! It was genius!

"Okay. Think *Amazing Race*," Levi said. "Our man travels around the world competing with other guys in all kinds of challenges—physical and daring challenges, but they have to find clues. Women are watching him and cheering him on and of course he's the winner at the end and celebrates with a beer. And a woman." He grinned.

"Around the world's not gonna fit in our budget," Scott said slowly. "Just saying."

"Right. Okay. But we could find places that make it look like he's traveling around the world, or just give us enough variety. Hawaii and Alaska could probably do it. Those aren't even out of the country."

Scott nodded, eyes alight with enthusiasm.

"Actually maybe it would be better if we kept it *in* the country," Levi said, suddenly hit with that thought. "Since it's an American beer. Add a little patriotism into the mix, along with the guy everyone wants to be. Good-looking, athletic, smart, competitive...a winner."

"Dude. That is freakin' awesome." Scott high-fived him.

They kept brainstorming, going online for some ideas, excitement building.

"We have to make this happen by next week," Levi said.

Scott looked a little ill at the thought.

"Come on, man, we can do it. We were going to work this weekend anyway. Now we have a focus."

"Yeah, yeah."

As usual pressure excited him, whereas it apparently made Scott want to puke.

They worked more on the idea all day Friday. By the end of the day he was feeling pretty good and looking forward to a fun night with his friends. And Sloane. It was cool that she was coming. She hadn't seen his friends since the wedding.

Since she was out at the Verhoeven head office, he texted her that he'd pick her up at her place in a cab at around seven thirty. They had a dinner reservation at the restaurant and then space booked in the dance club with bottle service. Jacob had told Levi everything was planned—which most likely meant Tara had everything planned.

Levi asked the cab driver to wait as he went to get Sloane. His jaw dropped when she answered the door. "Holy fuck."

She grinned. "I look okay?"

"Holy fuck." He swept his gaze down over her black lace dress, lined with black so you couldn't see through it, strapless, tight and short, down her killer legs to sky-high black stilettos, then back up, lingering on bare shoulders. "You look fucking amazing."

"Thanks."

He studied her face. She still wore signs of tension, a faint tightness at the corners of her eyes. But after the last two stressful days, that was probably understandable. She needed a night like tonight to chill.

She picked up a big scarf thing and a tiny purse, and then a square box wrapped in glossy red paper with a multicolored bow on top. It appeared heavy.

"What could this be?" he murmured, taking it from her.

"You just wait." She locked the door behind them as they left her condo.

In the back seat of the taxi, Levi continued to eye Sloane hungrily. "We could just skip dinner." He slid his hand up the inside of one bare leg.

She laughed. "You're the birthday boy. You have to show up at your own party."

"If I'm the birthday boy, I should get to do whatever I want. Or *who*ever I want." He nuzzled her ear. "Was that you who put the balloons on my chair today?"

"Maybe."

"Thank you. That was sweet." He breathed in her fantastic perfume, which created a spontaneous hard-on. "Let's make out."

She turned her face to his and they kissed until he was dizzy. And then they were there.

They entered V Bistro, with low lighting, lots of dark wood and brown leather banquettes. Sloane was hurriedly applying lip gloss since he'd pretty much destroyed what she'd had on.

The hostess showed them to the big table where Jacob and Tara sat, along with Tucker and Tara's best friend Brynn, who'd been maid of honor at their wedding. Despite Brynn passing out in Tuck's hotel room the night of the wedding, he'd asked her out and they'd apparently been out a few times. Luke and Cam weren't there yet.

"Happy Birthday, Levi!" Tara jumped up to hug him. Then she turned to Sloane with a big smile. "Hi again! Finally we get to spend some time with you."

Sloane returned the smile and they all slid into the booth. Levi again set his hand on Sloane's bare thigh as they ordered drinks and talked. Cam and Luke arrived soon after.

They all brought him stupid gifts, some golf balls that said *New balls for an old body* on the package, a beer mug that lit up and a gift box of all different kinds of gourmet bacon. He saved Sloane's present for last. He removed the thick paper, opened the box and found a set of four mugs, striped in bright colors.

He stared at them. "I don't fucking believe this."

He looked at Sloane, who was biting her lip.

Everyone else exchanged glances.

"Where did you get these?"

A smile trembled on her lips. "You know what they are?"

"Of course I know what they are! They're Charlie Harper's coffee mugs!" He lifted one out of the box and held it up reverently.

"Yeah."

"How'd you find them?" he asked again.

"On the Internet." She bit her lip once more.

"I can't believe you did that. I can't believe you even knew...wow." He slid a hand around the back of her neck and pulled her in for a kiss. "Damn, I love..." *you* "...them."

Whoa. What had that been that nearly slipped out? Eh, he was just happy about the present. And the pleased look on her face was as good as the present itself. Fuck. Fuck, he was crazy about her.

He gave his head a shake and got his shit together.

Dinner was fantastic, good food, lots of jokes, a few drinks. When they were done they moved to the dance club. It was relatively early, so not that crowded, but their VIP table was waiting for them. The DJ was spinning great mixes; they drank tequila and danced. Levi was the first to admit he was a little hammered, but he was having so much fun. Sloane surprised him by getting down and dirty on the dance floor, grinding against him.

"Who knew our star account director was such a bad girl?" he murmured into her ear, her body moving against his and making him hard again. "Wearing a sexy dress like that. Dancing dirty."

She smiled and lifted her arms, moving to the beat. His dick throbbed.

"Can't wait to get you home and peel you out of that hot little dress," he growled. "You're making me hard in public. You know what that means."

She pushed her ass into his groin. "Am I going to get spanked?" She cast him a sultry glance.

"Oh yeah."

The music shifted to a slower beat and he turned her to face him, hands going around her waist. She draped her arms over his shoulders and their eyes met as they danced. "I can't wait either."

They spent the night at her place. For some reason they always seemed to end up at his place. Probably because of Chuck. He'd had to make sure Colin would take him out in the morning so he could stay over at Sloane's place. He liked her place. He liked being surrounded by her things, the objects she chose to decorate her condo—the big black and white picture propped against the wall on the fireplace mantel, the scented candles and carved wooden bowls on the coffee table, the pottery painted with sunflowers in her kitchen, and all the girly things in her bathroom.

Since both of them were a little wasted, the sex was sloppy and uninhibited. They laughed and groped each other. He didn't actually spank her because she crawled between his legs and offered him a birthday blow job. How could he turn that down?

Her mouth on his dick was hot and luscious. He held her hair back from her face so he could get the visual too. Pleasure so blindingly intense swelled inside him, electricity racing through him, up his spine. So close... He held her head and stopped her.

"Stop," he panted. "Wanna come inside you. Wanna fuck you, beautiful girl."

"Yes, please."

He knifed up to sit. He lifted her onto his lap. It took a bit of inebriated fumbling but finally they together managed to fit their parts together and he was inside her, fuck yeah. Hot. Wet. And bare.

"Shit," he groaned. "Need a condom."

"Do we?" She met his eyes, her fingers threading through his hair.

"Oh baby." He gritted his teeth at the exquisite sensations rocketing through his body. His balls squeezed. "Are you on birth control?"

"Yes. And I'm clean."

"Christ, me too." He made sure of that, often, despite religiously using condoms.

"Happy bareback birthday." She kissed his mouth and he groaned again as he lowered her to her back without disconnecting their bodies, then fucked her hard. She slid a hand to her clit.

"Wanna fuck you all night. Christ, Sloane." His blood felt like liquid fire in his veins, his body burning up. Exquisite pleasure raced through him. She cried out her now-familiar orgasm sounds as her body contracted around him, so fucking perfect and beautiful it made him come too. His brain sizzled into blackness as he came hard inside her.

He wasn't sure how much time passed before he roused. He suspected they both might have passed out. "Baby," he murmured. "I kinda wish I'd been sober for that."

She giggled and kissed his shoulder. "We can do it again. I mean, when you're sober."

"Fucking right we will."

⊙⟋⟍⟋⟍⊙

It had been a late night. They'd left the club shortly after two, screwed around until nearly three thirty, then passed out. They were sound asleep when Sloane's doorbell rang.

It took a while for the noise to penetrate his slumber. Rousing himself, he nudged Sloane. "Sloane, baby, someone's at your door."

"Whuh?" She blinked her beautiful, bleary eyes at him. "The door. Want me to get it?"

"I..." She mumbled something incoherent. He took that as a yes and threw back the covers. He grabbed his boxer shorts and stumbled out to her front door. Bright sunshine stabbed his eyes and tiny hammers pounded against his skull. He yanked open the door, ready to give whoever was there a piece of what little was left of his mind for disturbing them so early on a Saturday morning.

A woman stood there. Her eyes went big as plates. Levi blinked. Long blonde hair, pretty blue eyes... Jesus, she looked like Sloane. Oh Christ.

"Uh, hi," she said. "Is Sloane here?"

"Yeah. You are...?"

"Her sister. Becca. And you?" One eyebrow lifted, just fucking exactly like Sloane's did.

"I'm Levi." She'd told her sister about him. Hadn't she? Apparently not.

"Levi Wolcott. Sloane's, uh, boyfriend."

"Whoa. I didn't know she had a boyfriend."

Fuck. He swallowed, still squinting at the bright light. "Ah, come in."

"Thanks." She stepped inside, pulling a small carry-on sized suitcase.

He reached for it and lifted it over the threshold then set it on the floor in the hall. "Sloane's still asleep. We had a late night."

"I see." Her gaze tracked over him and he remembered that he was pretty much naked. "I gather Sloane didn't tell you I was coming."

"Nope."

"I'm earlier than she expected." She paused. "I'm confused. Did she tell you that my brother's coming too? And we're all driving up to our dad's place this afternoon?"

"Nope." Uneasiness brewed in his gut. Or maybe that was last night's tequila.

"Did she tell you about our mom?"

The roiling in his belly intensified. "About your mom disappearing when she was fourteen?"

"I mean…" She hesitated. "I mean about them *finding* our mom. The other day."

Apparently there were a lot of things Sloane hadn't told him.

22

"Becca!"

Becca's gaze went past Levi and he turned to watch Sloane and her sister rush at each other and hug. He closed the door, as quietly as he could since his head was pounding.

He watched them hug each other tightly, taking in their obvious love for each other. He enjoyed seeing Sloane like that, kind of like she was with Chuck—soft and open. Except this was with a person. Duh.

"You're early!" Sloane said. "Why?"

"There was an earlier flight, and I managed to get a seat on it. I just took the train here from the airport."

"You should have called! I would have picked you up."

"Eh, I didn't want to bother you."

Levi crossed his arms and leaned against the wall in her foyer.

"Oh, Levi." Sloane looked at him. "I guess you two met."

"Yeah. We did."

A feeling of hot pressure built inside him. "What the fuck is going on?" he growled.

Sloane blinked at him.

He pushed away from the wall and advanced on her.

240

"Why didn't you tell me someone found your mom?"

"Uh...why would I?"

He frowned. "What?"

"It's not like you can doing anything about it," she said.

He picked up the way her body had tensed and her fingers twisted together. "When did this transpire?" he demanded. He looked from Sloane to Becca.

"Tuesday," Becca answered, since Sloane didn't.

"That's why you went to see your parents that night."

"Yes."

"That's why you looked like you'd been crying all night on Wednesday morning."

Sloane just shook her head, her face expressionless.

"Why didn't you tell me?" he asked again. Fuck, was he nothing to her?

A knife stabbed into his heart and twisted.

She hadn't even bothered to tell him something that happened in her life that was so significant. Something that had shaped her whole life. "Never mind."

He shook his head and strode past her down the short hall to the bedroom. He grabbed the black pants he'd worn last night and yanked them on.

"Levi."

She'd followed him into the bedroom. She closed the door.

He picked up his wrinkled shirt from the floor and thrust his arms into the sleeves without looking at her.

"What are you so mad about?" she asked.

He turned and stared at her, fingers going still on the buttons of the shirt. "Seriously? You're asking me that?"

She blinked.

Shirt half-buttoned, he sat on the side of the bed to pull on socks. "Fuck," he muttered. He stood and looked for his shoes. When he'd found them and laced them, he walked over to where she stood at the door. "Yeah, I'm mad," he said, the words clipped. "I...I care about you. I thought you cared about me too. I want to be there for you, no matter what. I want to look after you."

"I don't need looking after."

"I know you don't. And I admire that about you. But that doesn't change how I feel. I want to comfort you when you're hurting. You didn't even give me that chance. You didn't even *tell* me. Fuck, Sloane." He shook his head. "I knew something was going on. Christ."

He should have pushed harder, but dammit, he'd barely seen her the last few days. Although she'd come to his place Wednesday night and still hadn't said a goddamn word. That hot knife twisted in his chest.

She stared back at him, sucking on her bottom lip, her eyebrows sloped down over her eyes.

He sucked in air. "I thought we cared about each other. Was I wrong?"

Her eyes went wide. "I...I..."

"Obviously, I was," he said bitterly. "Otherwise you would have told me something that important. I could've...I don't know. You could have talked to me about it. I could've helped you deal with it."

"I'm dealing with it fine."

He stared at her. Was she seriously in that much denial about her own feelings?

He nodded. "Sure," he said. "Good. Great. You deal with it. You don't need me. I'm done."

He nudged her away from the door, grabbed the knob and yanked it open. He walked straight to the front door. Becca was in Sloane's kitchen apparently making coffee.

"Nice to meet you," he snapped before he slammed out the front door.

He started walking toward Lake Shore. Maybe he'd find a cab. Or maybe he'd just keep walking. Adrenaline burned through his veins, hastening his pace. He didn't even see what was around him, just kept walking past an ice cream shop and a CVS and a Starbucks. His face felt tight and his head still pounded.

Great. A great day to be not only hungover but heartbroken.

❀

"What just happened?"

Sloane looked at Becca. "I'm not sure." She rubbed the back of her neck. Tightness crawled up her scalp and made her head throb. "I think we just broke up."

"I didn't even know you were seeing anyone. Why didn't you tell me?"

"It…it wasn't that serious."

"No?" Becca gaped at her. "That dude looked pretty serious to me."

Sloane swallowed. "I need some Tylenol." She moved to the cupboard where she kept it.

"Are you okay?"

"Yeah, yeah. It was Levi's birthday yesterday… Oh no." She whipped around and saw the box with his Charlie Harper mugs sitting on the counter where he'd set them last night when they'd stumbled in laughing and horny. She closed her eyes. "Oh damn." Pain burst in her chest.

I'm done.

She covered her mouth, then drew in a long breath and let it out. She found the Tylenol and shook out a couple of pills then filled a glass with water and swallowed them.

"We were out celebrating with his friends," she said. "I might have a tiny hangover today."

Becca blinked. "Wow. Good for you."

Sloane frowned. "What does that mean?"

"It means your whole social life consists of business dinners. Good for you to go out and let loose and get a

243

little drunk. With your boyfriend who I didn't even know about."

Sloane picked up on the hurt tone in her voice. What was with everyone? Why did they expect her to tell them every freakin' private detail of her life? "Is that coffee ready?"

"Yeah."

Sloane poured herself a cup. She'd been sure Levi would be gone by the time Becca arrived, which wasn't supposed to be for four more hours. This should not have happened. Not that she'd anticipated Levi would be so angry.

"Call Eric and see when he's picking us up," she said. "I'm going to shower and get dressed."

The day was cool and cloudy so she dressed in jeans and a T-shirt. She scrunched her wet hair up into a messy knot and didn't bother with contact lenses. After she threw a few things into an overnight bag, she returned to the kitchen.

"Eric's on his way," Becca said, sitting at the kitchen table flipping through a magazine.

"Great."

"Why didn't you tell me you were seeing someone?"

Sloane slumped on a chair at the table and gazed unseeingly at her coffee mug. "I don't know." She sighed then sipped her coffee. "At first it was just…sex. I wasn't about to message you on Facebook and tell you I just had hot sex with the new guy at work. Especially since that first time I was convinced it was a huge mistake and was never going to happen again."

Becca made a face. "Okay, I get that. But obviously it turned into more than one time."

"Yeah. Somehow we're…dating. Or something." She pushed her glasses up on her nose.

"You seem upset. Did you two just have a fight?"

Sloane swallowed. "There wasn't much fighting. He said he's done, and walked out."

"Oh no." Becca's eyes scrunched up at the corners. "What was he so mad about?"

"Apparently he's upset because I didn't tell him about Mom being found."

"I don't get it, Sloane. You told him about Mom disappearing, which you hardly ever do, with anyone, and yet you didn't tell him that she'd been found? Or that you were going home to Oakville this weekend?"

"I didn't think it was something he needed to know."

"Seriously?"

"I don't want to talk about this."

"No. You don't get to do that. You always do that."

Sloane felt a defensive burn inside her. "I always do what?"

"You don't talk about your feelings."

"My feelings are my own business."

"I know, but I'm your sister. You can tell me how you're feeling."

Sloane gave Becca a sad smile. "I've always tried to protect you from that."

Becca's eyes widened. "Oh my God. Really?" She set her hand on her chest. "You always seemed so strong. No matter what happened, you were there for us. But inside you were hurting. Weren't you?"

Sloane grimaced. "Sure. We all were."

"Christ, Sloane! I love you. But you don't have to protect me anymore. I want to know what's going on with you. For real. This whole thing with Mom...how you're feeling about it. We need to talk about it, or we're never going to get past it."

Sloane nodded. "You're probably right."

"And Levi. You need to talk to him. I think you hurt him by not telling him what was going on."

Sloane blinked at Becca with a sinking feeling that she was right. "It's not like that between us. We're just...you know. I didn't mean to hurt him."

"I'm sure you didn't." Becca carried the coffeepot over and refilled both their mugs. "But he's probably not thinking that right now."

"I know." Sloane rested her head on a hand. "But it's too late to talk to him."

"It's never too late. You obviously care about him."

I thought we cared about each other.

"I do," she admitted. Why could she admit this to her sister and not to him?

"When you care about people, you share yourself with them," Becca said softly. "All of you, including your feelings, even if they're bad feelings." She paused. "Were you upset about Mom?"

Sloane remembered coming home that night she'd found out, remembered the bitter rage that had filled her. She was a little ashamed of how violently she'd reacted. That wasn't her. She was in control and collected. Always.

Well, not always. Levi liked to take control away from her and...ruffle her. Make her let go and come apart. And she loved it.

"Yeah, I was upset." Her stomach pitched and her head still hurt despite the painkillers. "I think I might be coming down with something. Maybe I shouldn't go see Dad and Viv with you."

Becca narrowed her eyes. "You're hungover. We're not going to catch a hangover from you."

It felt way worse than a hangover. More like the flu, with full body aches. Even her skin hurt. "Fine," she said wearily. "I'll come."

When Eric arrived, she climbed into the back seat of his car and let Becca sit up front. Once they were driving, Eric said, "So do we know for sure it's Mom?"

"The police had a picture." Sloane rested her head against the side of the car. "It's her. She looks terrible, though. Although it was a mug shot. Christ on a crutch."

"I can't believe this," Becca said. "I hardly even remember her." Her voice went sad.

Becca and Eric talked for a while and Sloane closed her eyes and tried not to see Levi's face as he'd stared at her. Eventually she fell asleep.

She woke up when they arrived at Dad and Viv's place and stretched her aching body. She felt disoriented and confused. She'd been dreaming about Levi, dreaming that she was chasing him and couldn't catch him. Her limbs felt heavy and stiff as she walked into the house.

She watched Eric and Becca exchange slightly awkward hugs with Dad and Viv. Then she hugged them, and this time it felt more comfortable.

"Are you okay, cookie?" Dad looked down at her with a notch between his eyebrows.

"She's hungover," Becca stated.

Sloane shot her sister a look.

"Also her boyfriend just dumped her."

"Becca!"

"Boyfriend?" Dad frowned.

"You didn't tell them either?"

Sloane sighed. If she was going to tell anyone anything, it would be Becca long before it would be Dad and Viv.

"We've only been seeing each other a few weeks," she said. "It was no big deal."

Becca coughed around the word "bullshit".

"He broke up with you?" Viv asked, concern creasing her forehead. "Are you okay, Sloane honey?"

The motherly tone and the endearment had Sloane's eyes stinging. She opened her mouth to say she was fine, but no words could get through her clogged throat. She blinked and swallowed.

"You're not okay." Viv moved toward her and wrapped her arms around her. "What happened? Come sit down."

The hug and the concern only churned up Sloane's

emotions even more. Tears slid down her cheeks as Viv led her to the couch in the living room. She sat and looked up to see her dad and siblings watching her with shocked confusion. Again, she started to tell them she was okay, but couldn't do it.

She wasn't okay. She was a mess. A melting-down, tear-stained mess. An embarrassing sobby noise escaped her throat.

Viv hugged her again, rocking her gently, and she let her head rest on Viv's shoulder as the tears flowed. Finally she sucked in a long shaky breath and lifted her head. She wiped her cheeks with her palms, glad she hadn't bothered with mascara. "I'm sorry," she said thickly. "This isn't what we came here for."

"No," Viv said softly. "I think this is exactly what you came here for. To be with people who love you when you're hurting. That's why we're all here."

Sloane looked at Viv. She didn't deserve such kindness from Viv, who she'd been at best guardedly friendly to all these years. Viv's warmth and generosity made her feel even more regret.

"Do you want to talk about this man?" Viv asked, her eyes soft.

"I don't think I can," Sloane choked out. "Right now."

"That's okay." Viv rubbed her back. "I understand. Art, why don't you tell them what you've learned from the police over the last few days."

"Uh. Sure."

Now Dad, Becca and Eric all took seats, and Dad filled them in on the information Mom had revealed to the police in California, more details about her life and the lies she'd been living. They were having a psychiatric evaluation done. She had a court-appointed attorney but was likely facing some kind of prison sentence for trafficking.

"Sometimes it feels like we're talking about someone

else's life," Dad said a while later. "This can't be our life. That can't be your mother."

"I know, right?" Becca nodded. "Maybe I'm weird, but I almost don't feel anything."

Eric shrugged. "I gave up on her a long time ago."

Sloane mostly listened. It was hard to sort out all her tangled emotions. But finally she confessed, "I always hoped she'd come back."

She started talking, about how hard it had been, how much she'd missed her mother, how painful it had been when she'd been declared dead. How angry she was. How much it hurt that her mother had walked out and never come back, knowing she left three children behind, abandoning them. She talked about how she understood with her head about mental illness but her heart still hurt.

Dad talked too. He told them more about how angry and scared he'd been when he'd been a person of interest. Everyone knew that the husband was going to be the first suspect in a case when a wife went missing. Especially when she'd disappeared for no apparent reason. He'd known he hadn't done anything, but even so, it had been a nightmare.

"I know I wasn't much of a dad after that," he admitted, his voice low. "I checked out of almost everything. I was lucky I didn't lose my job. I felt guilty about how much we'd lost and I couldn't face that either. I wondered if it was my fault that Cyn left. I was letting everyone down and I just wanted to hide."

Sloane nodded, her face hurting, her heart aching.

"Sloane," he said. "You were so strong. You were so brave and strong. I was scared for you, because I knew you had to be hurting so much. I let you take on way too much of the burden. I'm sorry."

She stared at her father. "Oh, Dad." Her throat thickened again. "We did what we had to do."

"I feel like you checked out too." His tone roughened.

"But please, cookie...don't live your whole life like that. If I didn't have Viv..." He cleared his throat. "Don't let it keep you from caring about people. You don't want to be alone for the rest of your life because you're afraid of getting hurt."

Her face flamed. This was so personal and she felt so vulnerable, talking about this in front of her whole family. She wanted to deny what he said. But she couldn't.

"That's what I was trying to say earlier," Becca added softly. "When we were talking about Levi."

"Levi," Viv murmured. She squeezed Sloane's hand. But she seemed to know that Sloane was on overload at that point. "I'm going to start dinner. Who wants to help?"

"I'll help." Sloane rose too and followed Viv to the kitchen, leaving Dad and Becca and Eric to talk.

The food preparation gave them a different focus, took some pressure off Sloane, who wasn't sure she wanted to think about the painful advice Dad had just given her.

"I was happy when you and Dad got together," she said to Viv as she snapped asparagus spears. "I really was."

"I know." Viv sliced beef into thin strips.

They both focused on their tasks and somehow that made it easier.

"And I didn't blame you for Dad having to declare Mom dead."

"I'm glad to hear that," Viv murmured. "I told him he didn't have to do that. I wanted to marry him, but I would have been just as happy if we lived together without being legally married. I just...loved him and wanted to be with him."

"Really?" Sloane looked up. "You told him that?"

"Yes. I know he agonized over it. But she'd been gone so long, and most people thought she couldn't be alive."

"I know." Sloane bent her head again. "Even though I hoped, I really thought she was dead too. Because otherwise, why wouldn't she come back?" Hurt burned through her once more.

"I kind of hate her for what she did to you."

Again Sloane's head snapped up.

"But I'm trying to be forgiving and understanding," Viv continued. "I'm sure she's not well. No woman in her right mind would leave three beautiful children like you. She couldn't help herself."

"That's what I'm trying to tell myself too."

"You can put the asparagus in that bowl and drizzle a little olive oil over it."

Sloane scooped up the asparagus.

"I'm also a little angry at this Levi guy," Viv added. "For breaking up with you."

Sloane sighed. "It was my fault. I screwed up. I'm no good at relationships."

"I don't think you've ever given yourself a chance to try."

Sloane nodded. She unscrewed the lid of the bottle of olive oil. "Even with you. I'm sorry, Viv."

"Don't be sorry. You can't make yourself feel things. Your feelings are what they are. Sometimes it just takes time to sort through them and figure things out and let your head and your heart come together."

"You're so nice," Sloane choked out. "And smart."

Viv laughed. "Eh, I don't know. I wasn't so nice the other day when Hazel Green asked if I'd put on weight."

23

Levi had holed up in his condo the rest of Saturday, lying on his couch watching TV, going from *E! True Hollywood Story* to *Ice Road Truckers* to *Mythbusters*. He didn't really care what he watched as long it stopped him from thinking about Sloane.

As if that was even possible.

What the fuck was the deal with her mother? A gazillion questions scrambled his brain. It had sounded like she was alive. Who found her? Where was she? Why had she never come back? Dammit. Were they going to see her together? Was that why Becca and Eric were coming?

Time for beer. So what if it was only two in the afternoon. Maybe that would help. An hour later he ripped open a huge bag of potato chips. By six o'clock he was toasted.

Then he recalled the work he needed to get done by Monday. He and Scott were supposed to work this weekend. Shit.

His career had always been the most important thing to him. Now…it felt like Sloane was more important than his career. But that was apparently stupid because clearly *he* wasn't important to *her*. And she was no longer in his life, which meant once again his career was his number one priority. He had to get his shit together and be ready for that presentation.

Sloane was going to be there. This was when he wanted to blow her stockings off—not that he'd ever seen her wear stockings. Imagining her in a black garter belt and stockings... *Fuuuuuuck. Stop already!*

He wanted to wow her with the ideas he and Scott had come up with for the various lines. This was the last step on the approval ladder. He was proud of what he'd come up with and he'd been looking forward to showing off for her.

But they had to *finish* the goddamn presentation. Instead he was going to be all bloated and hungover from too many salty snacks and beers.

He forced himself up off the couch, gathering up all the empties and carrying them to his kitchen. He found his phone and stared in dismay at the text messages and missed call from Scott. Shit.

He texted him back right away apologizing. *I'm really sick today, sorry. Feel like shit. Tomorrow? What time?*

They arranged to meet at the office at nine in the morning. Christ, on a Sunday, but oh well.

He'd better stop drinking. He looked around his kitchen. Did he even have anything healthy to eat? He surveyed his refrigerator. Nope. Nada. He moved on to the cabinets. Okay, there...a box of pasta and a jar of tomato sauce. That was healthy. He wasn't really hungry but he'd feel better if he put something wholesome into his stomach.

He chugged a big glass of milk while the water boiled. He went into his office and started his laptop so he could review things.

⌘

"Were you that hungover yesterday?" Scott asked as they arrived at the office the next morning.

253

"Uh. Yeah. Hungover." It wasn't a lie. "Sorry."

Isaiah and Hunter showed up around eleven to work on something. Otherwise the office was empty. Levi and Scott spent the whole fucking day working. But they did it. They goddamn well did it. They both slouched in their chairs at seven o'clock Sunday evening, empty water bottles and Subway sandwich wrappers littering their desks.

"Dude," Scott said. "I don't know how you pulled that out of your ass. I am seriously in awe."

Levi grinned. "Thanks, man."

The next morning his gut was like a rock as he walked into the office. But he looked good. He'd made sure of that. He had his pride. He was not walking into that meeting looking like something Chuck had barfed up.

"Morning, Levi!" Carly chirped at him.

"Morning, doll." He beamed a high-wattage smile at her and she winked at him.

Scott was already there, shooting a mini basketball into a small hoop mounted on the wall.

"Hey," Levi greeted him. "All set for our presentation this morning?"

"I'll be ready as soon as the Xanax kicks in."

Levi grinned as he threw himself down into his chair. "Little nervous?"

"You'd think I'd be used to this by now. The fear of rejection is making my bowels quake."

"Jesus Christ. I don't want to hear about your bowels."

"Fine. I'll be in the john. Last stall. Come get me when it's time."

Levi shook his head as Scott stalked away.

Yeah, he should be used to it. Every creative team faced rejection, rewriting and revising. It was part of the deal. Nobody liked it, but you had to accept it. That wasn't going to happen today, though.

At nine o'clock they gathered in the meeting room — Mason, Noah, Scott, Alia…and Sloane.

He was afraid to look at her.

This was probably why getting involved with someone at work was a bad idea. Hell, he'd never make that mistake again. For that matter he'd never make the mistake of getting involved with *anyone* again.

He picked the moment to sneak a peek at her exactly when she looked at him. Their eyes met and it was like a physical jolt of electricity to his body. He kept his face expressionless and looked away.

She was so damn gorgeous.

His heart contracted and his gut torqued with tension.

Her smooth blonde hair curved perfectly around her face. She wore the black and ivory dress that hugged her curves. Her lips were shiny with rose-colored gloss and her eyes... Even in that brief glance, he'd seen the shadows there.

He fucking hated that she was sad. He wanted to slam a fist on the table. He hated that she was sad and even more he hated that she didn't want him to be part of that. He'd take all her sadness if he could, if it would make her feel better. That sour ache in his gut started up again.

He and Scott went through their presentation.

The print ads were a success. Even Sloane smiled at the Natural Belgian Blonde ad. He'd hoped for a little more reaction, but if approval was all he got, fine, he'd take it.

Then they went through the television commercials for Cerone.

Sloane looked at Mason, then Noah. She shook her head. "I can't take that to the client."

Levi turned his head and gave her side eye. He hadn't heard that right. Had he?

Scott pressed a hand to his abdomen.

"What the fuck?" The words burst out of Levi, completely unprofessional. He sat bolt upright in his chair. "Why not?"

She met his eyes with cool assuredness.

"The concept itself is brilliant," she said. "It's big and bold. I love it all the way to the end. But at the end…those women…" She shook her head. "I know sex sells, but we have to stop the objectification of women."

His eyes bugged out. "Objectification? Are you fucking kidding me?"

"Calm down, Levi." Mason gave him a sharp warning look. "Listen to the feedback."

This wasn't feedback. This was an attack. This was personal. She was looking for any reason to torpedo his ideas because of what had happened. He fumed, pressure building in his skull, but he kept his mouth shut.

He looked at Mason. "You agree with that?" Surely to fuck Mason was going to have their backs. He'd already seen the storyboards and loved them.

"She has a valid point," Mason said slowly. "I think we do need to take the female perspective into consideration. And we need to be responsible advertisers."

Sloane threw up her hands. "Truth hurts."

Levi gave her a narrow eyed look. *Truth hurts?* What bullshit was that? She wanted to hear some truths that hurt? He could… He shook his head, lips clamped firmly together. "Fine. We'll redo them."

He and Scott exchanged glances. For some reason, Scott seemed less fazed by this than he did, and Scott was the one who'd spent the last hour in the bathroom. They gathered up their materials. Sloane had already left.

"Well," Scott said in Levi's office. "Back to the fucking drawing board."

"Fuck that."

"Yeah. Christ." Scott rubbed his face. "I knew she could be a bitch, but I didn't expect that kind of feminazi crap from her."

Levi blinked. A red filter appeared before his eyes as Scott's words sunk in. "What did you just call her?"

Scott opened his mouth, then looked at Levi and snapped it closed.

Too late. Levi was reacting, adrenaline, anger and aggression kicking into high gear. He lunged at Scott and took a swing.

"Hey!" Scott yelled, trying to defend himself from Levi's fist. They scuffled, both throwing punches, grabbing onto shirts and shoving each other around.

"Gentlemen!"

The booming voice stopped both of them. Levi's chest heaved as he turned to look at Joseph Huxworth standing in the corridor watching them. Mason stood right behind him. Levi's gut swooped and his blood turned to ice.

"What the hell are you two doing?" The Hux demanded. His face went ruddy. "This is a place of business, not a boxing ring."

Levi released Scott and stepped back, straightening his shirt. Fuck, fuck, fuck. "I'm sorry, Mr. Huxworth," he said quietly. "I overreacted to something."

Then of course Sloane had to appear. "What's going on?"

"These two idiots were trying to beat the crap out of each other," The Hux said. "Thank Christ we didn't have any clients here."

Shame slithered down Levi's spine. What the fuck had he done? He was such an idiot. He just felt so...raw. Strung tight. He'd overreacted in the presentation, and he'd overreacted to what Scott had said. Except the asshole had insulted Sloane, and that was *not* something he could stand for. Once again, he pressed his lips together.

"I'm on my way to a meeting," The Hux said to Sloane. "When I'm back, I want to see you in my office."

"Of course," she murmured.

Levi's face burned. Goddammit. He'd gotten her in trouble again.

"You two good now?" Mason asked in a low voice, looking back and forth between them.

Levi glared at Scott. "Sure."

"I don't even know what I did," Scott muttered.

"Perhaps you could discuss it like adults," Sloane said. She turned on a stiletto heel to walk back to her office. Mason followed her.

Levi faced Scott. "Apologize for what you called her."

"What? Why?"

"Because you insulted her and she doesn't deserve that. She is not a bitch and definitely not a feminazi, for Chrissakes."

"She just trashed our idea!"

Levi sank into his chair and rubbed the heels of his hands over his eyes. "She was right."

24

Mason followed Sloane into her office. She dropped wearily into her chair and blew out a breath. Sweet loving Lord. What a mistake it had been to get involved with Levi. Now she was making a legitimate business call and he was taking it personally because of what had happened between them.

She hated the way he'd looked at her before the meeting started. The tightness of his mouth, the set of his jaw, the anger still in his eyes. It made her want to throw up. She'd felt like that pretty much all weekend, and it wasn't the liquor she'd drunk Friday night.

"Why the hell were they fighting?" she asked Mason, leaning her head back.

Mason didn't answer right away and she lifted her head to look at him. A smile played on his mouth as he took a seat.

"What?"

"Levi was defending your honor."

She squinted at him. "What?"

"Scott insulted you. I won't repeat what he said. I'm sure it was said out of frustration. I happened to be just outside the office and heard it. I didn't expect Levi to physically attack him for it, but hey...I have to admire how he came to your defense."

Her body went rigid and her lungs seized up. She stared at Mason. She didn't know what to say.

"I sensed some tension between you and Levi this morning." Mason rested his elbows on the armrests of the chair and linked his fingers together. "Actually, I've sensed some tension between you two for a while. Only usually it's more...sexual tension. This morning it felt like angry tension."

She swallowed. Her throat stung. "Oh, Mason," she whispered. "Have other people noticed?"

He shook his head. "I just pick up on stuff like that."

"I know you do." She tucked her hair behind one ear. "We've been seeing each other. But we had a big argument on the weekend, and he...ended things."

"I'm sorry. Are you okay?"

She blinked, her vision having blurred. As usual her first instinct was to tell him she was fine. But the world hadn't ended when she'd told her family how she felt. On the other hand, the office wasn't the place to spill your guts...but Mason was a friend. "I'm really not. I'm a mess."

"Want to tell me about it?"

She drew in a shaky breath. "I think I may have hurt him."

"We all make mistakes. We hurt people we care about without meaning to. Then you say you're sorry and ask for forgiveness and move on."

She stared at him. "It's not that easy."

One corner of his mouth kicked up. "Why not? You're not sorry?"

"No! I mean, I am. I didn't mean to hurt him. I was...geezus." She bent her head. "I was just trying to protect myself. I'm not good at relationships. I don't know why I thought I could do it with Levi. But I..." Her heart rose into her throat and lodged there. She swallowed again. "I think I might be in love with him."

"Oh." He paused. "Doesn't that make it worth saying you're sorry?"

She lifted her gaze again. "Do you really think that's all it would take? That he'd forgive me?"

"I don't know. I don't know how he feels about you. Oh wait. He just punched a guy who insulted you."

A smile tugged at her lips.

"What happened with other guys you've dated?" he asked. "I know you always say you're no good at it. Why is that?"

She lifted a shoulder. "They just always lost interest after a few dates."

"See, I find that odd. Because you're a smart and beautiful and interesting woman."

"Uh...thank you."

"My suspicion is you never let people close enough to you to find out how smart and interesting you are."

"Ah..."

"I could be wrong. Something to think about."

He rose with a half smile and left her office.

She took a few deep breaths. Okay. She could think about that. But it would have to be later, because she had work to do.

She headed to Bailey's cubicle. "Hey," she said. "What happened with the billboard for Steel? Did Isaiah come through?"

Bailey smiled. "He sure did. It was on my desk when I got here this morning. I don't know when they finished it, but I know he and Hunter were here on the weekend."

Sloane smiled too. "Awesome. I knew they'd get it done."

Next she found Isaiah and Hunter. "Good work, guys. I just talked to Bailey. Thanks for the extra effort."

They nodded.

"Mason and I are taking you for lunch to show our appreciation," she said. "Does that work for you today?"

Their eyes widened. "Yeah. Sure. Thanks."

She started back to her office, then changed directions and returned to Bailey's desk. "Mason and I are taking Isaiah and Hunter for lunch," she said. "To thank them. Want to join us?"

Bailey tipped her head. "Well, sure. That's so nice of you."

"I don't like to see hard work go unrewarded."

Sloane wasn't exactly in a cheerful, socializing mood, but she was a professional. She could get through this day.

Because she still had that meeting with Joe.

He came to her office when he was back, walking in and closing the door. "Might as well talk here," he said.

She lifted her hands from her computer keyboard. "Of course."

He sat. He sighed. He looked at her with a piercing stare. "Did we make a mistake hiring Levi Wolcott away from AdMix?"

She snapped her mouth shut and blinked. There was only one answer to that question. She didn't even have to think about it. "No," she said firmly. "Absolutely not."

"You're sure?"

"I saw some of his work this morning. He's brilliant. He has that same sense that Mason has. He knows how to read people. He knows what they want and he knows how to reflect what people want back at them."

"Comparing him to Mason is saying a lot."

"I know." She held his gaze.

"What was with the fighting?"

She sucked her bottom lip briefly. This might not be the time to tell him she and Levi had just finished a brief affair. Honesty? Partial honesty? A lie?

She sighed. She was a good businesswoman and she could dissemble with the best of them when it was required. But she couldn't lie to Joe. "Apparently Scott insulted me. I sent them back to tweak their TV commercial idea for Cerone. He was frustrated. Levi took offense on my behalf."

Joe frowned. "Chivalry? He was fighting out of chivalry? Seriously?"

"That's what Mason said."

"Jesus Christ. He *is* like Mason."

Her eyebrows rose.

"Mason once gave an AD hell because he'd called a female copywriter a dyke." He grinned. "I thought they were going to come to blows."

Sloane smiled. "Really? Wow."

"Yep. However, that kind of behavior is still a problem. You're supposed to be keeping those guys under control."

Sloane looked past Joe at the framed poster on her wall, a quote from Albert Einstein.

She might be fucking up her career, but she had to take a stand. She had to tell Joe how she really felt. Coming down on those guys the last few weeks hadn't felt good. Hadn't felt right. It went against things she'd learned in the business, things she'd believed in. Nothing they'd done had caused any harm. And they'd produced a hell of a lot of good.

She read the quote on the poster aloud. "Creativity is intelligence having fun."

Joe frowned. "What?"

She focused on him again and sucked in a big breath, stiffening her spine. "Creativity is intelligence having fun. Joe. I get where this new concern about optics is coming from. I understand things have been tighter the last few years. Some of our biggest clients have cut the amount of advertising they were doing. Some of them have had financial struggles through the economic downturn."

"Yes, yes. That's it."

"But these guys who work for us are some of the best in the business. Including Levi. They work hard. They come through. I don't want to trample their creativity. Their spirit. Their fun. I want them to *want* to come to work every day, eager to do their best. It *should* be fun."

She watched his face as he frowned, considering her words. He pursed his lips. Shook his head.

She prepared to be fired for speaking her mind so bluntly. Or maybe offer her resignation. Her stomach tightened and her shoulders tensed.

"I'd argue with you," he said slowly. "If you weren't the best account person I've ever worked with."

Her eyes popped open wide. Did he really just say that? Her heart thudded into a rapid beat.

"I know you understand our clients," he continued. "And our staff. You have the right balance." He pursed his lips. "I trust you to do the right thing. Keep them out of trouble. But let them have some fun. Maybe just try to keep it...discreet. We have a staff lounge. They can let loose in there. But nowhere else."

She smiled, her heart now expanding. "Thank you. It means a lot to hear that from you."

Joe left her office.

Wow. Just...holy shit. A bright spot in her currently black and dismal life. Relief made her muscles lax and she slumped in her chair for a few moments.

Lunch turned out okay. Isaiah and Hunter appreciated the gesture. She managed to smile and laugh at the right times. Bailey seemed happy to be included too.

Sloane watched Bailey laugh at something Mason said. Sloane's feminine intuition spidey senses tingled at the way Bailey looked at Mason. Actually, Bailey watched Mason a lot.

Oh no. Bailey had a crush on him.

Mason was *so* unavailable. Sure, he was single, but he was definitely emotionally unavailable. He was also quite a bit older than Bailey.

Should she talk to Bailey about it? No. It wasn't her business, and it was just a hunch. Bailey had to know that

Mason dated a lot of women. A *lot*. And he had no intention of ever settling down with one woman.

Emotionally unavailable. Like her.

She swallowed through a suddenly tight throat, then sipped her coffee to ease the ache.

Of course Levi had walked away. Just like every other man she'd dated. And Mason had totally been right. She never let them get close enough to be really interested. Dad had said pretty much the same thing.

She'd let Levi get closer than anyone. But she hadn't let him all the way in. So of course he'd walked away. Why wouldn't he? She wasn't worth the hassle.

She'd pushed away this really great guy because she was afraid to care, the one guy who'd cared enough to stick with her even though she was a bitchy workaholic with no life. The one guy who'd wanted to be there for her even when her life was a mess. The one guy who really got her and knew what she needed. She'd screwed up so badly, and in trying to protect herself, she'd hurt him. And now she was miserable too, because she did care about him. She loved him.

Was Mason right? Would an apology fix things? Maybe if she got down on her knees and promised she'd try harder. Do better. Or was it too late for them?

25

Levi arrived at Madeleine and Bryan's place and was greeted by two excited ankle biters. "Uncalevi, Uncalevi!" He picked up both Emily and Elijah and propped one kid on each hip as he walked into their living room.

"Hey, rug rats," he said. "I hear you're babysitting me tonight."

They giggled. "Noooo! *You're* babysitting *us!*" Emily poked his chest.

"I am not a baby," Elijah protested.

"No, you are not," Levi agreed. "In fact, you're getting so big I can barely hold you." He pretended to drop them, bending his knees to catch them. They both screamed.

"Hey, don't get them all wound up. They'll be your problem if they won't go to bed." Madeleine fastened a bracelet on her wrist. "Thanks for coming at the last minute."

"No problem. Had nothing else going on."

Madeleine was super fussy about who she left the kids with. They had one babysitter who was now seventeen years old and not as available as she'd been when she was fifteen. This wasn't the first time Levi had been roped into childcare duty, but honestly, he didn't mind because his niece and nephew were the cutest kids in the world. And when he babysat them, he got to play with their cool toys.

"Stupid business dinner on a Monday night," Madeleine grumbled. "Okay, they can have a snack before bed. Something healthy." She outlined the bedtime routine for each kid. Levi ignored her because he already knew it. Or close enough.

"How's Sloane?" she asked.

He gave her a sour look. "Sloane who?"

She frowned. "You're not seeing her anymore?"

"Sloane's pretty," Emily said.

"Yes, she is," Levi agreed. "Very pretty." He sighed.

"Oh Levi." Madeleine shook her head. "When are you going to grow up?"

His eyeballs nearly burst from their sockets. "What the fuck?"

Emily sucked in a breath. "Oooh, that's a bad word."

"Fuck," Elijah said.

Madeleine rolled her eyes. "Thank you very much."

Levi set the kids down. "Go play. I'll be right there." He glared at his sister. "What the hell do you mean, when am I going to grow up? You assume I did something to mess things up with Sloane?"

"You never stick with one girl very long."

"True." He hesitated. "But she was different."

"Then what happened?"

"Long story. It wasn't my fault. She... Fuck." He rubbed his eyes. When he looked back at Madeleine her expression had changed from condemning to concerned. "Let me see if I can condense this. Did Mom tell you about Sloane's mother?"

Her eyes clouded. "Yeah. That's awful. It must have been so hard for her."

"Well, apparently they found her mom. Last week."

"Oh. Wow."

"Yeah. But Sloane didn't tell me. She was all torn up

about it, I could tell, but she didn't bother to share that with me."

Madeleine tipped her head. "Why not?"

"Fuck if I know." He shrugged. "Okay, wait I do know. She's…independent."

"Uh-huh."

"I mean independent to a fault. Like, sometimes you *need* other people, right?"

"Right." Her tone softened.

"Well, she doesn't need anybody, and she apparently doesn't need me. I could've been there for her. I could've helped her." He cleared his throat. "So. We're done." He tried to keep his tone nonchalant, but had a feeling his sister picked up on the hurt he couldn't quite hide.

"Oh, Levi." She touched her fingers to her throat. "Are you in love with her?"

"Fuck no!" His eyes popped open wide.

Madeline smiled slowly. "Little bro." She shook her head. "You brought her to the wedding."

"That was just because she needed to get out and have more fun."

"Uh-huh. And you wanted to be there for her and help her through a rough time."

"Well. Uh. Yeah."

She bit her lip. "Oh, baby brother. Maybe you have grown up."

"Whatever."

"It looked like she was really into you," she said. "At the wedding. I really liked her. You seemed so good together."

"I thought we were too," he said glumly.

"So you're just going to give up? Let her go?"

He frowned. "Uh…"

She smacked his shoulder. "You spoiled brat."

"Ow!" He lifted a hand to his shoulder and rubbed it. "What the hell does that mean?"

"Everything's been handed to you your whole life. Everyone's always done whatever you want. Now you run into an obstacle, you're just walking away? Even though you love her and your heart is broken?"

"What?" His mouth fell open, but her words stabbed into him.

"Jesus. Come on, Levi. I'm guessing she has some issues because of what happened with her mother. Show some empathy and understanding. Relationships take work."

"Okay, let's go." Bryan appeared, cell phone in hand. "Sorry, that call took longer than I thought. Hey, Levi. Thanks for coming."

"No problem," he said again, his head in a daze from Madeleine's crazy words.

"We'll be home around eleven," Madeleine said. "They better be asleep." She paused and gave him a long look. "Sack up, Levi."

He saluted her and watched them leave through the kitchen door to the attached garage.

He was not a spoiled brat.

And he knew relationships took work. Well, he'd never had a real relationship, but he'd *heard* that they took work.

In love with Sloane? Jesus Christ.

His distracted himself by playing with the kids. He took them out to the backyard and let them run around. They swung on their swing set and played with some dump trucks in the sandbox, and Elijah rode his tricycle around in circles on the patio, making engine noises. If he got them tired enough, they'd be asleep in no time.

Then Elijah tipped his trike over, scraped his elbow and started bawling. Levi carried him into the house. Madeleine had showed him where the first aid stuff was the first time he'd ever babysat the kids, and it was the well-stocked first aid kit of a paranoid, overprotective mom. He cleaned up the scrape, applied a SpongeBob bandage, hugged Elijah and dried his tears.

"Need another bandage," Elijah said. "On dis arm." He held up the other arm.

"Where?"

"Here." Elijah pointed at his forearm. It appeared fine to Levi.

"Okay." Levi shrugged and applied another SpongeBob bandage to the other arm. Elijah nodded in satisfaction.

"Let's wash up and get you in your PJs," Levi said. "Then we'll see if you have any cookies."

"Cookies!"

Probably not what Madeleine had in mind for a snack, but the kid was hurt. He had to distract him. They found oatmeal cookies, which were somewhat healthy, and the kids sat at the big kitchen island on stools to eat their bedtime snack.

"I cannot use that cup," Elijah said as Levi handed him a glass of milk. Levi raised his eyebrows.

"Is blue," Elijah said. "I ony like the red cup."

"Ooookay." Levi opened the cabinet door and found the red plastic cup, then poured the milk from the blue one into the red one and handed it to Elijah. He set the blue one in the dishwasher.

After cookies and milk, they read a couple of stories in bed and Elijah was nodding off before he'd even finished the second one. Emily wasn't far behind him.

Then Levi was alone in the quiet house, thinking about Sloane.

His anger had muted. So had the hurt. Yeah, it bothered him that she hadn't told him about her mom and what was going on. But maybe like Madeleine said, he needed to understand what was behind that. Sloane was very private. She kept her feelings to herself. She came across as tough and take-charge in the office. Away from work, he'd seen her softer side, and she liked it when he took control. He knew that.

Her mom had left her. Her dad had checked out after

that, basically leaving her too. She'd had to give up her dog — *Christ!* — her figure skating, and all her friends to move to a new school.

And he'd done the same thing. When the going got tough, Levi got going...right out the goddamn door.

What an asshole he was.

He'd let her down just like everyone else in her life she'd cared about.

Even she had told him not everything was easy. *Sometimes you have to work for what you want. And sometimes, the things you have to work the hardest for mean the most.*

She meant the most to him, the most of anything. She was worth anything, no matter how hard it was. Fuck yeah. Madeleine was right. He was in love with her.

He'd never been interested in one woman forever...but Sloane...yeah. She was it for him. Forever. And that didn't even make him want to vomit. Other than thinking that she might not feel the same about him.

Goddamn.

She hadn't been attacking him in that meeting this morning. After he'd calmed down, he recognized she was right about the commercial. And it took practically nothing to fix it, just change up the way the women acted at the end. Change up who the women were. He'd gotten carried away with the image they were trying to portray with their guy who met all these challenges to demonstrate his masculinity. They could still get that across without the objectification part. He and Scott had fixed it by the end of the day.

Hopefully.

He wanted to go to Sloane right then and there, but he was stuck in that house with his sister's sleeping offspring until she got home. So instead, he made plans.

26

Sloane wasn't going to try to contact Levi ahead of time. She'd just go to his place with the mugs he'd left behind and give them to him, and tell him how sorry she was. She was afraid to think too far ahead. Every time she remembered him saying *I'm done* and walking out, her heart felt like a knife was slicing through it. She wouldn't blame him if he didn't want anything more to do with her.

She asked the doorman to call up, but he shook his head. "He's not home, ma'am. Saw him going out about an hour ago."

"Oh." She bit her lip. Damn. "Okay, thanks."

She walked back out onto the sidewalk, the box still in her hands. Should she just leave it with the doorman? Or give them to him tomorrow? Or just forget the whole thing?

She didn't want to do it at work. But maybe that would be a safe place to have that conversation.

Safe? Safe from what? Did she think Levi was going to yell and create a big scene or something? Not likely.

Still undecided, she got back in her car and drove home with the mugs.

Now she wondered where Levi was. Out with friends? Maybe even on a date.

Her stomach cramped. Maybe she was too late.

Now she did understand that he hadn't been just angry. He'd been hurt. She'd hurt him and she hated herself for that. When had her own hang-ups mattered more than someone else's feelings? When had protecting her heart turned her into such a stone-cold bitch?

She missed him. She'd come to need him for so many things—comfort and companionship, laughter and joy. Needing someone that much scared her.

Face your fears, baby. That makes them so much smaller.

Okay, this wasn't a Ferris wheel, but Levi's words made her realize she needed to get over her fears and think about his feelings. If she loved him, she needed to make things right for him, even if it was just by apologizing.

✿

The next morning, Mason was in her office first thing. "When do you have time to have a look at Scott and Levi's commercial? They worked on it yesterday."

"Really? Already?"

"Yeah."

"Okay." She clicked to open her calendar on her computer and peered at it. "How about ten thirty?"

"That should work."

She walked into the meeting room at ten thirty with small birds beating their wings in her stomach. Levi was already there. She let her gaze roam over him while he was preoccupied, taking in his beautiful mouth, long dark eyelashes, that thick hair that was so wonderful to run her fingers through. He wore a casual short-sleeved golf shirt that hugged his broad shoulders and she admired his arms—the bulging biceps, the veins tracing down his lean forearms, his long fingers and neat nails.

She took a seat and Levi looked up. She caught his reaction. He kept his face neutral but a flash of…something…in his eyes told her she affected him. Somehow.

"Morning, Sloane," he said. "Before we start, we — I owe you an apology."

Her eyes widened. What was he talking about?

"For yesterday," he continued. "I was a little…stressed yesterday and when you gave us that feedback, I overreacted. I'm sorry. That was unprofessional."

She blinked.

"I'm also sorry for the, uh, fight that happened." He glanced at Scott. "That was also unprofessional. Again, I overreacted. I hope we didn't get you in trouble with The Hux. I mean, Mr. Huxworth."

Her lips twitched at his nickname for Joe. "You didn't."

"Good."

"I'm sorry too," Scott offered.

"Okay." Levi lifted his chin. "Let's go. Here's what we did."

They showed her the changes they'd made. And it was perfect. It really hadn't taken much. Happiness and pride bubbled up inside her. The commercial quickly moved from a surfing competition to shark diving to outrigger canoe racing, then a race through a pineapple maze and fire-knife dancing, moving to snow kiting and a snowmobile race across a glacier that culminated in the triumphant ending.

"I love it," she said. "I loved it yesterday, honestly. But now, I can't wait to show it to the client."

Levi grinned. "Great."

Their eyes met and something passed between them. Was it wishful thinking that he still cared? She dropped her gaze to the table as the others chattered and rose from their chairs. She followed the group out and returned to her office.

He'd apologized. That was sweet. And big. If he could do it, so could she.

She felt lame returning to his place that night. Maybe she was there for nothing again. Maybe he was out on another date. The doorman probably thought she was a big loser, stalking him after a breakup or something.

Hmm, she sort of was. She could have called and asked if she could come see him. But what if he said no?

She had to be prepared for rejection. But she wanted to apologize. And give him back his mugs.

The doorman called up and Levi was there. She shifted from one foot to the other as she waited for his permission to come up. The doorman nodded and let her in, and she took the elevator to the twenty-first floor.

Levi was at his door, dressed in jeans and a nice shirt, shoes on. "Hi," he said, an intense look on his face. Possibly surprise. Chuck was at his side, wriggling and jumping and whining.

"Are you just going out?" She took in his apparel and the leash in his hands. Crap.

"Yeah, goddammit."

She flinched back.

"I was just leaving to come to *your* place."

"Oh."

"Chuck and I were coming to see you. And bring you a few things."

"Wh-what things?" Her forehead tightened.

One corner of his mouth lifted. "Some things." His gaze dropped to the box in her hands.

She held it out. "Here. Your mugs. You left them at my place Saturday."

"I know," he murmured, taking the box from her. "I was bummed about that." He lifted his gaze back to her face. "Is that why you're here?"

She inhaled a long breath. "Partly. I also came to…apologize."

He looked at her intently. Then he stepped back. "Come in."

She walked in and he closed the door. Chuck still danced around, crying.

"I'm sorry, little buddy. No car ride right now." Levi set the leash in the drawer of the small table in his foyer. "When the leash comes out, he goes nuts. Jesus, maybe if I give him a biscuit he'll calm down." He strode over to the jar on the counter she remembered from her first night there.

But Chuck was now distracted, as Sloane crouched down and reached for him. He set his front paws on her knees and tried to lick her face. "I missed you too," she crooned to him, rubbing his silky head. "You're so handsome."

"Thank you."

She tried to stop her smile as she looked up at Levi. "I was talking to Chuck."

"Oh." His lips twitched. "Damn."

She straightened and faced him. "Well, you're handsome too."

"What are you apologizing for?"

Her head tilted. "For not telling you about my mom." She tried to gather her thoughts, which was difficult because her brain was suddenly as empty as balloon. "I never meant to hurt you, Levi. I was...pretty upset. Well, that's putting it mildly."

He folded his arms across his chest and leaned against the counter. "I know you were," he said quietly. "I could tell something was wrong. I've been kicking myself ever since for not pushing it with you, digging deeper to find out what it was." He paused. "I have something to apologize for too."

"No." She frowned. "That wasn't your fault."

"Yeah, it was. It was my fault for trying to just coast along with everything all smooth and easy. Something went wrong, and I didn't have the guts to find out what it was. And then when I found out you'd held out on me with something so important, I was pissed...and I bailed. Instead of making you talk to me and tell me what happened. Even if I was mad at you, I should have stuck around to work through it."

"Oh." Her heart swelled up. "Oh, Levi. I didn't blame you for walking away."

"Because you expect that, don't you? From everyone."

She drew her bottom lip between her teeth as tension stiffened her spine. "Yes," she whispered. "I'm afraid to care too much. Because it hurts so much to lose people you love."

His mouth softened and his eyes warmed. "Are you saying you love me?"

27

ah. Her throat quivered. Her lips trembled. Okay. She could do this. This was something that scared the ever-loving crap out of her. Admitting her feelings for someone, who could then stomp them into a pulp.

But it was Levi. And the way he looked at her, all calm and reassuring and steady...

"I do. I love you, Levi."

His eyes closed briefly, relief sweeping across his features. Then he said, "I knew it."

She burst out laughing. "You cocky ass. You did not."

He moved toward her, prowling on long legs, reaching for her. "Okay, there may have been a tiny bit of doubt. But that was why I was so confused. I was sure you cared about me. And then you kept something like that from me. I couldn't understand why. But I think I do now. I just needed to have my head smacked around."

She slid her arms around his waist and leaned into him. God, he felt so good. So strong and secure. "Who smacked you around? Besides Scott?"

"Hey. He never even landed a punch. I totally won that fight."

She laughed. "If you say so."

"It was my sister. Madeleine. I was babysitting Emily

278

and Elijah last night and told her what had happened."

"You were babysitting? Seriously?"

"Yeah. I do it all the time."

She felt another rush of love for him. "I came by last night, but you weren't here. I never thought you were babysitting."

"Aw, babe. Sorry I wasn't here."

"I'm glad you weren't out on a date."

He snorted. "As if. I'm pretty hung up on this girl." He bent his head and touched his lips to hers. "You. I love you too, Sloane."

Relief loosened her tense muscles and she sagged against him, holding on tighter. "Even though I hurt you and made you mad?"

"Yeah." He kissed her again, slow and sweet. "Madeleine reminded me of something a very smart woman told me once."

"What's that?"

"That not everything is easy. And important things are worth working hard for."

"Um. I think *I* told you that."

"That's right. Like I said, a very smart woman." He kissed her nose. "Madeleine put that into the context of a relationship and gave me shit for just walking away. Which is why I was coming to see you tonight. To tell you I love you. And I'm not giving up on us. I was going to say that maybe you haven't accepted how you feel about me, but I'm going to make you accept it. Or else."

"Ooh. You know how that bossy stuff turns me on."

"Oh yeah. I do." He nodded meaningfully. "I'm going to show you more of that. Face it, Sloane. You're mine now. I may not have to tie you up and spank you until you tell me how you feel after all."

She choked on a laugh. "Do you know how very wrong that sounds?"

He grinned.

They smiled into each other's eyes for a moment, a warm hum building between them.

"Will you tell me now?" he asked quietly. "About your mom. What happened...and how you're feeling about it."

"It's really awful, Levi."

"Hey." He nudged her chin up with his fingers, eyes narrowed. "Are you afraid I'll think less of you because of what your mom did?"

She gave a little grimace. "Maybe."

"Fuck that. Your mom's not you. And I know what she did hurt you and marked you forever, but damn Sloane, you're an amazing woman. I know it wasn't easy and maybe you have some wounds that are still healing, but you're smart and successful and confident—"

"I'm confident about business," she corrected. "Not so much about personal things."

"You love your brother and sister," he continued. "And they love you. I could see that when I met Becca. You sacrificed a lot of your own life for them. I know you do care about people. I've seen it. Even with Bailey at work, helping her out. And I heard you took Isaiah and Hunter out for lunch to thank them for meeting a tough deadline. You do care."

Her throat thickened. She nodded.

"Come on. Let's go sit down and you can tell me all about it. See, this is me, working at a relationship."

She huffed out a laugh and let him lead her over to the couch.

Snuggled in his arms, she told him the whole ugly story about her mom turning up, where she'd been, what she'd done. She told him how she felt, as much as she could name the feelings—anger, hurt, betrayal. And she cried. Having Levi's arms around her, holding her as she sobbed, was the best feeling ever.

When the tears had slowed, she said, "The one good

thing that came out of this is that I kind of warmed up to Viv." She sank her teeth into her lip briefly. "She's a nice person. I always felt guilty that I couldn't love her. But I do like her, and I felt so bad for her when this happened...and I realized I wasn't *letting* myself love her."

"Aw, beautiful girl." He kissed her hair and caressed her face. "See, you are smart."

"I've been keeping my distance from my dad too, all these years. It hurt that he withdrew, but now I understand more about what he was going through. The police investigated him as a suspect at that time. I knew that, but it never really clicked with me how awful that must have been for him. We talked about a lot of stuff on the weekend, and weirdly, Mom turning up has actually brought our family closer together."

"Are you going to see your mom?"

"Not right now." She sighed. "At first I said no way, never. Viv told me I should just think about it. Take my time. So I will. I don't know. I don't know what my mother would say if I saw her. I know I probably need to forgive her and just move on, and I'm afraid if I don't forgive her I'll be stuck in this place—this angry, bitter place—forever. I don't want to be like that."

He nodded. "I can't tell you what to do," he murmured. "But whatever you want to do...I'm with you, baby. You have to know that."

She shifted in his arms to look into his eyes. "Thank you. I didn't realize how much I needed you until I screwed up and thought I lost you. I do need you, Levi. I could handle this all on my own...but it feels so good to know I don't have to."

"I wanted to be there for you. I hated that you were hurting and wouldn't tell me." He searched her face. "I was so fucking stupid, I didn't realize that meant I love you. I'd do anything for you, anything to make you happy."

She loved that. So much. Warmth filled her. "We can't always be happy."

"I guess that's true. Life has ups and downs. My life has been easy and I guess that means I'm spoiled. As Madeleine so helpfully pointed out. But the bad shit maybe is easier when you have someone who's got your back. I'll always have your back, Sloane."

"I know. I heard the reason you fought Scott is because he insulted me."

His eyebrows pulled together. "You heard that?"

"Mmhmm. That was really nice, Levi." She touched her fingertips to his stubbled jaw. "And I've got your back too. When The Hux talked to me about the fight, he asked if we'd made a big mistake hiring you. And I said no. Definitely, emphatically, no. You're brilliant and talented."

"You called him The Hux." His lips curved.

"Yeah. I better be careful I don't call him that to anyone else."

"I love you so goddamn much."

"I love you too." They kissed again. "So. What were you bringing me?"

He grinned. "Well, first of all...Chuck. He missed you."

"Aw. I missed him too." She looked at Chuck, lying on his side on the rug, feet stretched out in front of him, snoring lightly. "I love that little guy. I was thinking about getting a dog. But it's hard when I work so much."

"You can share Chuck," he said solemnly. "I was never good at sharing my toys growing up—I never had to—but I'll share my dog with you. That's how much I love you."

Laughter bubbled up her throat. "Thank you."

"I'll get the stuff." He slid his arms from around her and she pouted but watched him walk into the kitchen. He returned seconds later with a big bouquet of flowers—

sunflowers! Her favorite. Also a small glossy black Sephora bag. And an opened bag of Bits & Bites.

"The flowers are beautiful," she murmured, taking the cellophane-wrapped bunch from him. He handed over the Sephora bag next. "What's this?"

She peered inside and pulled out a bottle of her favorite Givenchy perfume. She looked up at him. "Thank you."

"Yeah, you better thank me," he muttered. "That fucking little bottle cost two hundred and fifty dollars. I was going to buy you a gallon jug of the stuff, but it's a good thing they don't make it in gallon jugs or I'd be broke. Also, I didn't know there was more than one kind of Givenchy perfume. The girl asked me which one I wanted and I had no clue. Christ, I hate that fuckin' store. It's all full of makeup and girl shit."

She rolled her lips in to repress a smile. "Yes. It is."

"So I sniffed every one. But as soon as I tried that one, I recognized it. It gave me a stiffy."

She fell back into the couch cushions, laughing. "Well, good. Every time you meet a woman wearing that perfume you're going to get an erection."

"Nah, babe, it's just *you* wearing that perfume." He grinned.

She picked up the other bag. "And a half-eaten bag of Bits & Bites. Thank you."

"It's not half-eaten." He looked wounded. "It's two bags. I took out all the Cheerios and stuff and it's just the pretzels and the cheese bits combined into one. The ones you like."

The hot softness in her chest made it hard to get her breath. She stared at the bag. And swallowed. "Thank you," she whispered. "Levi. You're such a great guy."

"I tried to tell you that. Remember? When you were all pissed about that girl from the Kitten Club being in our hotel room, worried about her?"

She rolled her eyes. "Oh yeah." She didn't want to know any more details about that night.

"I *am* a great guy." He leaned over and kissed her. "And you love me."

"Yes. I really do."

She was his.

He was going to look after her and take care of her, hopefully for the rest of her life, whether she liked it or not.

He picked up the bag of Bits & Bites and the bottle of perfume and set them on the table. Then he lifted and turned her so she was straddling his lap facing him.

Luckily she was wearing a dress that had a loose skirt, a pretty pink sundress with tiny straps and a snug bodice. She touched her fingertips to his face as their eyes met.

"I love you," he whispered. He slid a hand up the side of her neck and into her hair and pulled her face closer for a kiss. A long, slow, sweet kiss. He poured his goddamn heart into that kiss to show her how much he loved her.

She gripped his shoulders as the kiss went on and on. They lifted their mouths then joined them again, licking, sucking at each other with feverish hunger. His other arm wrapped around her back and he lifted her off him, turning his ass so he could lie down with his head on the armrest. He pulled her down with him, still straddling his hips, the skirt of her dress riding up around her thighs.

Their mouths met again, long, lush kisses of relief and yearning. Her hips rolled against him in a needy rhythm, right where he was hard and aching. "Seems like you need something, sexy girl," he murmured against her lips. Her eyes opened and met his again. "Need this?" He lifted his hips and bumped his erection against her.

"Yes," she breathed.

He pulled her mouth to his again, tongue sliding inside to play with hers. His hand swept down her back, bunched the skirt higher and then grabbed her ass. He squeezed a firm cheek, her hips still rocking against him.

"Love this sweet little ass," he muttered. "And I love doing this." He popped her ass with a firm swat. She moaned and he did it again, then rubbed over soft skin.

He cupped a breast through the fabric of the dress, gave it a squeeze and a rub. She whimpered and pushed upright.

"Yeah, that's it," he said. "Show me those pretty tits." He pulled the tiny straps down then grasped the bodice of the dress and tugged it down. "Oh yeah. Oh Christ, baby." He used his abs to raise himself and take a nipple into his mouth. He drew it in and sucked and sucked as she made soft little pleasure sounds, then switched to the other one and did the same. He drew back and studied the puckered peaks, all shiny and deep pink. "Beautiful."

Now he pushed her to her back, her head on the other armrest, and moved over her. He touched his forehead to hers as together they undid his jeans and shoved them down his hips. His aching cock sprang out and Sloane's slender fingers circled it. Excitement whipped from his groin up his spine. He kissed her forehead, his eyes closing as heat and pressure built. Her fingers caressed and stroked, tickled his balls. Lust spiraled higher inside him.

"Gotta be inside you, baby. I need to fuck you."

"I need you too."

He set his hands on the armrest and pushed to straighten. On his knees, he let his hand linger on her pretty face, their eyes joined again in that unique connection. Soft skin. His thumb brushed her bottom lip. Then he whipped his shirt off and tossed it away. She rose onto her knees and tried to wriggle her panties off. With a noise of impatience, Levi yanked at the thong underwear and snapped the side string. With his pants around his thighs and her dress bunched around her waist, he gripped his cock and pushed inside her.

Her breathing went choppy but she kept heavy-lidded eyes focused on him as her body closed around him, hot heaven. He lowered back down to kiss her again, his hand playing with her pussy as he slid in and out.

Her tongue stroked over his. She bent her leg up to press against his thigh as he fucked her, slow and sweet. Electricity buzzed up his spine and shorted out his brain. Heat burned over his skin, and love for her filled his chest. He held her head as he sought her mouth again, then stayed like that, breathing the same air, mouths barely touching, eyes fastened on each other.

"So fucking hot," he whispered. "Love that pussy. Tight and so wet for me."

"Oh, Levi."

He hugged her bent leg, bracing her as he moved faster, his thrusts deeper and harder. He pushed hair off her face and kissed her once more, then buried his face in the side of her neck.

"Is this gonna do it for you?" he mumbled. "Want you to come."

"I'm...going to come." Her voice came out breathy. "Keep doing...that."

"Aw yeah, baby. I love you so much."

"Ungh..." Her pussy contracted hard around him and her body went tight.

He pumped faster, his blood racing, his balls squeezing. "There you go, beautiful girl. So gorgeous. Yeah...there it is. Fuck, gonna come too...inside you. Fucking love that." Ecstasy exploded at his groin and surged through his body as he came inside her tight, succulent pussy. He went rigid for a moment, breathing hard, his mind blank. Then the words filled his head, over and over again. *I love you. I love you.*

"Oh baby." He caressed her face and looked down into her eyes. "We didn't even get our clothes off."

The sweet curve of her mouth made his heart turn over in his chest. "I love that," she confessed. "I love how hot you get for me."

"Christ. Do I ever." He closed his eyes briefly. "Can't get enough of you, Sloane. But not just your hot little body. All of you. Want you with me, all the time." What had happened to his belief that sex with only one woman for the rest of his life was wretched, torturous hell? Now, he *only* wanted her. Mind. Blown.

"I know. Me too." She pushed her fingers through his hair, her eyes anxious. "Me too. But I told you…I'm not good at relationships. I still have all these mixed-up feelings. I know I almost lost you because of them, and I'm afraid it will happen again."

"We'll probably both screw up. I've never done this before either. We'll help each get past it, right?" He stroked her face. "I won't walk out on you again. I promise."

"I know you say that, but…" She sucked in a breath. "Sorry. I don't want to be all negative."

"It's okay. We're gonna get past that. I know words are easy. I'm going to prove to you that I won't give up when things get tough. Eventually you'll believe it and trust me."

"I do trust you. I really do. It's just hard to get past those fears. I've been like this for so long."

"I know, baby. I know." He pushed hair off her face with his fingertips. "I've been a spoiled jerk for so long too. You call me on that shit whenever you see it."

She smiled. "I can do that."

"I know you can." His smile went wry.

She laughed. "And you still love me."

"Yeah. I still love you."

28

The following week, Levi sat in the large meeting room at the offices of Huxworth Packard while the creative team presented to the brand managers from Cerone.

He appreciated being included in this meeting. He'd asked to present his own stuff, which they originally hadn't wanted to happen because they didn't want all the creatives in the room overwhelming the client. But since it was only his and Scott's campaign going forward they'd agreed he and Scott should be there.

A good idea could sell itself, but sometimes it also helped to have the people who'd birthed the baby there to explain it. No one loved that baby like he did. Sure, Mason was good, and he could probably sell anything, but Levi also liked selling his work. He could convince a hesitant, fearful client that the risk was worth the reward.

They'd all rehearsed this pitch. They all had to be on the same page—him, Scott, Noah, Mason and Sloane. They all were ready to speak to how and why they came up with the idea, what the benefits were, what the potential costs were and how long it would take to produce. They were ready to answer any tough questions Ross and Greg threw at them. None of them wanted to look like unprepared or unprofessional idiots.

Mason had cautioned him that this was going to be big and bold and scary for them. Levi knew better than to expect the client to jump up and down with excitement. These commercials were going to cost big bucks. Levi was prepared for them to go away and discuss the plan and probably come back and ask for changes, especially ones that would save them money.

So his mind was blown when Ross and Greg looked at each other, nodded and looked away.

"That is amazing," Greg said.

The tightness in Levi's chest eased but he didn't let himself get too excited.

"Cost is going to be an issue," Ross said. "But damn, I want that."

Levi looked first to Sloane. As if sensing his gaze on her, she glanced his way. And smiled.

Then he looked at Mason, who was leaning forward and talking about ways they could keep costs down, knowing he had them hooked and just had to reel them in. And then he looked at Scott who was grinning like a fool. Scott met his eyes and Levi understood his desire to jump up and do a celebratory dance to the tune from Kool & the Gang.

The discussion went on a while longer. Sure, they could make small changes and Levi was happy to provide some input on ways that might be cheaper without taking away from the impact of the ads. But it looked like it was going to be a go.

After the client had left, he and Scott exchanged a high-five and sagged back into their chairs.

"Good work, boys," Sloane said crisply, though her eyes were warm. "Let's hope we hear back from them quickly. Then we can start working on budgets and timelines."

"Hawaii here we come," Scott said.

Excitement rose in Levi. Goddamn it was going to be fun to see this idea come to life.

Soon he and Sloane were the only two left in the room.

"You did it," she said quietly. "Wow, Levi. That really was amazing."

He tried for casual nonchalance with a self-deprecating smile and shrug. Then he lost it. "Fuck yeah!"

She grinned, stood and walked over to his chair to slide onto his lap. She curled her arms around his neck and kissed him. His hands went to her hips and pulled her closer.

"You were amazing too," he murmured against her lips. "I love watching you handle clients. So smooth. I love how you totally respect their fears but talk them out of them."

"You did that too," she said. "You made a compelling case for doing something a little risky."

"In this economy, being safe is even riskier."

"Yep." She smooched his mouth again. "You made them want to stand out and do something really bold. That takes some skills."

"Thank you. We make a good team."

"We sure as hell do. And not just here in the office."

Someone cleared his throat and Sloane lifted her head. They both looked at Mason at the door of the meeting room. "Sorry to interrupt, kids, but this room is needed for another meeting in five minutes. You might want to…get a room."

Sloane laughed and rose to her stiletto-clad feet. She tugged her skirt down so the hem was just above her knees. Levi shifted in the chair. Dammit, the guy downstairs was stirring due to Sloane's sweet little ass on his lap, and he had to get up and walk to his office.

He liked it that people knew about them now. Now everyone knew she was his. Most importantly, *she* knew she was his. She knew he was going to be there for her no matter what and he was determined to live up to that, no matter how hard things got. Because she was worth working for.

Enjoy this sneak peek at

NO
OBLIGATION
REQUIRED

Brew Crew Book 2

by Kelly Jamieson

*H*ow many times could she turn down these invitations without trashing her career?

Bailey sighed inwardly, her stomach knotting. She loved socializing and meeting people, and she knew attending this work event was important, but damn, it wasn't that easy for her.

"It's important to get to know people in other departments." Sloane crossed her arms, leaning against Bailey's desk, her eyes curious but compassionate. "That was a mistake I made when I first got into the business. You can't just focus on your own little niche, you need to network. Build relationships."

"I get that, I really do." But what the hell was she supposed to do about Maya? Thursday night was Maya's last swimming lesson of the summer, but even if they skipped that she'd need to find a babysitter. She could ask Crystal again, but she'd just done that last week when she'd ended up leaving work late one day. Crystal, who looked after Maya before and after school, or right now summer day camps, was sweet and helpful but she had things to do with her own family in the evenings.

Sloane tilted her head. "But...?"

Bailey had never told anyone at work that she was raising her little sister. She'd seen what happened to working mothers who talked about their kids all the time and left early to attend school concerts or soccer games. Nobody took them seriously. And she had enough problems being taken seriously.

But in the end, people were questioning her anyway.

Her lips tightened. "It's just...I have other plans already."

Sloane regarded her thoughtfully. "Well, okay. I'm not being critical, Bailey, but some might question how dedicated you are to the agency and to your career if you don't come to this. People notice that you rush out of here every evening."

"I get my work done." Bailey tried not to let defensiveness creep into her tone.

Sloane nodded. "I know you do. In fact, you go above and beyond. That program you developed is brilliant. You must have put a lot of time into that."

"I did." She'd put in a lot of time at home, working on her laptop late into the night when Maya was asleep.

Pressure built inside her, a hot swelling that made her curl her fingers into her palms. Life had been such a battle the last few years and she was working her ass off. Even so, she was being questioned and doubted.

She'd thought it would be enough if she did a good job. Knowing she wouldn't be able to stay at the office late, she'd become ruthlessly efficient and often took work home with her. But face time was apparently just as important as doing a good job.

"I don't know how you do that," Sloane continued. "But I can't argue with the fact that you do a good job. It's just...people form perceptions about you."

"I'll rearrange my plans," Bailey said quietly.

"Is everything okay, Bailey?" Concern pulled Sloane's eyebrows together.

Bailey pulled out her brightest smile. "Of course! I'm sure it will be a fun evening. I'm looking forward to it."

Sloane had been great to her at Huxworth Packard Advertising, mentoring her, giving her career advice, helping her solve problems, like when idiot art directors ignored her deadlines. Bailey appreciated all that, she really did. She wanted to move up at Huxworth Packard. She loved her job as media buyer, but it wasn't what she wanted to do for the rest of her life. She wanted to work in accounts, liaising between clients and creatives, learning about the clients' businesses and helping them achieve their objectives.

In a couple of years, Maya would be old enough to stay home alone and Bailey could start putting in more hours, but right now, her ten-year-old sister needed her and that had to be her priority. But, damn, she couldn't afford to lose this job or the opportunities she had here at Huxworth Packard.

She'd figure it out. Like she always did.

"Thank you, Sloane. I appreciate all your advice."

"You're welcome." Sloane smiled and straightened. As usual, she looked elegant and professional, her blonde hair smooth, her makeup understated, her sleeveless purple dress fitted to her slender body. But she still eyed Bailey with faint curiosity, as if she suspected Bailey was keeping something from her.

Which she was.

Should she confide in Sloane? Maybe she'd have other advice for her. But Sloane wasn't married and had no children—what would she know about being responsible for a child, trying to balance work and home?

And it shouldn't have anything to do with work. It was her personal life and she wanted to keep it personal. The details of how she'd ended up raising her little sister weren't exactly something she was proud or eager to share.

"I better go. I have to call Ben at Channel Seven about adjusting our ad schedule. We need to make some changes based on the most recent audience numbers."

As she left Sloane's office, copywriter Levi Wolcott passed her in the corridor, no doubt on his way in to see Sloane. He and Sloane had been dating for a few weeks now—actually longer than that, according to office gossip, but they'd kept it on the down low. It had been interesting to learn that Sloane and Levi were a couple, since a lot of people at Huxworth Packard thought Sloane and executive creative director Mason Ward had something going on.

Levi was super sexy and charming and smart, and he made Sloane relax and smile a lot more than she'd used to. Not that Sloane was a bitch. She was just focused and driven. And Bailey envied that.

Damn.

In her cubicle, she dropped her head into her hands. What the hell was she going to do about tomorrow night?

"You okay, hon?"

Bailey looked up to see fellow media buyer, Phoebe. She smiled. "Yeah, I'm fine. I have a bit of a headache, that's all."

Phoebe moved to her own desk in the next cubicle and pulled open a drawer. She handed a tiny bottle to Bailey. "Here. Sniff this."

Bailey blinked. "What is it?"

"Peppermint oil. Sniffing it will help your headache."

"Uh, that's okay." She didn't really have a headache, but even if she did she wasn't sure she wanted to sit there snorting peppermint oil.

Phoebe shrugged and dropped the bottle back in her drawer. "If you change your mind, it's right here. Just don't take drugs. Drugs are bad for you."

Right.

"Thanks, I'll keep that in mind." She reached for her phone and Phoebe returned to her own desk.

As media buyer, Bailey's job was to determine how to best expose their ads to the desired targets. She did research and analysis to help figure out the best combination of TV, radio, magazines, billboards — and these days digital media like YouTube videos and native advertising — to reach as many target consumers as possible at the lowest cost. Then she worked with those media outlets to buy space, whether print, digital or air time, for the ads the creative teams developed.

This morning she dealt with changes to the TV ad schedule, retrieved a couple of voice mails and played phone tag with the sales guys who'd been trying to reach her, one of them from a new local magazine wanting to pitch to her about placing print ads with them, the other from the marketing department at Steel, one of Verhoeven's big beer brands. Then it was off to a meeting with one of the creative teams to strategize on a new campaign for Ammen and Ammen Light, more of Verhoeven's big brands.

Bailey knew she was lucky to be working with the "Brew Crew", the creatives who handled the Verhoeven Brewery accounts. Everyone wanted to work on the sexy beer account. She'd made a point of learning all she could about beer and the beer industry in what little spare time she had. And the guys who worked on the Brew Crew were awesome—smart and creative and talented. Of course they had huge egos and attitude, but she still couldn't help but like them.

Especially Mason Ward.

As the executive creative director, he was responsible for the large creative team working on the Verhoeven accounts. He assigned work to the copywriters and art directors and made sure it got done. He worked closely with Sloane, the account director for Verhoeven. While Sloane was involved in the overall direction of campaigns, she liaised with the clients while Mason oversaw the creative work. Sloane was the one who could help the client understand why a particular strategy was good for their business, while Mason was the expert at getting inside the head of a target audience. He had a unique ability to understand their hopes and fears, dreams and aspirations, which enabled him to successfully guide the creative process at Huxworth Packard.

Bailey knew she was creative—just not in the kind of way the copywriters and art directors were. But she did have a good business head and knew she could do well on the account side of things.

Mason sat at the long table in the board room, looking at some papers, most likely the creative brief that Noah had prepared. Noah, the account manager for the Ammen brand, and copywriter Dash were already there as well, but as usual, Bailey's gaze went immediately to Mason and also as usual, a shiver worked down her spine as she took her seat. He was just so damn gorgeous.

Thick eyebrows drawn down over dark eyes, he studied the papers. His lustrous dark hair made her want to run her hands through it, his lean jaw clean-shaven. His face was sculpted into almost elegant lines, although his nose was strong with a faint bump on it, but his mouth was sensual, the bottom lip full and the top lip curved in a perfect arc.

She'd never seen him naked but she'd fantasized a lot about what was beneath his impeccable suits. She'd heard that he'd been a football player in college, destined to turn pro until some kind of injury had knocked him out, and his wide shoulders and hard body definitely gave the impression of a fit athlete, even though his college days were far behind him.

He was thirty-six years old, eleven years older than her. That sounded like a lot, but he didn't seem old...just mature and experienced and definitely brilliant in his field. And she felt a lot older than twenty-five most of the time. So the eleven-year age difference didn't stop her from crushing on the sexy executive creative director.

He looked up from his paper then, catching her looking at him. Damn. She gave him a bright smile. "Morning, Mason."

Even though she'd had a crush on him forever, she didn't want anyone to know that.

"Morning."

"I'm here." Renzo Tagarelli rushed into the room and threw himself into a chair next to her.

Sloane strode in moments later, looked around as if taking roll and closed the door behind her.

Noah, Dash and Renzo had met with the client to discuss what they were looking for. Often, a campaign started as a way to solve a particular problem for the client. In this case, Ammen's problem was that drinkers, particularly Millennials, weren't consuming enough of it. Especially Ammen Light.

"Wine and spirits continue to make gains," Noah said. "And although the craft beer brands are growing, the gains aren't enough to overcome declining sales of Verhoeven's stalwarts like Ammen and Ammen Light."

Bailey nodded. Verhoeven had recently been buying up some of those craft breweries in an attempt to capture those sales. "Are they looking for something like the big campaign they just approved for Cerone?" Levi and Scott had developed an amazing campaign idea and Bailey didn't think she'd ever seen a client so in love with a campaign right from the start. Levi had only recently joined the firm, headhunted away from AdMix because of his brilliant copywriting skills, and had quickly proven his value. Or maybe that would depend on how well the campaign actually did once it was launched. But so far everyone seemed impressed.

Noah sighed. "Yes and no. Of course they'd love something big and bold like that one, but they don't have the budget for it. Something on a smaller scale."

Noah's creative brief included competitive analysis, research and some input from Bailey's supervisor, Kaleb, the media planner. Noah continued to talk, briefing them all on the timelines, budget and proposed media. Bailey's input at this early stage was limited, but she took notes of their discussion.

"I've heard that the big light beer brands that launched in the early eighties have dropping sales because kids these days don't want to drink what their parents drank," Dash said.

Mason nodded, leaning back in his chair. "Well sure. That makes sense. I don't want to drink my father's beer."

Bailey absorbed this detail about Mason. Did he even really drink beer? He seemed like a martini kind of guy. Or maybe expensive scotch...

Focus, girl.

"And he didn't want to drink what his dad did," Mason continued. "It's the product life cycle theory—all big brands will eventually mature and begin to falter."

"That's depressing," Dash said.

Mason smiled. "No. Not at all. It's an opportunity. It means they need us."

After a short pause, Dash pumped a fist in the air. "Booyah!"

"So do we focus on lifestyle marking?" Renzo asked. "Younger lifestyles?"

Mason tapped a pen on the table. "No."

Eyebrows rose but everyone was hanging on his next words.

"There's a perception that light beer equals light quality. Those craft beers are all pushing that stronger taste means higher quality. That's where we need to focus—on the quality of the product. Embracing who Ammen and Ammen Light really are."

"And if we focus on digital advertising, we'll reach the younger people we need to draw in," Bailey added. She had a particular interest in digital advertising lately and had been gathering data and analyzing the results of their efforts.

"Excellent point." Mason nodded approvingly.

Bailey sucked in a breath, her heart thumping wildly. She kept her face neutral and dropped her gaze to the papers on the table in front of her.

The meeting ended after an hour, with Dash and Renzo prepared to spend the next couple of weeks working on ideas. While they worked on the campaign, Bailey would be researching and considering best options for where to place the ads.

The rest of her day was hectic with more phone tag, emails to deal with and a meeting with a salesman from the largest Chicago newspaper. Huxworth Packard placed a significant amount of business with them, and Bailey felt they deserved better pricing considering that, so the meeting involved some rigorous negotiating, which she enjoyed. It was like a game and she loved being one move ahead of whoever she was dealing with and, in the end, getting exactly what she'd wanted.

Late in the afternoon she sent one of her two best friends a text message. Kate and Lauren had both looked after Maya for her from time to time, but it wasn't easy for them either. Kate had gone back to school and now had classes on Thursday evenings, so that wouldn't work. Bailey just hoped that Lauren wasn't working. As a nurse, her shifts varied, which sometimes was great if Maya was sick and Lauren was off during the day, but more often than not, things didn't work out.

Luck was with her this time when Lauren quickly texted back that she could babysit Maya Thursday night, although it would be best if it wasn't too late as she started work at seven in the morning. So fine, Bailey would leave the party in good time, but at least she'd be able to put in an appearance.

She shoved a USB drive into her purse with spreadsheets she would work on later at home and left the office at five o'clock as usual, since she had to pick up Maya from the babysitter's by six. Today she was smiling and energized after the meeting that had gone so well.

Mason stood at the elevator on their floor and she nearly skidded to a halt at seeing him. Her heart gave the usual lurch it did when she encountered him. "Oh hi," she said a little breathlessly. Her voice sounded breathy at the best of times, another curse that made people look at her as a little blonde ditz, but around Mason she almost always did lose her breath.

"Hi, Bailey." He smiled at her. "Heading home?"

Was it her guilty conscience, or did she just imagine the hint of censure in his tone at the fact she was leaving early?

She gritted her teeth briefly but kept a smile in place. "Yes. You too?"

"I have an early dinner meeting."

"Of course." No doubt with one of the many gorgeous women he was often seen with.

A bachelor at age thirty-six, Mason dated an endless string of women. He kept his private life very private, but office gossip was rampant, rumors started by people who'd seen him out with one sexy woman after another. He'd had girlfriends, but never any that lasted more than a few months at the most. Apparently he wasn't into commitment or settling down.

Nobody knew much about Mason other than he used to play football, dated a lot of women and was a brilliant ad man. He'd worked for Huxworth Packard for six years, and before that he'd worked for a big advertising agency in Los Angeles.

The elevator doors slid open and Mason gestured for her to enter first. A gentleman.

Awareness prickled over her skin as he stepped in too and they began the descent from the thirty-fifth floor to the lobby of the Lachman building.

"Great input in the Ammen meeting this morning," Mason said to her, his intent gaze focused on her.

She blinked and tried to get her galloping heart back under control. "Thank you." She flashed what she hoped was a professional smile.

"Sloane was telling me about some kind of program you designed for us." His forehead creased. "She was pretty impressed."

"Oh. She told you about that?" Bailey resisted the impulse to jump up and down. "It's been working well for me."

"Technology can be our friend. We need to make use of that."

"Absolutely."

She knew what he was thinking—little blonde media girl Bailey had done something smart? She sighed inwardly but lifted her chin and met his eyes.

Her belly fluttered. He regarded her with a curious intensity. Her hand wanted to lift to her hair to smooth it back but she kept it pinned to her side, working to appear casual and professional.

"I liked what you said too," she blurted. "About big brands maturing and falling, but that's an opportunity." The corners of his eyes creased up, though his lips barely moved. Heat slipped through her veins at how damn attractive that was. "Thank you."

Other Books by Kelly Jamieson

Heller Brothers Hockey
Breakaway
Faceoff
One Man Advantage
Hat Trick
Offside

Love Me
Friends with Benefits
Love Me More
2 Hot 2 Handle
Lost and Found
One Wicked Night
Sweet Deal
Hot Ride
Crazy Ever After
All I Want for Christmas
Sexpresso Night
Irish Sex Fairy
Conference Call
Rigger
You Really Got Me
How Sweet It Is

Power Series
Power Struggle
Power Play
Power Shift

Rule of Three Series
Rule of Three
Rhythm of Three
Reward of Three

San Amaro Singles
With Strings Attached
How to Love
Slammed

Windy City Kink
Sweet Obsession
All Messed Up
Playing Dirty

Three of Hearts

Loving Maddie from A to Z

Brew Crew
Limited Time Offer
No Obligation Required

Aces Hockey
Major Misconduct
Off Limits
Icing
Top Shelf
Back Check
Slap Shot

Last Shot
Body Shot
Hot Shot

Bayard Hockey
Shut Out
Cross Check

Dancing in the Rain

About the Author

Kelly Jamieson is a best-selling author of over forty romance novels and novellas. Her writing has been described as "emotionally complex", "sweet and satisfying" and "blisteringly sexy." She likes coffee (black), wine (mostly white), shoes (high heels) and hockey!

Subscribe to her newsletter for updates about her new books and what's coming up, follow her on Twitter @KellyJamieson or on Facebook, visit her website at www.kellyjamieson.com or contact her at info@kellyjamieson.com.